RESURRECTION BAY

EMMA VISKIC is an award-winning Australian crime writer. Her critically acclaimed debut novel, *Resurrection Bay*, won the 2016 Ned Kelly Award for Best Debut, as well as an unprecedented three Davitt Awards: Best Adult Novel, Best Debut, and Readers' Choice. It was also iBooks Australia's Crime Novel of the year in 2015.

Emma studied Australian sign language (Auslan) in order to write the character of Caleb Zelic, whose adventures will continue in *And Fire Came Down*, coming soon from Pushkin Vertigo.

[A] stunning debut... original and splendidly plotted [with] a superb cast of main characters'

The Times Crime Book of the Month

'More than lives up to its hype... Fierce, fast-moving, violent... it is as exciting a debut as fellow Australian Jane Harper's *The Dry*, and I can think of no higher praise'

Daily Mail

'Adds to a bumper year for quality Australian crime fiction... The dialogue is excellent... [it] zooms along'

Sunday Express

'Distinctive flavour'

Herald Scotland

Viskic really ramps up the tension... Fantastic conclusion'

Col's Criminal Library **(blog)**

'A very impactful thriller... distinctive... a hero you will want more of in future'

The Book Bag

'*Resurrection Bay* is a really enjoyable crime thriller: punchily written and snappily paced, with a vivid cast of characters'

David's Book World **(blog)**

'In a packed genre the author has succeeded in creating an original lead character... The denouement is bloody with an excellent twist... Enjoyable and compelling... A recommended read for all crime thriller fans'

Never Imitate **(blog)**

'Delivers a rush that does not let you go. A thrilling debut... with many twists and turns'

The Last Word

'Fast-moving narrative... Recommended'

Mystery People

'Gutsy, original, with a devilishly tricky plot... Spare, flawlessly paced writing... A stunning crime debut'

Thriller Books Journal **(blog)**

'Wow! What a debut novel!... Captivating, quirky and absolutely riveting'

Crime Book Junkie **(blog)**

'Viskic's novel is the reason I love reviewing. This is a truly gripping debut which feels as though written by a seasoned writer. Mesmerising'

Crimesquad

'Excellent debut novel... certainly a name to watch'

SHOTS

'In her research for *Resurrection Bay*, the author studied Australian sign language to add to the authenticity of the novel and that work really pays off here'

Crime Fiction Lover

'I was hooked... There is so much to love about *Resurrection Bay*'

Northern Crime **(blog)**

'A truly rock and roll writing style... riveting... banging brilliant... A perfect storm of a read... Highly recommended'

Liz Loves Books **(blog)**

'Accomplished, original and utterly riveting, so much so that I read it in pretty much one sitting'

Raven Crime Reads **(blog)**

'The drama added by Caleb's deafness is what makes the book'

Action on Hearing Loss

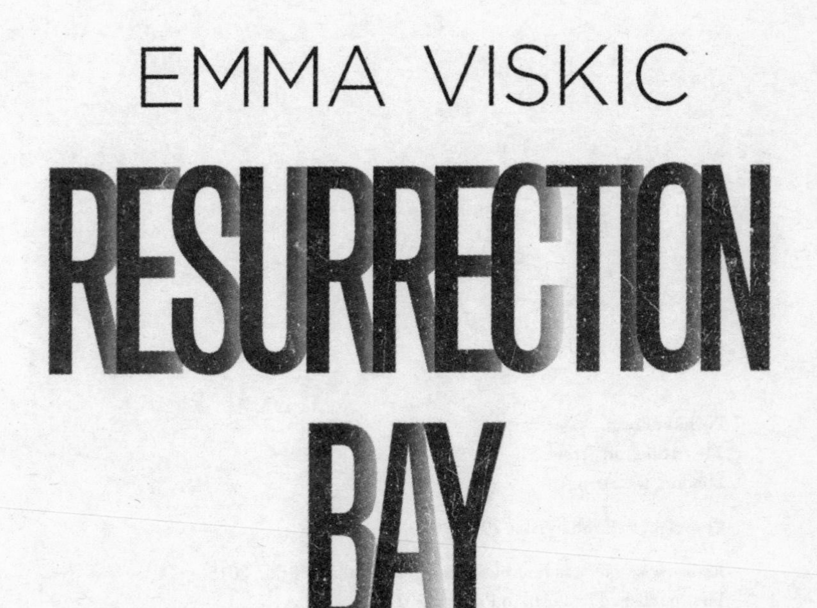
EMMA VISKIC
RESURRECTION
BAY

PUSHKIN VERTIGO

Pushkin Press
71–75 Shelton Street
London, WC2H 9JQ

Resurrection Bay was first published in Australia by Echo, 2015
First published by Pushkin Press in 2017
This edition first published in 2018

9 8 7 6 5 4 3 2 1

ISBN 13: 978-1-78227-391-2

Offset by Tetragon, London
Printed and bound by CPI Group (UK) Ltd, Croydon CRO 4YY

www.pushkinpress.com

For Mum

1.

Caleb was still holding him when the paramedics arrived. Stupid to have called an ambulance – Gary was dead. Had to be dead. Couldn't breathe with his throat slit open like that. The ambos seemed to think so, too. They stopped short of the blood-slicked kitchen tiles, their eyes on Gary's limp form in his arms. A man and a woman, wearing blue uniforms and wary expressions. The woman was talking, but her words slipped past him, too formless to catch.

'It's too late,' he told her.

She stepped back. 'You got a knife there, mate? Something sharp?' Speaking slowly now, each syllable a distinct and well-formed shape.

'No.' The tightness didn't leave her face, so he added, 'I didn't kill him.'

'Anyone else in the house?'

'No, but Gary's kids'll be home from school soon. Don't let them see him.'

She exchanged a glance with her colleague. 'OK, how about you put Gary down now, let us check him out?'

He nodded, but couldn't seem to move. The ambos conferred, then ventured closer. They coaxed his hands loose and laid Gary gently on the floor, their fingers feeling for a pulse that couldn't be there. Blood on their gloves. On him, too – coating his hands and arms, soaking the front of his T-shirt. The material stuck to his chest, still warm. Hands gripped him, urging him up, and he was somehow walking. Out through the living room, past the upended filing cabinet and slashed cushions, the shattered glass. Away from the terrible thing that used to be Gary.

He blinked in the pallid Melbourne sun. The woman's voice hummed faintly, but he gazed past her to the street. It looked the same as always – a row of blank-faced houses; trampolines in the front yard, labradoodles in the back. There was his car, two wheels up on the curb. He'd been finishing a job down the Peninsula when Gaz texted: a great result, back-slapping all round. It had been an hour before he'd read the message, another two in the car, stuck behind every B-double and ageing Volvo. He should have run the red lights. Broken the speed limits. The laws of physics.

Police lights strobed the street as dusk turned to darkness. Caleb sat on the back of the ambulance tray with a blanket around his shoulders and the company of a pale and silent constable who smelled of vomit. His own stomach churned. He couldn't rub the blood from his hands. It was in his pores, under his nails. He scrubbed them against his jeans as he watched strangers troop in and out of Gary's home. They carried clipboards and bags, and wore little cotton booties over their shoes. Across the road, the lights from the news vans illuminated the watching crowd:

neighbours, reporters, kids on bikes. He was too far away to see their expressions, but could feel their excitement. A charge in the air like an approaching storm.

The constable snapped to attention as someone strode down the driveway towards them. It was the big detective, the one who'd searched him and seemed a little disappointed not to find the murder weapon. Around Caleb's age, mid-thirties at most, with short-cropped hair and shoulders that challenged the seams of his suit. Telleco? Temenko? Tedesco.

Tedesco stopped in front of the young policeman. 'Move the reporters back from the tape, Constable. If you feel the urge to up-chuck again, aim it at them rather than the crime scene.' He turned to Caleb. 'A few more questions, Mr Zelic, then I'll get you to make your statement down the station.'

The easy rhythms of a dust-bowl country town in his speech, but his face was half-hidden by shadows. Caleb shifted a few steps to draw him into the light.

Tedesco glanced from him to the nearest streetlight. 'If it's too dark for you we can move closer to the house.'

Metres from Gary's body. The stench of blood and fear. 'Here's fine.'

'I take it you had more than just a business relationship with Senior Constable Marsden.'

'He's a friend.' No. No more present tense for Gary. From now on, only past: I knew a man called Gary Marsden, I loved him like a brother.

Tedesco was watching him: a face hewn from stone, with all the warmth to match. He pulled a notebook from his pocket.

'This urgent call he made, asking you to come, can you remember his exact words?'

'I can show you, it was a text.' His hand went to his pocket, found it empty. Shit. He patted his jeans. 'I've lost my phone. Is it in the house?'

'A text, not a call? Not too urgent, then. Could just be a coincidence he asked you to come.'

'No. Gaz always texted me, everyone does. And he was worried. He always used correct grammar, but this was all over the place. Something like, "Scott after me. Come my house. Urgent. Don't talk anyone. Anyone." All in capitals.'

Tedesco flicked slowly through his notebook, then wrote. Careful letters and punctuation, a firm, clear hand. He'd be able to read that back in court without a stumble. Gaz would have approved.

He kept his pen poised. 'Who's Scott?'

'I don't know.'

'I don't care what dodgy dealings your company's involved in, Mr Zelic. I'm homicide, not fraud, not narcotics. So what are we talking about here? A deal gone wrong? In over your heads with someone?'

'No, there's nothing like that. Trust Works is legit. We do corporate security, fraud investigation, that sort of thing. My partner's an ex-cop – Frankie Reynolds. Ask around, half the force can vouch for her.'

'And Senior Constable Marsden? How does he fit in?'

'He was just helping out on an insurance case, earning a bit of extra cash.'

It had been a flash of fuck-I'm-good inspiration over Friday-night beers with Gaz. A solution to a job that was way too big for them. One that Frankie had tried to talk him out of accepting. Why the hell hadn't he listened to her?

Tedesco was talking again, asking if Gaz had... something. Many problems? No, that couldn't be right.

'Sorry, what?'

'Money problems,' Tedesco said. 'You said he was earning extra cash. Did he have money problems?'

'No, but he's got a young family, money always comes in handy. Look, the case has to be connected. It's a couple of big warehouse robberies. Gaz thought the thieves had an inside contact.'

'Constable Marsden wasn't killed by some dodgy warehouse manager, Mr Zelic. He was executed. Executed – that's a word you don't hear thrown around the outer suburbs too often.'

A happy-looking word: a little smile for the first syllable, a soft pucker for the third.

'Blood all over the walls and ceiling.' Tedesco waited a beat. 'All over you. That's someone sending a message. Who? And what?'

'I don't know. He was just talking to people. Nothing dangerous, nothing... I don't know.'

The detective's eyes pinned him. Grey; the colour of granite, not sky. If the silent stare was an interrogation technique, it was wasted on him: he'd always found silence safer than words.

'Right,' Tedesco finally said. 'Come this way. I'll get someone to take you to the station.'

'Wait. The dog, the kids' dog, I didn't see it. Is it...?'

The detective's words were lost as he turned away, but Caleb caught his expression. A flash of real emotion:

sorrow. Fuck. Poor bloody kids. Tedesco was halfway across the road, striding towards the crowd. Later, deal with it all later. Just hold it the fuck together now. He jogged to catch up and followed Tedesco under the police tape. Cameras turned their black snouts towards him. Lights, thrusting microphones, a blurred roar of sound. He froze.

Tedesco was in front of him, his mouth moving quickly. Something about parachutes? Parasites?

'I don't understand,' Caleb said, then realised he was signing. He tried again in English.

The detective gripped his arm and hauled him towards a patrol car, half pushed him inside. The door slammed shut, but couldn't block the hungry faces.

Caleb closed his eyes and turned off his aids.

Scott. A soft name, just sibilance and air. Who the hell was he? And why had Tedesco taken twenty seconds to flick through a clearly blank notebook when Caleb had mentioned his name?

2.

He showered and dumped his bloodied clothes in the apartment block's rubbish skip, showered again. A glimpse of something Halloween-like in the bathroom mirror: skin white against dark hair, black pits for eyes. What now? Try to sleep? Eat? He wandered into the living room. The pink walls and striped orange furniture jarred, even in the dimness. They were remnants of the previous tenant, along with the purple carpet and lingering scent of incense. Frankie had winced at the colours when she'd first visited, and given him a tin of white paint as a housewarming present. In the eighteen months since, he'd got as far as moving it from the floor to the hall table. Ten litres. Would that be enough to re-paint Gary's kitchen? Have to hose it down first. Scrub the walls and ceiling. The floor.

Something terrible rose inside him, clawing to get out. Move. Move and keep moving. He strode from the room and was halfway to the front door when the strobe lights began to flash: someone ringing the doorbell. It was Frankie. She was wearing her usual jeans and battered leather jacket; her short, grey hair purple-tipped and scarecrow-wild.

'Cal.' She hefted her backpack onto her shoulder and opened her arms. 'Fuck, mate. I'm so sorry.'

He leaned into her bony embrace, blinking against the sudden burning in his eyes.

She squeezed hard, then let go. '...home? I've...hours...'

'What?'

She peered at him, then flipped the light switch. He flinched in the sudden brightness.

'When did you get home?' she said slowly. 'I've been texting you for hours.'

'I've lost my phone. I'll look for it later, I have to go now.' The words caught on his tongue; too fast for his mouth. 'I have to talk to everyone. Somebody has to know who Scott is.' He stepped forward, but Frankie was blocking the doorway, her face oddly blank.

'Cal, it's one a.m.'

'Oh.' He looked at his watch. His hand was shaking.

She draped an arm across his shoulders, tall enough for it not to be too much of a stretch.

'Come on,' she said, and steered him into the living room. 'Sit down. I'll be back in a sec.' She disappeared into the kitchen.

He dropped his head into his hands. Three days ago, he'd sat on this couch and convinced Gaz to help with the case. It was an insurance job – a couple of professional hits on a Coburg warehouse and the theft of two million dollars' worth of cigarettes. Gaz was just doing a few interviews, hunting around for similar cases. Three days. Seventy-two hours. What the fuck could have happened in that time?

'Executed... Blood all over the walls and ceiling.'

A touch on his shoulder. Frankie was standing over him, holding a mug that smelled like cat food.

'Creamed mushroom,' she said, setting it on the coffee table.

He stared at it: Frankie's idea of food preparation was to open a bag of salt and vinegar chips.

'You made soup?'

'Made? Give me a fucking break, it's from a tin. It was either that or Weet-Bix.' She slumped onto the chair opposite and nudged her backpack with her foot. 'I brought Johnny along, too. Figured you wouldn't have anything stronger than beer here.'

A drink would be good. Bad. Terrible for Frankie. She'd been dry for six years, but when they'd first met, back in his early days as an insurance investigator, she'd worn the scent of whisky like perfume.

'Maybe later,' he said.

'Fuck, Cal, I don't know what to say. You found him? Jesus.' She ran a hand through her hair, standing it on end. 'And the phone – how'd you manage to call the cops?'

Clutching Gary's phone. Speaking into the silence, praying someone would hear, someone would come.

'I dialled and talked. The lead detective's a guy called Tedesco. Know him?'

She squinted, then shook her head. 'Must be after my time. What's the story? Are you a suspect? The bastards told me fuck-all.' She looked a little bewildered by her ex-colleagues' lack of love.

'I don't think so. Everyone calmed down a lot when they realised I didn't have a knife.'

'You don't think so? Jesus Cal, why didn't you ask for an interpreter?'

Heat flushed his face. 'Because I didn't need a fucking interpreter.'

'Don't get your dick in a twist. You and I both know you struggle sometimes. Like when you're tired, or distressed, or people are throwing questions at you. I'd be surprised if you got half of what they said.'

'I got everything. Tedesco thinks Gaz was into something dodgy. Us, too. He wouldn't listen to me about the insurance case.'

'The warehouse job? What's that got to do with it?'

'Gaz texted, said someone called Scott was after him.' He swallowed. 'I didn't get it until it was too late.'

'He called me, too.' She looked away. 'I let it go through to voicemail. I was in the middle of... Fuck.'

God, who else had Gaz tried to reach out to?

'What did he say in the message? Anything about the job or Scott?'

'Nothing, just to call back. But Cal, there's no-one called Scott involved in the case.'

'Are you sure? There are a lot of employees at the warehouse. Then there's the security company, the...'

'Mate, I've been so far up those guys' arses I know who needs more fibre in their diet – there's no Scott. And nothing about the job makes me think the thieves are violent.'

'You said a security guard was hurt in the second robbery.'

'Mild concussion, barely had a bump. Almost feels like they went out of their way not to hurt him.' She tapped the arm of her chair, an arrhythmic pattern that involved every finger. 'How was Gary... Was he... Did it feel professional? How'd they get in?'

'Broke in the front door.' No, that wasn't right. Standing on Gary's porch, the winter sun behind him, shining on an undamaged lock. 'God. He opened it. He opened the door to them.'

'Would he have checked before opening it?'

'A cop with young kids? Every time.'

'So it was someone who looked harmless – a charity collector, a delivery guy.'

But he'd taught Gaz how to watch, back when they were kids. How to read people's hands and eyes. How to know when a sideways glance meant he should run, when it meant he should throw the first punch. Could he have got it that wrong? Opened the door to some guy carrying a clipboard and a knife?

He met Frankie's pale eyes. 'It was someone he knew.'

She stayed silent. Sitting very still now, her hands folded in her lap.

'Two people,' he said. 'Maybe three. Gaz knew how to fight, but there was no damage in the hallway. One on either side, one for his legs, straight to the back of the house, away from the neighbours. They killed the dog to shut it up, then wrecked the place. Took a fair while doing it – ripped every cushion, tipped out the drawers, smashed the TV and computer.'

What had come first, the killing or the destruction? Don't think about Gary's sprawled body, his blank eyes, just the room. Books strewn across it; the spray of blood across the pages.

'They wrecked the place, then killed him. I think they made him kneel.' A fist in his hair, the soft skin of his throat exposed. Did he plead? Bargain? A flash of silver and the cold burn of the blade. 'He didn't die straight away. The blood… it sprayed.' He blinked and refocused. Frankie's eyes were wet. 'Why wreck the place?' he said. 'Why risk the time?'

'Looking for something.'

'They wouldn't have had to search – Gaz would have given it to them. The kids were due home. Sharon, too. Nothing would have been more important to him than keeping them safe.'

'Maybe the killers were sending a message.'

'Detective Tedesco agrees with you.'

'Smart man.'

'Not that smart if he thinks Gaz was bent.'

She didn't say anything, but the tapping started up again.

'Just say it,' he said.

'Why did Tedesco jump straight to that?'

'Because he's an idiot.'

'Mate, in thirty years on the force, I never met a stupid homicide cop. Arseholes, sure, but no idiots.' She patted the air. 'Settle down. I'm not saying Gary was bent, just that you should back off and let Tedesco do his job.'

'I can't just… I asked him to do it, Frankie. I dumped him right in the middle of it and I didn't have a fucking clue.' Something squeezed his throat.

'No-one did. Because it's not connected.'

She kept talking, but he let his gaze drift away. Words, more words, but none of them could change the truth.

She smacked his arm. 'Fucking look at me when I'm talking to you. What are you? Three?'

'I don't need a pep talk, Frankie.'

'I'm not giving you a bloody pep talk, I'm setting you straight.' She dropped her gaze to his hands and he realised he was rubbing them on his jeans. He held them still.

'Look,' she said. 'If it'll help set your mind at ease, we can have a poke around tomorrow, ask a few questions. OK? Great. Now eat that soup so I can stop looking at it. The colour of fucking cat sick.'

A layer of grey scum had formed across the soup. He should eat it: not eating was the first sign. Then not sleeping, then not functioning. If you were lucky, it ended with a friend helping you start again in a tiny apartment with pink walls and striped orange furniture.

He forced down a mouthful. 'Thanks.'

'You like it? I've got some stale Weet-Bix for dessert.'

3.

Gary was gripping his shoulders with bloodied hands, shaking him.

'They killed the dog, Cal. Why did you open the door?'

He wrenched awake, his breath coming in panicky gasps. Gary kept shaking him. A flailing moment trapped inside the nightmare before he worked it out: six a.m. and his pillow alarm was vibrating. Christ. He fumbled for the off-switch, then swung his legs out of bed and stumbled into his running clothes; there was no way he was getting back to sleep now.

Into the bathroom for a quick piss and a handful of water. His aids lay like tiny pink snails on the vanity. Expensive enough to put a serious dent in his bank account, small enough to hide under his hair. They changed the silence in his ears into distant sounds; blurred and directionless, like the murmurings of an underwater world. His hand hovered over them. Stupid not to use them: a chance to catch a warning horn or accelerating truck. And every other untranslatable hum and rumble. No, not yet. A long run by the river first. Nothing but footfall and breath, the cold sting of the wind in his face. He turned, almost expecting to see Kat in the doorway, eyes heavy with sleep, but carrying the clear warning to be careful on the roads.

Funny how an absence could carry so much weight.

He found Frankie sprawled on the couch. She'd sent him to bed around two, saying she might as well stay for the 'few fucking hours' sleep' she was going to get. He was pretty sure she was snoring. Her mouth was open, hair matted: an oddly reassuring sight. Starting Trust Works with her five years before had been one of his smarter decisions – there wasn't much in the world Frankie hadn't already faced and survived. Possibly due to her capacity to sleep through anything.

He set her phone to go off at 7.30, added a few five-minute reminders, and bent to put it by her ear. Paused. Something wasn't right. He could smell... He scanned the floor, then dropped to his hands and knees. Under the couch lay a bottle of Johnny Walker Red. He pulled it out: half empty. Fuck. Fuck. Six years on the wagon and she had to choose now to fall off. His fist tightened around the bottle. What now? Leave it out to confront her? Pour it down the sink? Over her head?

He shoved it back under the couch and went for a run.

They were on their way by 8.30, Frankie driving while he skim-read the case notes she'd printed out. At regular, terrifying intervals she attempted to sign with him. She'd picked up a handful of Auslan over the years, most of it profane. And slow. So slow.

'Man good,' she signed as she turned north onto St George's Road. 'Twenty years.' She abandoned the wheel to make the X shape for 'work'.

Probably talking about the security guard they were on their way to interview, but he wasn't about to extend the conversation by asking.

'Hurt. No remember. Sad head.'

Good facial expressions to accompany her signing, a big improvement. Pity it meant she was looking at him instead of the road. His foot pressed against an imaginary brake as they drifted into the path of an oncoming semitrailer.

'We'll both have sad heads if you don't look at the fucking road.'

She nudged the wheel with one hand and used the other to give him the universal 'fuck you' sign. He was definitely driving next time. Except his car was still parked outside Gary's house. It was going to be a while before he could face going back there for it.

'His name...' She wedged the wheel between her elbows and began finger-spelling at a glacial speed. One fist on top of the other – G. A stab at her middle finger – I.

He glanced at the folder: Giannopoulos. They were going to die.

'Arnie Giannopoulos,' he said. 'Sixty years old. Been with City Sentry Security for twenty years. Has mild concussion and can't remember anything about the robbery.' He pointed out the window. 'Thompson Street's the next right.'

Frankie gave the road a cursory glance and turned in front of a speeding delivery van.

When he opened his eyes again, they were pulling up outside a dilapidated Californian bungalow.

'OK if I do the talking?' Frankie asked as they got out of the car.

Code for '*Are you with it enough to follow two people in a conversation?*'

'Sure.'

'Because he took a bit of a shine to me.'

'Shit, really?' That meant he was playing bad cop to her good, a role reversal that never sat well.

He eyed the house as they walked to the door. It needed re-stumping, re-roofing, and some serious attention paid to the weatherboards, but there were new security bars on the windows. Sawdust from the drill holes still specked the window ledges. He nodded towards them as they waited for someone to answer Frankie's knock.

'New locks, too,' she said.

The sun caught her face as she turned. Frankie could usually pass for a cranky sixteen-year-old boy, but every one of her fifty-seven years showed this morning: sagging skin and pink-rimmed eyes, a hollowness to her cheeks. The bottle had been gone by the time he'd returned from his run. Neither of them had mentioned it.

The door opened a few inches and a man peered at them past a security chain. His long face was a mess of yellowing bruises. One ear was swollen and butterfly tape held together the raw edges of a scar that ran from his bloodshot eye to his lip. A deliberate cut, straight and deep.

Caleb glanced at Frankie – that was a lot more damage than the single blow to the head the police report had detailed.

'New,' she mouthed.

'Not the police again,' Arnie said. Going for disgruntled impatience, but he was scanning the street behind them. A lot of twitching and blinking.

Frankie gave him an obvious once-over. 'You're not looking too good there, Arnie. What's happened?'

'Bit of an accident.'

Caleb missed Frankie's reply, but Arnie clutched his tattered blue dressing gown to his throat. 'No,' he said. 'Not here. Come in.' He unchained the door and ushered them inside, locking it securely behind them.

'Police?' Caleb signed to Frankie as they followed the guard down a dark hallway. Former Sergeant Francesca Reynolds just grinned.

Arnie led them into a dimly lit living room and slumped into an armchair. The room smelled of ancient potpourri and unwashed skin. China kittens and puppies crowded the mantelpiece and framed tapestries of farmyard scenes lined the walls. Even the lounge suite continued the theme: cows and horses, a gentle sunrise across green pastures. Either Arnie had once had a wife, or he was struggling with a split personality.

The guard was mid-rant, his arms crossed awkwardly across his chest '... to be... people and... got rights...'

Shit. He'd miss half the conversation in this light. Time to put his bad-cop powers to good use. He crossed the room and stood over Arnie. He held the guard's blinking gaze, bent down and switched on a table lamp. A rosy glow illuminated Arnie's face. Not quite the intimidating wattage he'd envisaged. The kittens on the lampshade didn't help much, either. Avoiding Frankie's eye, he went to lean against the mantelpiece.

'Sorry, Arnie,' Frankie said. 'Do you mind if I sit down? It was a long day yesterday.'

'Oh.' Arnie lowered his arms. 'Sorry, love, of course.

You're in a hard job for a girl, eh, lady.'

Frankie smiled demurely and settled herself next to the guard. 'Not as hard as yours. You look like you've been in the wars since I saw you.'

Her sweet-little-thing act always freaked Caleb out: he kept expecting her head to rotate 360 degrees. He let her work her dark magic while he watched Arnie. Short, choppy sentences, dry lips pecking at his words like a hen's beak. Clear consonants apart from the dropped Gs. An easy read, but why the nerves? Most men settled quickly on the rare occasions Frankie opted for charm, but Arnie looked ready to cry. Be interesting to see how he'd respond to a little snooping. He watched for a few more sentences, then peeled himself from the mantelpiece and wandered from the room. Arnie shifted restlessly in his chair, but made no move to stop him.

Master bedroom first. More cutesy figurines on the dressing table. He picked up a dense-looking shepherd, then wiped a thick layer of dust from his fingers. Not the treasured shrine to a long-gone wife then, just the belongings of a man who couldn't find the energy to change unwanted surroundings. Moving right along – no personal comparisons to be made here. Wardrobe next. No wall safe behind the sour-smelling clothes or scuffed shoes. None behind the tapestry of gambolling lambs. Into the kitchen. An ancient stove and fridge, no microwave. If Arnie was on the take, he was being remarkably disciplined about spending the money.

He moved towards the back door, then stopped. A paler patch shone on the floorboards. An area the size of a man's body had been scrubbed clean. Dark stripes still showed where something had seeped between the planks. This was where Arnie's attackers had caught up with him. A lot of blood for one cut. Maybe Arnie was a bleeder. A cold sweat broke out across his forehead. He took a moment, then shoved his hands in his pockets and strolled back into the living room. Frankie looked at him and frowned.

He took up his place by the mantelpiece and focused on Arnie.

'... last Tuesday,' the guard was saying. 'Just a stupid accident. Had a few drinks down the pub with me mate, Pearose. Can't hold it like I used to. Fell over on the way home. Flat on me face, blood everywhere. Pearose reckons it's lucky I didn't kill meself.'

Pearose? That couldn't be right. He made a mental note to check it with Frankie.

'You went drinking two days after the robbery?' Frankie asked.

'Yeah, couple of drinks with a mate. Nothing wrong with that.'

'While you were concussed?'

Arnie's mouth hung open for a moment 'Mild concussion.' He attempted a smile. 'I've got a thick skull.'

Frankie shook her head. 'Arnie, we know what happened – someone bashed you. You witnessed something during the robbery and someone hurt you to shut you up.'

'No, I...'

'He really hurt you, didn't he? Punched you, kicked you.' She laid her hand on the guard's. 'Used a knife.'

'No.' Arnie clutched the neck of his dressing gown. 'I fell. I fell and, and there was, there was glass.'

Enough.

'One of his mates held you down while he cut you,' Caleb said.

Arnie's eyes locked on his. 'What?'

'In your own home. Where you thought you were safe. What do you think he'll do to you when he finds out that you've informed on him?'

'W-what?'

'Because that's what I'm going to do the minute we leave here – put the word around that you're a dog. Those shiny, new bars on the window won't stop him. Or the expensive new locks. A sledgehammer to the door, down the hallway, and he's in your room. With that knife.'

Arnie's hand twitched towards his cheek. 'I fell over.'

'I've seen what he can do with a blade, Arnie. He killed a cop yesterday, a friend of mine. Slit his throat. Did it nice and slow, so Gaz knew what was happening. So he could watch his blood pump all over the walls and the ceiling. All over his kids' toys.' And he was somehow across the room, leaning over the cowering guard. 'Do you know what that looks like, Arnie? What it fucking smells like?'

A pain in his wrist: Frankie pulling him away. He stepped back, his breath heaving in his chest. Frankie shot him a back-the-fuck-off look, but Arnie was reaching a hand towards him.

'Please, you can't tell him. He'll kill me.'

'Who, Arnie? We can't protect you if you don't tell us.'

The guard shook his head like a cornered animal.

'We won't tell anyone it came from you, Arnie. Not your employers, not the police. No-one.'

Arnie jerked back. 'You're not cops?'

Shit. Amateur fucking mistake.

The guard struggled to his feet. 'Bastards, coming around here. Get out.'

Frankie was speaking, her hands making soothing motions.

'Get out. Get the fuck out.' Spit flecked Arnie's mouth. He flung an arm towards the door and his dressing gown fell open to reveal a pale and hairless chest. A red scar marred his skin, a hand-span wide. He yanked the gown closed, but not before Caleb had made sense of the mark. Bile rose in his throat.

Someone had carved the letter S into Arnie's chest.

4.

He'd made a serious misjudgement with the cafe, taken the flying ducks and formica tables as tongue-in-cheek kitsch when they were obviously original fittings. Probably bought around the same time the coffee machine had last been cleaned. Not happy sitting with his back to half the room, either: a dozen people behind him, including a group of young mums wielding enormous prams. Odds were, at least one of them would scare the crap out of him by creeping up in his blind spot.

Frankie's mouth puckered as she tried her latte. 'Jesus. My choice of cafes next time, country boy.' She nudged it away from her. 'What's your take on Arnie?'

'A follower, not too bright. No obvious new money. If he's working for Scott, he's low on the food chain and very well trained. You almost had him there. Sorry for the fuck-up.'

'Yeah. Remind me to smack you for that later.' She rubbed absently at her breastbone. 'Branded. Fuck.'

'Yeah, that's weird.'

'Weird? It's fucking perverted.'

'Assumed that was a given. I mean the timing's weird. If Scott did it to warn Arnie to keep quiet, why do it two days after the robbery? Why not do it on the night?'

'Maybe Arnie did something afterwards – talked to someone, or tried to blackmail Scott. Huh. Do you think Gary…? I mean, no stupid ideas, right?'

'There are definitely stupid ideas, and that's one of them.'

'Then why kill him? Arnie's obviously in trouble with Scott, but he's still alive.'

Gary as a ten year old, back in Resurrection Bay. Always by his side, even when the local mouth-breathers decided it was bash-the-retard time again. Twig-armed and trembling, but never backing down.

'Because Gaz wouldn't scare off.'

Frankie took another sip of her coffee and grimaced. There was a film of sweat on her forehead. Either her latte was even worse than his long black, or she was feeling the effects of half a bottle of Johnny Walker. They'd never discussed her drinking. Never talked about her battle to get dry, her brief foray into painkillers, her broken marriage. Most of it had happened before his time, but he'd gone into their partnership knowing the stories.

'You OK?' he asked.

'Mate, I'm not the one yelling at witnesses.'

Fair point. 'Did you talk to the other guard? The one from the first burglary?'

'Yeah, he was a last-minute ring-in.' She reached for a paper napkin and began shredding it. 'I checked – there's no way he could have known he'd be at the warehouse that night. And a witness has the truck rolling through the warehouse gates about fifteen minutes after he left.'

A thump. He swallowed a startled 'fuck' and turned around. A harried-looking mother was trying to push her pram past his chair, while clutching a screaming baby. He returned her grimace-like smile and moved his chair. Something to be said for not registering higher frequencies.

'Reliable witness?' he asked Frankie.

'Shift worker getting home. Said he took note of the time because they've been fighting the warehouse about noise. The truck came in at 1.06.'

'So our guys knew how to disable the CCTV and alarm system, knew the guards' schedules, and had keys to the warehouse doors. What are you thinking? An insider at the warehouse or at the security company?'

'Warehouse,' she said. 'The security firm feels solid. It's a small firm called City Sentry, been around for about twenty years. The manager thinks he's better than Jesus, but he runs a tight organisation. The guards don't have the alarm codes or keys to warehouse doors. And...'

'And?'

'And Gary was looking into the warehouse when he was killed.'

A thump. Shit, another pram. Should have been prepared for that; they always travelled in pairs. He checked over his shoulder to make sure the remaining mothers weren't carrying out stealth manoeuvres behind him.

Frankie tapped the table to get his attention. 'You want to move?'

'No.'

'Then stop twitching, I feel like the Gestapo's after us. Any chance we can get our hands on Gary's laptop? It'd cut out a lot of work if we had his notes.'

'The police haven't got it – they kept asking me about it.'

She abandoned her napkin and started in on his. 'Then I guess we'll just have to talk to everyone at the warehouse again. You right to start on that by yourself? I want to chat to a few mates, see if I can find out anything about Scott.'

A lot of new people. Some with moustaches or accents; gum-chewers and smokers. And in a noisy environment, the soft murmur of voices lost as his aids amplified every revving engine and clanging pipe. Probably have to turn them off. Hard to speak without them, even harder to lip-read.

'Sure,' he said.

'Great. Have you found your phone yet?'

'No.'

'Jesus. Can't you do a GPS search or something?'

'I haven't got location services on. Remember that little chat we had about cyber security?' He could probably pinpoint where it was without GPS, anyway: in the back pocket of his jeans, which were currently being bulldozed into the Reservoir tip.

'For fuck's sake. Well, get yourself a pre-paid until you find it. I don't want you wandering around without any means of communication.' She scattered the napkin pieces on the table and poked at them. There was a faint tremble to her hand.

An uncomfortable thought wormed its way into his brain. Was she really going to spend the day talking to old colleagues, or was she planning another drinking session?

'Frankie.'

'Yep?'

'I saw the bottle.'

A slow flush crept up her neck. 'Just a slip. Won't happen again.'

'It hasn't happened in a long time.'

'Exactly.' She glanced at her watch and stood up. 'See you back at the office around six. Actually, why don't you go straight there instead of the warehouse? You could get some paperwork done.'

He stiffened. 'Why?'

'The warehouse is pretty noisy. And it's a lot of new people for you to follow – eighteen including the cleaners.'

'You saying I'm not up to the job?'

'I'm saying your abilities would be of more use elsewhere.'

Abilities. He loosened his jaw. 'Are you unhappy with the standard of my work?'

She buttoned her jacket, took a bit of time on the bottom hole.

'Frankie? Do you have a problem with the quality of my work? With my *abilities*?'

Pink-rimmed eyes met his. 'No, Caleb, you're doing fine.'

He watched her go, a hollowness in his chest. *Doing fine*. He took a swig of cold coffee to rinse the bitter taste from his mouth. Eighteen people. If he got a move on, he could get them all done today. He pushed back his chair, felt it slam into something solid. Another fucking pram.

A tiny woman with two enormous babies. She scowled at him.

'... the hell's wrong with you?'

He was back in the city by five. He paid the taxi driver and stood on the footpath, an iron band squeezing his forehead. Eighteen interviews and all he'd gained was confirmation that warehouses were noisy, and some very specific directions on how he could go fuck himself. There was obviously a bit of pilfering going on at the place, but no-one had struck him as a criminal mastermind and no-one had blinked at the name Scott.

He looked up at the darkened office windows. An hour until he had to meet Frankie. Sixty minutes of silence, maybe a couple of beers. Or, seeing as he'd achieved fuck-all today, he could walk the two blocks to Lonsdale Street and catch City Sentry's manager before he left for the day.

'If your best isn't good enough, try harder.'

His father's voice. The low rumble of it still in his head, even after all these years. One of a handful of auditory memories, along with whole sections of Chopin's Études. Fucking strange, the human brain.

He headed up the hill for Lonsdale Street.

City Sentry's reception area ran to faux-wood panelling and nylon carpet, but a glimpse of the open-plan office beyond showed state-of-the-art computers. The place was empty except for a young receptionist with metallic-red hair and awe-inspiring nails. According to her star-shaped badge, her name was Elle and she was happy to help him.

'Sean?' she said to his request to speak to the manager. 'Yeah, he's still here, hang on.' She phoned through, giving

Caleb a little wave as she caught him watching her nails.

'You like?' She wriggled her fingers, making the embedded crystals glint.

'They're great.'

'A friend of mine did them for free. They'd cost a packet otherwise.'

He edged a hip against the desk. 'Handy friend.'

'I know, right? She's the nail technician at the hairdressers' I did my apprenticeship with.'

'You're a hairdresser?'

'Nah, it was so boring.' An expressive roll of her mascara-caked eyes. 'All I ever did was wash hair and sweep floors, you know?'

'You like it better here?'

'It's a bit quiet, but Sean says I can do some other stuff when I've been here longer.' She tapped a nail against the desk. 'Your accent – can I ask, are you Danish or something?'

It happened when he was tired; all those hours of speech therapy, slipping from his tongue. His brother called it his cotton wool voice.

'Good guess,' he enunciated.

'My boyfriend's mum's from there. She's got more of an accent, but. You must've been here a while.'

'Years.' Since a bout of meningitis as a five-year-old. A very observant young woman, the fluffed and painted Elle. Definitely worth talking to again.

She bestowed a brilliant smile on someone behind him. 'Sean. Caleb Zelic from Trust Works for you.'

Sean Fleming was in his late forties, with a body that had seen some serious time in the gym. His skin glowed orange against the white of his shirt and he'd brushed his hair forward to disguise the beginnings of a receding hairline. He winked at Elle and encased Caleb's hand in a knuckle-bruising grip.

'Caleb, mmmm mmmmm?' A thin stream of sound escaped his rigid lips.

The band around Caleb's head tightened. Shit, a letterbox-mouth.

'Just a few follow-up questions about the Altona warehouse robberies, Sean.'

The manager glanced at Elle and folded his arms across his chest, tucking in his hands to make his biceps bulge. 'Mmmm finished with that?'

A big swinging dick. Step up or step back? A big swinging dick playing up in front of a pretty young audience? Better step back.

He opened his hands, palms outwards. 'Yeah, sorry, we're getting a bit of heat from the bosses. Insurance companies, you know. Don't like parting with their money.'

'Mmm mmmmm, Frankie mmmm.'

His left eye gave a dull throb. 'Sorry, I didn't quite catch that.'

'Frankie Reynolds said mmm mmmm OK.'

Christ. He nodded, scratched his head, and flicked up the volume on his good ear. It wouldn't make Sean's words any clearer, but at least they'd be audible. The manager was looking at his ear, frowning slightly. That was sharp: not many people would have caught the move; even fewer would have spotted the pale plastic through his hair. He braced himself for the usual flustered response, but instead, Sean's shoulders loosened and a faint smirk lifted his mouth. Relieved. Which meant he had something to hide.

Caleb suddenly wasn't tired any more.

'Just a few quick questions, Sean.'

'Right. Sure.'

'Does anyone at City Sentry have the code to the warehouse alarm?'

'No.'

'And the guards only have keys for the perimeter gate?'

Sean's attention wandered to Elle. 'Mmmm mmm.'

Do it. Suck it up and play the game. 'Sorry, I didn't catch that.'

Another knowing grin. 'Yeah, just the keys to the gates.'

'But not to the warehouse?'

'No.' Sean's eyes were on Elle again.

'What can you tell me about Scott?'

The manager's attention shot back to him. 'What?'

'Scott. What can you tell me about him?' Easy smile, open hands.

'I don't know any Scott.'

'Oh sorry, I thought they said...' He pulled out his notebook and found an old shopping list. 'Yeah, here it is – they all said, "Ask Sean Fleming at City Sentry about Scott."'

'Sorry, Caleb, I don't know any Scott.' The manager was finally speaking clearly.

'We believe his gang robbed the warehouse.'

'First I've heard of it. Now if you don't mind, I've got work to do.' He was turning away.

'How many of your clients' properties has Scott hit?'

Sean swivelled back. The condescending smile was

gone. In its place was the same snake-eyed look Caleb used to see on the kids who cornered him in the playground. Boys driven by fear and testosterone and a fierce desire to crush.

'They not working, mate?' He jerked his chin towards Caleb's ear. 'I said, I don't know any Scott.'

Big swinging dick: step back.

Caleb lifted his hands. 'Sure, sure. But a guy like you, you'd be on top of everything, you'd know what's going on in the industry. Have any of your competitors been targeted by his gang?'

Sean stepped in too close. The smell of sweat fought with his musk deodorant. Elle raised a hand to her mouth and gnawed on a thumbnail.

'Still having trouble hearing me?' Sean's voice rose to a painful level. 'HOW ABOUT NOW?'

Step back.

'Just point me in the right direction and I'll get out of your...'

'I. Don't. Know. Any. Scott.' The manager prodded Caleb's chest with each syllable.

He was going to snap off that finger and shove it up Sean's arse.

Step back.

'Do. You. Under. Stand?'

'I understand that you're fucked, Sean. Going by your reaction I'd say he's hit your clients multiple times. And you've let it happen. What'd he do to make you so scared? Call you names? Tease you about your bald patch?'

Sean rocked onto the balls of his feet, fists bunched.

Caleb tensed for the blow. From the corner of his eye,

he saw Elle's mouth move. A single word. Sean's knuckles whitened, then released and he exhaled with deliberate slowness.

'Sorry I couldn't be of more help, Caleb.' He strode to the door and shoved it open. 'Bye now.'

As he left, Caleb caught a glimpse of Elle's fingers lifting in a sparkling wave.

5.

He bought a cheap phone on the way back to the office and tried to program it as he walked. No point in reading the instructions – they were written in a language that looked a lot like English, but clearly wasn't. By the time he'd reached their block he'd managed to text Frankie his new number, a process he wasn't entirely sure he could repeat.

The office was empty and mercifully quiet. He edged around his desk to Frankie's and banged an elbow on a filing cabinet. They'd rented rooms in a soulless tower block in order to attract corporate clients, but the lease was calculated with a complex algorithm, which took into account glass and chrome, but ignored square footage.

He wedged himself behind the biohazard of Frankie's desk and moved a mouldy banana from the mouse-mat so he could bring up her file on City Sentry. Pages of dry and thorough detail about credit ratings, employees and reputation. How could such a slob produce such painstaking work? It was one of the great mysteries of the world. According to her research, Sean had been with City Sentry for twelve years. He'd worked his way up from general dogsbody and survived a recent change of ownership even though a third of the staff were made redundant. So the man was an arsehole, but he was good at his job. Which left two very large questions: what did he know about Scott, and why was he hiding it?

Caleb sat back. What could silence a man like Sean? That fake tan and sad haircut – maybe the threat of humiliation? Financial woes, a gay lover, a bad sex tape. No. Everything about this case was dark. It was in Arnie's trembling hands and Sean's vicious expression. It had seeped between the tiles in Gary's kitchen and into his family's lives. So what darkness had touched Sean?

He brought up the manager's Facebook page: good security settings, but his profile picture showed him with his arms around a child. A boy of around six years, with the same stocky build and straight brown hair as Sean. Caleb fixed on Sean's face. He was smiling at his son, his I'm-too-sexy grin replaced by something open and vulnerable. The nightmare of the security worker: '*Do what I want or I'll hurt the ones you love.*' Eighteen months separated, divorce papers waiting in a drawer, and that particular horror still visited him in his dreams. He closed the page and scrubbed his face: they wouldn't be getting anything more out of Sean.

A weight dragged at him. So tired. He needed Frankie to get here so he could debrief, then go home and crash. He checked his watch: 7.30. She was an hour and a half late, but hadn't bothered to text him to explain why. Fuck it, was he going to have to babysit her now? Make sure she stayed sober, took her vitamins, didn't get hurt? Hurt... Something cold slithered into his heart.

He shot to his feet.

There were lights on inside Frankie's house, but no-one answered his knock. Nothing to freak out about – the door was shut; no damage to the mortice lock. He did a quick tour of the building: a detached red-brick Edwardian Frankie had bought back in the days when houses in Brunswick could be had for a spit and a promise. The peeling windowsills were at his eye height. All closed, blinds down. Slivers of light appeared at the edges, but there were no shadows moving inside. The small courtyard held two dead pot plants and an empty washing line. Security lights flicked on as he approached the back door. Securely locked. He looped back to the front door and gave it another bash. Would it be overstepping the bonds of friendship to use the spare key she'd given him? He didn't care.

A faint tremble to his hand as he opened the door. The air felt cold, un-breathed.

'Frankie, it's me. You OK?'

Bedrooms to each side; jumbled clothing and sheets. Past the bathroom, down the hall. No-one in the study or kitchen, the living room. Haphazard piles of papers and books on every surface, clothing dumped on chairs. But no friend lying dead, no blood pooling on the floor. On the coffee table lay an empty bottle of Johnny Walker and an upended glass. Christ. He'd just put himself through seven hells because Frankie had gone for a fucking grog run.

He lowered himself onto the couch. When he was sure he wasn't going to throw up, he shifted to remove the book he'd been sitting on. Not a book; a photo album. It was open to a page of wedding photos: a much younger Frankie smiling up at him. She was clutching a bouquet and looking unusually elegant in a cream dress and with shoulder-length honey-blonde hair. The grinning boy next to her was just recognisable as her ex-husband. A small cast of people were gathered around them, including a teenage girl with Frankie's blonde hair and crooked smile. A sister. How could Frankie never have mentioned she had a sister? And it was definitely Frankie's fault, because otherwise he'd have to examine why, after working with her for five years, he hadn't known a pretty basic fact about her.

So she'd been drinking while reminiscing over old wedding photos. Maudlin behaviour he was embarrassingly familiar with, but wouldn't have picked for Frankie. What had set her off? And when? Frankie had the cleaning habits of a fourteen-year-old – nothing was put away that could be dumped, nothing washed that could be rested – but the house was looking chaotic even for her. There were at least two weeks' worth of dirty clothes strewn around the room, and more than that in newspapers. Could he have missed the signs of her drinking? Not noticed her bloodshot eyes or booze-laced sweat? No.

But there were other ways to dull pain.

He fought the decision, then went to the bathroom and searched the cupboard, ran his hand along its dusty top. It wasn't the first time he'd checked a bathroom cabinet; he was a real fucking hoot at parties. Nothing in the vanity or shelves, nothing in the bedroom. Where did his brother keep his stash? Living alone, no need to hide things... top of the fridge. The kitchen was disorganised, but relatively clean. No little bottles of pills on the fridge or bench tops. Nothing except a single plate and spoon lying on the draining board. A sudden flush of shame at his snooping. Poor bloody Frankie: trying so hard and still he doubted her. No wonder she'd smacked him down this morning; she must have had dozens of self-righteous pricks casting judgement on her through the years. Some of them probably featured in that photo album of hers. One of them was definitely in this room. Time to go.

And then he saw it. Stark red against the white wall. The bloody imprint of a hand.

6.

Caleb's right leg was jiggling in time with the interview room's flickering light. Strangely airless in here. The grey walls seemed to lean inwards. Tedesco had been gone a long time, more than an hour. Did that mean good news, or bad? A single handprint, no arterial spray, no signs of a struggle. Maybe Frankie had had an accident – coordination affected by a too-liquid diet. She'd be in emergency, getting her hand sewn up. She'd turn up in a couple of hours, bandaged and cranky, and smack him across the head for panicking. Please, God, he couldn't lose her too.

He jumped as the door opened. Detective Tedesco strode in. There was something different about his walk, a stiffness to his shoulders and neck. Coming through the door behind him was a ginger-haired man in his mid-forties. Pale and heavily freckled, with a stocky-legged strut. He'd been at the police station last night, leaning against a wall, separate from the bustle of the place. The younger cops had darted nervous glances at him. A feared senior officer, perhaps. And a fellow watcher: his green eyes had followed Caleb into the interview room, followed him out, hours later.

'Detective Sergeant McFarlane will be joining us,'

Tedesco said, without looking at the newcomer. He edged his chair slightly away as he sat down.

Shit, internal politics. That was going to slow things down.

'Can we get you anything?' McFarlane asked as he settled in his chair. He had oddly plump lips, like an overgrown cherub. 'Water, coffee?'

'No. Have you heard anything about Frankie?'

'You're not too cold?'

'No. Did you call her local police station? She might have gone there.'

'You look cold,' McFarlane said. 'Would you like me to turn the heating up?'

Caleb looked at Tedesco, but was met by blank, grey eyes. No help there; he was going to have to play McFarlane's power game.

'I'm fine.'

'And you can follow me all right? You can understand what I'm saying?'

'Yes.'

'Because I've reviewed the interview tapes from last night and I don't think you quite got everything, did you, Caleb? Don't get me wrong, you did well. Really well. But maybe we should get an interpreter in here now, make sure you can keep up?' His pale eyebrows lifted.

It was just an interview technique, the three Ds: distract, disarm, dismay. He wasn't above using it himself when faced with a difficult interviewee. So focus on the important part: why was McFarlane using it on him?

'I'm fine.'

'Good, good.' McFarlane pulled out a bound notebook,

spent a bit of time finding the right page and smoothing it down. Small hands with neat, square nails. 'Now, what exactly did Senior Constable Marsden tell you about Scott?'

'What about Frankie? Have you looked for her?'

'Let's just concentrate on Scott for the moment, shall we? What did Gary tell you about him?'

'Just what was in the text – that he was after Gary.'

'Come on, Caleb. You don't mind if I call you Caleb, do you? Your mate texts you, says he's scared. You don't just hop in your car and drive halfway across town – you ring him first. So what did he say?' He held his pen poised above the page.

'I can't...' The back of his neck burned. 'Look, I went through this with Detective Tedesco last night.'

'What exactly did you go through?'

The heat travelled up his neck and into his scalp. 'I can't use a phone.'

McFarlane nodded. 'You know, Caleb, my old nanna's as deaf as a post. Sharp though, wants to know what's happening with all the kids. Makes going to a restaurant an interesting experience, I can tell you. We end up yelling all sorts of private information across the table at her. And you know what? She's great on the phone. Just flicks the setting on her hearing aids, and she's right to go.'

'That's nice for her.'

A hairline crack showed in the detective's smile. 'Come on, Caleb, you managed to call emergency services yesterday. You can handle a phone.'

'I can talk, I just can't hear.'

'Senior Constable Marsden received a call from a phone

box five minutes after he texted you. Are you saying that wasn't you?'

'Yes.'

'Bit of a coincidence, don't you think?'

'Not really.'

McFarlane turned down his thick lips like a disappointed father. 'All right, Caleb, let's say it wasn't you. But immediately after he received that call, Constable Marsden made two phone calls to Resurrection Bay. Do you know who he called?'

'No.'

'We're talking about your hometown, Caleb. Come on, take a guess.'

'I don't know – his mum? Why's it relevant, anyway? No-one in the Bay's got anything to do with his death.'

'Relevant.' McFarlane's head bobbed. 'That's good. You speak really well, you know. I can hardly tell you're disabled.'

It would be stupid, very stupid, to punch a cop in a police station.

'Thanks. Your consonants could do with some work.' He turned to Tedesco and caught a brief tightening at the corners of the big man's eyes. Maybe a smile, maybe just a reaction to the flickering light. 'Did you even look for Frankie?'

'Yes.' Tedesco paused as McFarlane's head swivelled towards him. 'No-one matching her description has been found. Alive or dead.'

McFarlane lifted a hand to hide his mouth and spoke.

Tedesco's eyes took on a flat, unfocused quality. 'Sir,' he said, his lips barely moving.

A very subtle game of good cop/bad cop? More likely a real rift. Maybe there was a way to use it to get Tedesco on side.

McFarlane turned his attention back to him. 'Right then, tell me about vinceovac.'

'What?'

'Vinceovac. Tell me about him.'

So a who, not a what. But he still couldn't make sense of the words. Fuck it.

'Can you write the name down?'

McFarlane smoothed the notebook and slowly formed each letter; large printing, as though for a child. He underlined the words and spun the notebook towards him. Vince Kovac. A familiar name, but one he hadn't thought of in years. A tall guy, with white-blond hair and eyelashes so pale they were invisible. His personality was a little invisible, too. No reason for his name to come up in a Melbourne police station.

'Is that who Gary called?' he asked McFarlane.

'What can you tell us about Mr Kovac?'

'Not much. He's a year or two younger than me, a quiet guy. Never really had anything to do with him.'

'When was the last time you spoke to him?'

'I don't know, ten years. Maybe more.'

'And your phone records will confirm that, will they?'

'Yes.'

'And your brother?'

Brother? He must have misread him. 'Who?'

'Your brother, Caleb. Does he know Mr Kovac?'

Both of them were fiercely focused – they'd reached something important.

'I guess. They're about the same age and both went to the local high school. Why do you want to know about Anton?'

McFarlane gave him the flat cop stare. Caleb waited it out by counting his freckles. A lot of sun damage for a man of his age – his Gaelic ancestors hadn't immigrated to the kindest climate. When he reached the man's left ear, McFarlane cracked.

'Senior Constable Marsden was spooked enough to ring his wife and say they needed to take off. He was packing their bags – stuffing little kiddie clothes into suitcases. Soft toys, little love-heart pyjamas. But in the middle of all that, he took the time to have a chat with your brother. A minute and a half, that's a long time when you're shit-scared. Why would he do that?'

'Why don't you ask Ant?'

McFarlane's smile was unconnected to anything else happening on his face. 'Because I'm asking you.'

'They're friends, I guess they talk on the phone.' Except that Anton was friends with Gary in the way he was with everyone: with charm and ease, and no thought at all. He wouldn't be at the top of anyone's list in a crisis.

'Anton. Luka. Zelic.' Each syllable dropped from McFarlane's fleshy lips like a ripe plum. 'Possession, B and E, stolen goods. Cops in Resurrection Bay had a fair bit to say about him. And here's his big brother, best pals with a cop who's been killed in what looks suspiciously like an underworld execution.' The smile reached his eyes this time. 'That doesn't smell too good, Caleb. In fact, from our side of the table, it fucking reeks.'

Caleb's leg started jiggling again. Maybe he should call

a lawyer. Maybe he should have called one a couple of hours ago.

'What are we going to find when we go through Marsden's financial records, do you think?'

'Your financial records?' Tedesco added.

'Drug money?'

'Prostitution...'

'... laundering.'

'Blackmail...'

They bounced the words between them; impossible to follow.

Caleb let his gaze drift to the wall. 'I'd like to speak to a lawyer.'

McFarlane leaned across the table and snapped his fingers in his face. His breath smelled of coffee and peppermint mouthwash.

'Pay attention, Caleb, because a lawyer isn't going to help you now. Do you know what they did to your mate before they killed him? They broke his fingers. Every one of them.'

Caleb stopped breathing. 'What?'

'Then they sliced him open. Eleven separate wounds. I was at the autopsy this afternoon – he was a mess. Laid open like a carcass.'

'Don't. Just, just don't.'

'You'd better hope the same guy hasn't got Frankie Reynolds, because whoever carved him up is very handy with a knife.'

Caleb closed his eyes, but the images were behind his eyelids. His leg jiggled faster.

McFarlane's stubby fingers pressed a business card into

his hand. 'Have a little think about the kind of people you've pissed off, Caleb. Give us a call when you realise just how fucking scared you should be.'

Caleb pushed back his chair and walked out. The floor was unsteady beneath his feet.

7.

He caught a taxi back to his apartment. Somehow managed to pay the driver, drag himself up the three flights of stairs.

'*… sliced him open…*'

The light on the landing flicked off as he reached his door. Slow. Could usually do that with seconds to spare. He switched it back on, but it still took a few attempts to get the key in the lock.

'*Laid open like a carcass.*'

He opened the door and dropped his wallet and keys on the hall table. Stopped. The flat was dark, but the air felt wrong: the scent of stale cigarettes and cheap deodorant.

Someone was there.

He turned to run. Hands grabbed him, dragging him back. An arm crushing his throat. Air. He needed air. Solid muscle behind him, another man in front, light from the landing throwing shadows across his thin, grey face. Mouth moving fast. Yelling. Questions? Orders? Just noise, too dark to read. The arm jerked tighter against his neck. He pulled uselessly at it: blood pounding in his skull. Another squeeze and the pressure eased. He sucked in a breath.

Grey-face spat more words at him.

'Don't. Understand.'

The man raised his arm, a flash of silver in his hand – a knife. Christ. Get a weapon, something sharp. Keys on the hall table. He flung out a hand and scrabbled blindly for them. Fuck, where were they? His fingertips touched something cold and smooth – the paint tin Frankie had given him. Ten litres, that'd do a bit of damage. Stinging pain as Grey-face smacked him. Blood in his mouth. Another blow. Now. He let himself sag towards the table, felt his captor's weight shift. There, the tin's handle. He grasped it and heaved it over his head. Jarring contact. A gush of cigarette breath and his throat was released. He sunk an elbow into the man's groin and threw himself sideways as Grey-face lunged. Fuck, wrong direction, should have run for the door. He sprinted into the living room, towards the bathroom. A razor in there, scissors, a lock on the door.

The light on the landing flicked off.

Empty darkness, the stuff of childhood nightmares. Cold, clutching panic. He stumbled backwards and fell against the edge of the couch. A breeze as Grey-face swiped. Get away, crawl. Behind the couch. His chest was heaving. How loud was his breathing? Could Grey-face hear it? Was he creeping up behind him, following the sound of his gasping? He pressed himself against the floor and held his breath. A dull thud vibrated against his cheek, and another. Footsteps, but where? Moving closer? Further away? Be still, feel it. Another thud, fainter now; must be moving towards the bedroom. Not enough movement for two people; the guy he'd hit must still be down. What was in the room? Paper, chairs, coffee table, books. Table. A glass-topped thing; solid, but light enough for him to lift.

He got to his feet and felt for the light switch. Flicked it. A searing light flooded the room. A man doubled over by the front door, Grey-face running from the bedroom. Get to the table – heavier than he'd remembered. Grey-face was nearly on him. He heaved the table up and flipped it over. Shattering glass, flailing limbs. And Grey-face was down. He sprinted for the door, then skidded to a halt: the guy he'd hit was blocking it, hands clasped to his groin. A broad face, with a flattened nose like a boxer. Blood dripping down his forehead, looking a little groggy. A flick-knife on the floor by his knee. No way he could get past before Boxer reached it. A movement in the corner of his eye; Grey-face was getting to his feet. Fuck. Do something.

The light on the landing flicked on: someone coming up the stairs. Make a noise, scream. Couldn't remember how. He tried again, got something out. A young man holding a six-pack of VB appeared in the doorway. Grey-face stepped back into the bedroom.

VB was looking at Boxer, his mouth moving. Jesus, asking if Boxer was all right.

'Get the police,' Caleb yelled.

The young man's head jerked up. 'What?'

'Police. Get the police.'

VB shuffled backwards, but he was pulling out his phone.

Boxer still hadn't gone for the knife. Maybe he didn't want to commit murder in front of a witness. Maybe he was waiting for Caleb to get closer. Only one way to find out. He sprinted past. Out through the door, down the corridor, banging on doors. He should yell. Not enough breath, just run. Down the stairs, two at a time. Footsteps pounding behind him. Had to be Grey-face, Boxer couldn't be up and running yet. Out onto the street. He needed people, a crowd. He turned the corner into Nicholson Street. Shit, where was everyone? Major thoroughfare – empty.

He ran south, pressing a hand to his side. A stitch, he had a fucking stitch. Unbelievable. A quick backwards glance. No sign of anyone. Down an alleyway. Dead end. Fuck. He slipped behind a bank of rubbish skips. Was Grey-face still following him? Creeping down the alley, knife in hand? Wouldn't feel his footsteps on the concrete. Wouldn't know anything until he appeared in front of him. A slow count to fifty, then he risked a look. No-one. He leaned against the wall and let out his breath. Thank God he'd learned to fight dirty as a kid.

'*Go for the nose and kidneys*,' his father had always said. '*But never the privates. No-one will respect you for that*.'

Something like a laugh in his throat. Or maybe a sob.

That knife. Was it the same one that slit Gary's – no. No good could come from that line of thinking. The pain in his side was getting worse. He pressed his hand to it. Wet. How could it be wet? He lifted his fingers and peered at them in the dim light. Blood. A vision of Gary's mutilated flesh swam before him. All right, get it together. He'd know if the knife had done any major damage. Wouldn't he? Shit. He slowly lifted his top. The cut ran long and deep along his ribs, but his intestines seemed to be tucked safely away where they belonged. He lowered himself to the ground and concentrated on breathing for a while.

Cold now, a misting rain settling on his hair and clothes. He should get up and go to the cops. Another round of questioning, another round of accusations. McFarlane's punchable smile. Go to a hotel, face it all in the morning. Except that his wallet was back at the flat with Grey-face and Boxer. Fucked. Just totally fucked. Where could he go? And the answer, when it finally came, was blindingly obvious: Kat. Kat would help him, no matter how much she hated him.

He was pretty sure.

8.

He caught the 86 tram to Collingwood, his appearance gaining him no extra personal space. Wild hair, crazed eyes, blood-stained clothing – nothing new to the late-night Smith Street tram experience. Kat's house was one of a small row of not-quite dilapidated Victorian maidens on a quiet side street. The tiled veranda lay directly behind a hip-high brick fence, deep and smudged with purple shadows. Why didn't she have a globe in the outdoor light? Anyone could lie in wait behind the fence or the potted palm in the corner. A lurking junkie; a mugger. Worse.

A bell hung by the door. Hand-cast by Kat, no doubt. Solid brass, with what felt like a filigreed pattern around its scalloped edge. A thing of beauty. And nothing any home of his could have. He rang it and pressed his hand to the door. After a moment he felt the thud of footsteps against his palm, the even rhythm of a long, smooth gait.

He waited until they stopped and called, 'Kat, it's Caleb.'

A beat, two, three, four.

The door swung open.

Her hair was longer. She'd gathered it in a loose bun that tumbled dark curls down her neck. Dressed in black jeans and a rust-red jumper, she was a study in tones: her skin a smooth wash of burnt umber, sienna touches to her hair, the unexpected flash of blue eyes. The genes from all her Koori ancestors distilled to a heady perfection.

His mouth was suddenly dry.

She lifted her hand and, for a moment, he thought she was going to sign 'hello', but she jabbed a finger at him, then the ground, followed by a quick brush of her thumb down her chest.

Why was he here? Shit, he hadn't thought this part through.

Her hands flew, but he could have read her words by her expression alone. 'You can't just turn up here without warning. That's seriously not OK. Text next time.'

She was closing the door.

'Kat, please. I need...' He got the words out. 'I need help.'

She halted, then swung the door wider. Light from the hallway shone on him, a bright blade in the darkness.

Her eyes dropped to the red stain on his T-shirt. 'You're bleeding.'

'A couple of guys... they had knives.'

'Knives?' She stepped towards him. 'Cal.'

'I think the people who killed Gary... I think they've got Frankie.'

The shakes were suddenly back, his knees dangerously unstable. He braced himself against the wall. A touch on his shoulder, the warmth of Kat's hand against his cheek. She lifted his face towards hers.

'Ambulance?' she said slowly. Her eyes were wide.

'No. I'm fine. Just a bit wobbly.'

She slipped her hand into his, anchoring him. 'Come in.'

She led him down a hallway of honeyed floorboards

and arched doorways, into a small room that smelled of lavender and linseed oil. It was gently lit by beaded table lamps, and filled with books and jewel-hued rugs. One of her sculptures stood in a corner – a near life-size nude of flowing timber and bronze.

His eyes fell on a sketchbook that lay open on an armchair. 'You're doing trees again.'

She pulled her hand from his. 'Not really.'

She closed the pad and sat, leaving the high-backed couch to him. The burgundy velvet upholstery was new, but it was the couch they'd bought together on Sydney Road. Their first purchase as a couple. It was ridiculously oversized, with deep cushions and clawed wooden feet, but they'd happily lugged it to each of the three homes they'd shared. They'd lazed on it with the weekend newspapers and pots of tea, talked, dozed, read.

Kat's eyes were on him. 'What did you mean, someone's got Frankie?'

'I can't find her.' He told her everything: the case, the unsettling police interview, Boxer, Grey-face. But nothing about Gary's broken fingers, nothing about his butchered body.

'They're not looking for her? Even after Gary?'

'I don't know. Tedesco said they were, but they didn't seem too keen.'

'Do you want me...?' She stopped, unusually hesitant. 'Do you want me to make some calls?'

His kneejerk 'no' came out before he could stop it. He tried again. 'That'd be great, thanks.'

She unearthed a phone book and started with the hospitals.

'Give a description, too,' he said as she began spelling out Frankie's name.

'About five foot eight,' she said. 'Short, grey hair.'

'Purple tips.'

She flapped a hand at him. 'In her late fifties.'

'Fifty-seven.'

She swivelled away.

A restlessness propelled him to his feet. 'She'd been drinking. They might have just put her down as a drunk. Make sure you...'

She uncurled from the chair and padded out.

Fuck.

He prowled the room, picking up books and small wooden carvings. A lot of white-bellied sea eagles, Kat's totem animal. Some she had made, but most were gifts. He picked up a large stone bird with a misshapen head and heavy wings. It scowled back at him. No family member would have given her something so ugly, none of her female friends, either. Which left him with a very uncomfortable thought. He shoved it behind a large candle and kept moving.

Seventeen endless minutes later, Kat reappeared carrying a first-aid kit and a mug.

She set them down so she could sign. 'Nothing. I've called all the hospitals with emergency departments within twenty kilometres of her house. And all police stations. I gave them her description, name and age.'

'Did you...'

'Emphasise that she may not be using her real name? Yes.'

'OK. OK, thanks.' He lowered himself to the couch. No news was probably good news.

Kat passed him the mug. 'Sweet tea, good for shock.'

She knew the right tea for every occasion: Irish Breakfast to start the day; Darjeeling to end it; Earl Grey after languid afternoon sex. The day she'd left, she'd made cup after cup of Oolong. The smell of it still turned his stomach.

'Thanks,' he said. 'And thanks for not hitting me with the phone.'

'I rise to a challenge.' She knelt and opened the first-aid box. 'Let's get this cut cleaned up.'

Dark tendrils of hair brushed the skin of her neck as she leaned forward. She smelled of sawdust and beeswax and that other indefinable scent that was only hers.

He edged away. 'It's fine. It's stopped bleeding.'

'It's me or St Vincent's,' she said, suddenly sounding like the doctor's daughter she was.

While he was still weighing the options, she eased the T-shirt from his side and began poking at him with something, possibly broken glass. He held his breath. Less embarrassing all round if he didn't beg her to stop. When she started in with the sandpaper, he jerked involuntarily. She didn't look up, but her hand briefly touched his; the barest of caresses. Tears started unexpectedly in his eyes.

She deftly bandaged the cut and sat back on her heels. 'You OK?'

His skin was cold where her touch had been. 'I am now you've stopped.'

A small smile flickered and went out. 'You'll have to get a few stitches tomorrow. A tetanus shot, too. But that'll do you for now.' She stood up. 'I've made the spare bed.'

'It's OK, I can…'

'Just come.'

The spare room was warm and smelled like Christmas; the combined aromas from the pine cones stacked in one corner and the river red gum branch propped by the window. Light from a rose-coloured lamp gently illuminated the sketches pinned to the walls. Preliminary works for a project, by the look of them. There were pine trees and wattles, but mainly eucalypts: saplings with spindly limbs and a touch of fire to their new-growth leaves. How would she capture their reddened tips? With metal? Timber? He felt her stiffen as he moved to examine them, so turned away. A crack in the curtain revealed the darkness outside.

'You need a globe in your outside light.' Security spots, a chain, a big slobbering Doberman.

'What?'

'It's not safe, anyone could hide on your front porch. I'll do it for you in the morning.' Change her locks, too. The front one was a piece of crap.

'No.'

'It's all right, it won't take long. I think…'

'I don't care what you think.' Speaking now, not signing.

'I just meant…'

'No. You don't get to have an opinion about my porch, or my house or what I eat for breakfast. Understand?'

He nodded.

She turned her head as she left, but he'd caught the shine of tears in her eyes. The fabric of the universe was wrong. Kat didn't cry often, but when she did, she cried openly. Hers was a family of sharers; her sisters, mother and father all airing emotions with a casual ease that had often left him feeling stunned after family visits.

He turned out the light and lay staring into the darkness; Kat's scent was on the pillow.

9.

Caleb eased himself from the bed and dressed with wincing care. Strange how things always hurt more the next day: cuts, break-ups, sorrows. He found the bathroom, then followed the greasy smell of frying eggs towards the kitchen. His stomach did a slow, rolling loop. Maybe just dry toast for breakfast. He came to a sudden halt in the kitchen doorway. The cabinetry, table, and chairs had the matching blandness of an Ikea catalogue, but every accessible inch of wall was covered in pencil sketches; everything from lone figures to fully worked street scenes. He wondered if Kat was renting and, if so, how much her bond was.

A pot of tea and plate of fried eggs were on the table, but Kat was busy drawing. Hard, jabbing strokes – not a happy pursuit. He ventured closer. A white-bellied sea eagle was forming beneath her hand, swooping on a man with dark hair and eyes. Who knew a bird could look so menacing?

'Morning,' he said.

The pencil flew from her fingers and she spun around. 'God, don't sneak up on me like that.'

Her hair was hanging loose to her shoulders, still damp from the shower. Bare feet, faded jeans, and a light cotton top that brushed her breasts when she moved. She never seemed to feel the cold. Her blouse was patterned with tiny flowers in the red, yellow and black of the Aboriginal flag. Sunshine against the soft dusk of her skin. She'd obviously been busy the past eighteen months: designing fabrics, casting bells, creating new sculptures. Moving on. That was good, that was how it was meant to be.

He bent to pick up her pencil, had to pause for a moment on the way back up.

'Is the cut sore?' There was nothing but polite interest in her expression – the courteous inquiry of a dutiful host.

'It's fine.'

'I've called everyone again. There's still no word on Frankie.'

'Oh.' Shit.

Her face softened. 'That's probably good. The police would know if she was...'

Lying on a slab in the morgue. 'Yeah.'

'Is there anyone else you want me to call?'

'No. I mean, thanks, I'll email the rest.'

Neither of them spoke for a long moment. Kat's eyes slid away and he began to feel uncomfortably like a regretted one-night stand. He pulled out a chair.

She plucked her keys from the table. 'I'm off to the studio. Do you need anything before I go?'

He froze, arse halfway to the seat. That was a surgical cut: quick and muscle-deep. He kept his eyes from her uneaten breakfast as he straightened: lies worked best if everyone pretended to believe them.

'No thanks, I'd better get out to Broadmeadows and tell the cops about last night. Thanks for, ah, thanks for everything.' He turned for the door, patting his pockets. No car keys, no wallet: that was going to make things difficult. Kat's studio was out that way... No, that would be pushing it.

'My wallet's...' He cleared his throat. 'Could I could borrow money for a taxi?'

She looked at the keys in her hand. 'Broadmeadows?'

'Yeah.'

'I can...' She screwed up her face. 'I can drop you on my way if you like.'

Peak hour. It'd take at least thirty minutes to get there. Inches from her in the car. He should say no – clean breaks always heal faster.

'Thanks, that'd be great.'

Kat's ancient Beetle had a top speed of sixty, and an eye-popping mural that covered every inch of duco. It had been painted by someone with a deep love of the female form and very few inhibitions. Drivers slowed as they passed, often gesticulating. Hard not to imagine the sort of pervert she attracted every time she went out in it. He glanced at her. Unlike Frankie, Kat could drive and sign at the same time, probably knit a blanket and julienne vegetables too, but her hands hadn't left the wheel for the past half-hour. Before the second miscarriage, their lives had been filled with silences as soft as an embrace. No speech, no sign, just her hand in his, the rhythm of their breathing. This was the bruised silence that had come after.

She was turning off Pascoe Vale Road. Nearly there.

Ninety seconds if the traffic kept crawling. Say something. Anything.

'How long have you had the Beetle?'

'About a year.'

'Good?'

'Cheap.'

The police station was looming closer: a two-storey monolith of red brick and tinted windows.

'And the, ah, mural, is that what I think it is?'

'If you think that it's an empowering celebration of womanhood, then yes.'

Well, no, he thought it was an orgy. 'Not your work?'

'A friend's.'

A very close friend. A very close male friend? Maybe the same idiot who'd given her that fuck-ugly bird. The traffic began to flow and they were suddenly metres from the police station, pulling into a no-standing zone. Out of time. He was breathless.

She turned to him, but kept her hands on the wheel. 'I hope it works out with Frankie. With everything.'

Her mouth formed such perfect shapes: gently catching the Fs against her lower lip, kissing the Ws. He could watch her all day.

'Maybe email,' she said. 'Let me know?'

'I will.' A deep urge to hug her goodbye. Bad idea. Kiss her cheek? Shake her hand? And now he'd been staring at her too long. 'Take care.' He sketched a wave and got out.

He watched the Beetle edge back into traffic. A wave. A fucking wave. Seven years of marriage, a lifetime of yearning, and he waved goodbye. The car was moving pretty slowly; if he ran he could catch her. He turned for the police station. It was peak hour on the footpath as well as the road. Dark-suited people jostled each other, their elbows jabbing dangerously close to his throbbing side. Maybe he should write to her and apologise. A quick note. *Sorry I'm such an arsehole. All the best with your life.*

A familiar figure up ahead. Walking slowly towards him, head down, texting. Whippet-thin, with pasty, grey skin. His heart slammed against his ribs.

Grey-face.

Don't stop, don't attract attention. He lifted one foot, then the other, swung his arms. What the hell was Grey-face doing here? Had he followed them? He seemed oblivious, his eyes on his phone, no tell-tale glances or hesitations. Five seconds until they passed each other. Too crowded to run. Pedestrian barrier blocking the road. Three seconds. Walk past, hope it was a long text. Hope he wasn't carrying that knife. Two.

Grey-face looked up.

Caleb tensed, shoulders squaring. But the man was turning, looking over his shoulder. Caleb followed his gaze: a uniformed officer was sprinting from the police station towards him, waving a piece of paper. An arrest? The young man came to a halt in front of Grey-face, chest heaving. Caleb closed the last few centimetres, his eyes on the constable. He was holding out the paper, saying something. Saying...

'I'm sorry, Detective Sergeant, I forgot this.'

Detective Sergeant.

Easy movements, steady pace. Detective Sergeant. Don't look back. At the intersection: a crazy choreography of cars turning left and right, impossible to cross. Detective

Sergeant. And there was Kat's Beetle, just beginning to move at the green light. He strolled towards it and climbed in.

Kat turned to him, her eyes a little too bright.

'You should lock your doors,' he said. 'Anyone could get in.'

10.

Back at the house, Kat immediately set about making tea. A more involved process than usual. She fussed with strainers and spoons and plates of toast, and when she'd done all she could to avoid sitting with him, brought it all to the kitchen table.

'Thanks.' He grasped the mug with both hands; it was freezing in the kitchen, but Kat seemed oblivious.

'You're sure it was the same guy?'

'Yep.' No need to explain his bowel-loosening certainty. 'Sorry about the panic. He wouldn't have done anything outside a police station.'

'God, Caleb, the man tried to kill you! I think you're allowed a bit of a reaction. The other guy wasn't there? The boxer?'

'No.'

'Just as well. You think he's a cop, too?'

'He didn't have the look, but what would I know? I would have put Grey-face down as a mortician.' He was shivering now, but Kat had kicked off her shoes. 'Aren't you cold?'

'No.' She slathered butter on a slice of toast. White bread.

'What would your mother say if she saw you eating that junk?'

'I think she'd have more to say about who I was eating it with.'

They'd fallen into their old pattern of mixing sign with speech. He'd forgotten how easy it could be.

'On the bright side,' she said, 'at least Tedesco will believe you didn't have anything to do with Gary's death once you tell him about Grey-face.'

'No. He thinks I'm bent. If I rock up saying some cop tried to kill me, he'll show me the door. Or worse, go straight to Grey-face. They work in the same station, they could be mates.'

'The investigating officer just happens to be friends with a suspect? That'd be a pretty big coincidence. Detectives don't get to choose their cases, they're assigned them.'

'Coincidences happen. Hence the word.'

'Paranoia, too.' She took a bite of her fibre-free bread. 'But OK, maybe you shouldn't go there in person. Want me to ring?'

He was already shaking his head. 'I'll email, I've got his card.' He dug a hand into his jeans and pulled out a business card. Not Tedesco's, McFarlane's.

Detective Sergeant Hamish McFarlane, Ethical Standards.

Ethical Standards. That didn't make sense.

Kat was waving to get his attention. 'What?'

He showed her the card.

'Ethical Standards,' she said. 'Why would a detective from Ethical Standards be involved in a homicide investigation?'

Good question. Why? The information was all there; he just needed to sort it out. Pity his brain had turned to mush. Too little sleep maybe, or too much adrenaline. He pressed the heels of his hands to his eyes: they felt gritty. Think it through. Ethical Standards didn't investigate homicides; he knew that much from Frankie. So why had McFarlane muscled in on Tedesco's interview? Wrong question. Why had McFarlane been there the night Gary died? Leaning against the police station wall; watching, waiting. Long before anyone knew anything about the victim except his name. Oh, shit.

He lowered his hands. 'McFarlane was already investigating Gary.'

'What? Before his death?'

'That's the only reason he would've been there straight after Gaz was killed. And it explains why Tedesco was so quick to start accusing me and Gaz of being crooked – he walked into that house already thinking Gaz was bent.' He thought back to the airless interview room, the questions the detectives had lobbed at him.

'Drug money?'

'Prostitution...'

'... laundering.'

'Blackmail...'

'They were watching him, but they don't know what they're looking for. They were throwing around theories just to see my reaction. Stupid things, like...'

'Like?'

He hesitated. 'They were asking about Anton. Gaz called him that day.'

'You're thinking drugs?'

'Gaz wouldn't. Not drugs. Not anything.'

She held his gaze. 'Do Ethical Standards investigate anything except crooked cops?'

Crooked cops.

A series of previously unconnected thoughts lined up and clicked into place.

'It's not just Grey-face,' he said.

'What?'

'Gaz's connections were one of the reasons I asked him to work for us. He would have talked to his colleagues, asked if they knew anything about the robberies. And Frankie... Frankie spent yesterday talking to all her old mates.'

'Not a coincidence,' she said. 'An organisation.'

'And Gaz knew.'

Of course he knew, otherwise his family would have been under the protection of burly men with guns, and Gaz would have been down the station giving a statement. The ground dropped away beneath him: Kat's car idling outside Broadmeadows police station while he agonised over how to say goodbye. OK, no need to panic. A single car in peak-hour traffic, no reason anyone would have noticed it.

Except for the pornographic mural.

'You have to get out of here,' he said. 'Someone might have seen your car. Jesus, Grey-face might have seen it.'

'So what? It's just a car.'

'Just a car? People were taking photos of it!'

'Yeah, they do that sometimes. But you said Grey-face didn't see you. And no-one followed us from the station. At least, I assume that's why you spent the drive here with your head on backwards? Then relax, it's fine.'

'Just...' He dug his fingers into his aching skull. 'You need to go. Go to the Bay or something and stay with your parents.'

'It's a three-hour drive, I can't just up and leave. I've got a life, I've got work.'

Why could she not see the danger? 'It's too big a risk. You have to go. Just until I work out what's happening.'

She narrowed her eyes. 'I know you've got a problem understanding where your responsibilities begin and end, so let me make it easy for you. I'm not your brother, I'm not your partner, I'm not even your wife, so back the fuck off.'

'Kat. For God's sake.' He stood up. The room pitched and his stomach slid into his throat like leftover kitchen grease.

'Shit. Are you all right?'

He slowly lowered himself to the chair. 'Not really.'

'You're not going to throw up, are you?'

Clammy, sweating. Hold it together. 'Not if I can help it.'

'Because I'm not cleaning it up.' She dumped a mixing bowl unceremoniously in front of him and placed a cool hand on his forehead. 'You're running a temperature. Do you think that cut's infected? How's it feel?'

Infected. Right. That's why it hurt so much. A lifetime ignoring all sickness and this was when it had to backfire.

'God, Cal, you could have said something. Come on, I'll take you to St Vincent's.'

'No. They'll know I'm hurt. They'll be checking the hospitals.'

She was still for a long moment. 'OK. Stay there.'

She left the room and returned a moment later holding something that looked like a laser-gun from a bad sci-fi film.

'What's that?'

'A digital thermometer. Mum gave it to me.'

'Maria? So you're going to stick it up my...'

She pulled out his hearing aid and shoved the thermometer into his ear with unnecessary force.

'Christ, did you get your bedside manner from your mother, too?'

She winced at the readout. 'Right, well that's high enough for me to be worried about septicaemia. Come on, we'll have to risk the hospital.'

Hours in the waiting room, waiting for someone to slip a knife between his ribs. 'No. I'll go to a GP.'

'And they'll send you straight to hospital.'

An idea came to him, as practical as it was unappealing. He said the words before he could change his mind.

'What about Maria?'

'Mum?' Her mouth hung open for a second. 'You want Mum to treat you?'

No, he'd rather take his chances with whatever septicaemia was. A local girl made good, Maria Anderson was respected by all and feared by many. Resurrection Bay's first Koori doctor, Maria was an ER specialist who'd returned home to raise a family and run the local clinic. As a mother-in-law, she'd been briskly accepting of his inability to either hear or be black, but she'd never been shy in pointing out his other shortcomings. Which now included his indefensible failure as her youngest daughter's husband.

'Absolutely,' he said. 'She's an outstanding doctor with excellent credentials.'

'You just want me out of Melbourne.'

'Happy coincidence.'

She sighed. 'Damn it. All right.'

He woke with a start: bones aching, shivering.

Kat touched his arm. 'We're here.'

He squinted against the brightness. They were parked in front of Kat's family home, a long stone and timber building designed by her father. The lush garden that surrounded it was Maria's domain. She'd planted every tree fern and native orchid, made fruit trees grow where the ground was pure clay, and pounded crushed rock into smooth paths. Caleb wondered if she still owned the compactor.

'Is your dad here?'

'No, he's in New Zealand for some conference. None of my sisters are here either, so you'll have to face Mum undefended.'

Losing the moderating influence of Kat's gentle father was a major blow, but the absence of her three sisters probably worked in his favour. He was pretty sure they'd all have a bit of vitriol saved for the man who'd made their baby sister cry.

'You're looking pretty pale, even for a gubba. How are you feeling?'

'Been better.'

'Come on, Mum'll fix you up.'

He opened the door and eased himself upright, but the ground swooped up to meet him. On the gravel path, looking up at the sky. Too bright. Kat was there, kneeling over him. Her eyes were wide.

'Cal. God. Hang on.' She sprinted away.

He screwed his eyes shut. There didn't seem to be enough air. Where had all the air gone? Rhythmic pounding – people running. Fingers pressing against his neck. He brought their owner into focus. Blue eyes, grey-streaked black hair, a look of irritation: Maria. He tried to apologise for lying on her driveway, but couldn't quite get the words out.

'What were you thinking, bringing him here? He should have gone to the ER hours ago.'

'He was all right,' Kat said. 'He wasn't this bad, he really wasn't.'

Maria's mouth tightened. 'All right, Caleb, we're going to sit you up to ease your breathing a little.'

They hauled him up and propped him against the car. Blades of something hot stabbed his side and the sun shifted and dimmed. Hands held him upright.

'... won't be safe in hospital. They've killed people, Mum. They killed Gary.'

Maria didn't move. She was going to leave him here to die. Hopefully, she'd speed it up a bit, hit him on the head with something hard.

'Use a rock,' he said.

She frowned at him. 'Can you stand up, Caleb?'

He gave his head a small shake; regretted it intensely.

'Come on, we can't carry you.'

They pushed and pulled and somehow got him to his feet. Once there, he wanted nothing more than to be lying on the cool ground again. His feet stumbled, only distantly related to his body. Inside. Blessedly darker. And he was lying down, the pain chewing at his side with sharp little teeth. Someone tapped his shoulder, kept tapping. He peeled open his eyes. Maria was talking, something about treatment and hospitals.

'No hospital.'

'Well I'm not risking... or septic shock... so I'll be taking you... or the antibiotics don't work... Do you understand?'

The teeth were gnawing on his bones now.

'Do. You. Understand?'

'Yes.'

Splintering his ribs.

Kat came into view, her hands moving slowly, soothing. 'Did you really understand?'

'Think so.'

Spitting out the shards.

She put an icy hand to his cheek. 'Hang on, she's getting you something for the pain.'

Something wrong with his eyes. Or was it her mouth? Her lips were sliding down her face. Dripping. Oh God, she was hurt. He shot up, heart pumping furiously.

'I'm fine,' she said. 'Lie down.'

'There was blood.'

'There's no blood. I'm fine. Everything's all right.'

Thank God. His eyelids closed.

'Gary, too? He's all right?'

11.

Kat was stirring something on the stove, her hips moving to a driving beat. Probably eighties Aussie rock. A bag of Arborio rice stood open on the bench, along with scattered mushroom ends and garlic skin – looked like it was mushroom risotto today. That was new. As were the soups she'd been making the past few days. Kat could cook: she made a great lasagna and her laksa was perfection in a bowl, but that was it. She'd mastered both recipes in high school and seemed to decide that they, along with a can opener, were enough to get her through life.

She gave a double-fisted salute to celebrate the end of the song, and added salt to the pot.

'You've got to let the eighties die sometime,' he said.

She whipped around. A smile started in her eyes, but died before reaching her mouth. She glanced at his hand.

'So you convinced Mum to take the drip out.'

He flexed his wrist. 'Yeah, free at last. She said I'll be good to go in a couple of days.' Seven to be precise, but that was splitting hairs.

'Great.' Kat's face wore the same polite mask it had that morning in Melbourne. And every time she visited the room where he'd sweated out the past four days. The longer he stayed, the more distant she seemed to become.

He looked at her phone lying on the kitchen table. 'Have you…?'

'Five minutes ago. She hasn't called.'

He'd lost a couple of days, but as soon as he'd been lucid he'd started emailing everyone he could think of: Frankie's neighbours, old work colleagues, ex-husband. No-one had seen or heard from her. No-one seemed to care. He'd even managed to track down the sister he'd seen in Frankie's wedding photo. It had taken Maggie Reynolds two days to craft a three-word reply: *We don't talk*.

'Have you checked your voicemail?' he asked.

'Every half-hour, but I'll know if she rings.'

Maybe she just hadn't read any of his texts. Too busy drinking to bother checking messages. Except that Frankie's bond with her phone was her most stable relationship. She slept with it, took it to restaurants, on holidays.

His pulse kicked up a notch. Of course.

'Her phone,' he said. 'I can track her through her phone. There's a website that does it, for God's sake.'

'You'd need to know her password, wouldn't you?'

He thought of Frankie deciding to upgrade all her passwords one slow Monday afternoon, growing increasingly irate over the different security requirements.

'That's not going to be a problem.' He grabbed Kat's laptop from the table and opened it.

'She told you her passwords?'

'Not told, shouted. And just the Apple one.'

Please let her not have changed it in the intervening six months. He brought up the webpage and typed Ihatefuckingpasswords. She'd also yelled something along the lines of, 'How do you like that, you fucking fucks?' but he had the feeling that had just been an aside.

Incorrect password.

Think it through. Even pissed off, Frankie would have been security conscious. Swap some numerals for letters.

1hatefuck1ngpassw0rds

Incorrect password.

1hatefuck1ngpa$$w0rds.

Incorrect password.

Damn. Had he got the words wrong? Picture Frankie at her desk, her face reddening as she shouted at the computer. Shouted.

1HATEFUCK1NGPA$$W0RDS!

And he was in, the little phone icon flashing happily on the map. Where was it? In the Yarra River? The local pub?

Mary Street, Brunswick.

Frankie's address.

Not too many scenarios where Frankie would willingly leave her phone behind.

'It's only been five days,' Kat said. 'I know that feels like an eternity to you, but it's not long if she's off on a bender. How long's she been back on the grog?'

'She's been dry for six years.'

'You don't have to defend her. Not to me.'

No, of course he didn't. Kat had grown up witnessing the sway alcohol could hold over people. Over whole communities. There was a reason her whole family had a one-drink policy.

'I thought she started the night Gary died. She was holding it together for me, but she was pretty shaken up.' He paused, then told her the whole truth. 'But then I saw her house. It was pretty chaotic, looked like she hadn't picked anything up in weeks. I'm worried she's been drinking for a while and I didn't notice.'

'No, you would have noticed. It's what you do.'

'I don't know; my head's been pretty far up my arse lately.'

A smile tugged the corner of her mouth. 'Most of the time. But you seem to get a pretty good view from up there.' She squeezed his shoulder and went to fill the kettle.

He didn't move, didn't look where her hand had been.

'I've been meaning to ask,' she said. 'Do you still use your old Gmail address?'

'Not really. I don't think Frankie's even got it.'

Still, it was worth checking. He pulled the computer towards him. '*I've been meaning to ask*'. Awkward phrasing for Kat. Awkward posture, too: arms folded, leaning against the sink like that. Uneasy, and maybe a little bit... guilty?

'What's up?' he asked.

'Don't freak out, OK?'

Jesus, what had she done? 'OK.'

'I rang Detective Tedesco a few days ago and told him about Grey-face. He said he'd email when he had news.'

Her words washed over him like cold water. He opened his mouth a few times before he could catch his breath.

'The point – God, Kat, the whole point of you coming down here...'

'Was to prevent you from dying.'

'... was so no-one knew you were involved.' His hands stabbed out the words. 'And. Now. He's. Got. Your. Number.'

'Don't you use that tone with me.'

He took a moment, then crafted his sentences with slow and even movements. 'What if he's bent? What if he's legit but talks to the wrong person?'

'If you'll stop frothing at the mouth for a minute, you'll realise there's nothing to worry about. He doesn't know my name, or my phone number, or anything about me. I rang from a phone booth and pretended I was a relay operator.'

That was brilliant. And totally feasible. Tedesco didn't know he never used the phone relay service. Would rather chew off his own arm than have some stranger speak his words for him.

'It was still a risk. Why didn't you come and talk to me about it? I was five metres away, for God's sake.'

'You were five metres away puking up your guts and hallucinating that the walls were bleeding. Look, if he's bent, he's bent, but if he's straight, he needs to be on your side and hunting for Boxer and Grey-face. This way he's had four extra days to look for them.'

'How can he look for them when he doesn't know what they look like?'

'He does. I emailed some sketches from your Gmail account.'

'What? How did you…' A flash of the nightmare that had twisted through his waking dreams: Boxer and Grey-face at the door, Kat opening it to them. He'd grabbed her arm and refused to let go until she could repeat their descriptions. He had a feeling he'd done it several times. Fuck, fuck.

'This is where you say, "Great idea, Kat. Thank you."' There was a warning fire in her eyes.

'It's not great. It's not smart. It's reckless. I don't want you talking to anyone about any of this.'

'Well, lucky I don't give a flying fuck what you want then, isn't it?' She walked out.

When he'd calmed down enough not to throw the computer against the wall, he opened his old Gmail account. The inbox was filled with the e-version of dust bunnies, but among messages promising him sex with hot single mums was a string of emails from uri.tedesco@police.vic.gov.au.

The messages were as blunt as Tedesco was in real life.

– *Call immediately*.

He hit reply.

– No phone. Have to use email. Have you heard something about Frankie?

He sent the message and stared at the blinking cursor. 'Call immediately': that had to mean news. Maybe Tedesco had found Frankie in a squat with a week's worth of empties. Maybe he'd found her in a shallow grave, dirt filling her mouth and eyes. He hit refresh. When he'd hit it a couple more times, he went outside to do a lap of the house. New-foal wobbly and ridiculously short of breath. How often would Tedesco check his email? He'd used his phone a few times outside Gary's house; not a screen-gazing stroker, but definitely a regular user. It was 1.05 p.m. Odds were, he'd check them over lunch. He sped up the last few metres.

There was an email waiting for him.

– *What took you so long? It's been four days. I need to be able to contact you more reliably than this. Give me a phone number*.

He wiped his palms on his jeans as he sat down.

– This works best. Have you heard anything about Frankie?

– No.

He closed his eyes a moment, then read the rest of the message.

– Detective McFarlane would like you to come in for another interview.

– Why?

– Further questions about Gary's movements the day he died.

Gary, not Senior Constable Marsden. It was the first time Tedesco had called him by his first name. A salesman-like attempt at empathy, or had he known Gary? It felt genuine.

– Did you know Gary?

Tedesco's reply took a full minute to come, but was as short as his previous ones.

– Not well. We were stationed in Nhill together for a few months.

Seven or eight years ago. Tedesco would have been on the fast track to detective even then, Gary happy to just keep his head down and do the job. But two young cops in a town where heavy rain counted as entertainment? They would have been drinking mates at the very least.

– So you know what he was like. You know he never used the patrol car for personal chores. That he paid the caffeine kitty on time, in full every month. That he drove the other cops crazy with his pain in the arse adherence to every law that's ever been written. You know he couldn't have been involved in anything criminal.

There was a brief pause, then a new email.

– We need to meet. When can you get here?

– Not interested in seeing McFarlane again.

– No McFarlane, just me. But it needs to be in person, not online.

– Why?

....

....

....

Had Tedesco gone? He was about to type another message when the reply came.

– I have photos that may match those sketches you sent.

So the big man was taking him seriously. Thank God.

– I'm not in Melbourne. You'll have to email them.

– No. We have to do it in person, or not at all.

Tedesco was definitely loosening up, despite his stick-up-arse language. How to get him fully on side?

– I can't get there until tomorrow. Probably the day after. If you want to wait, fine, but it'll be quicker if you email them. You can trust me not to send them on to anyone. I need you on my side. On Gary's side. I won't fuck that up.

A long wait this time. He stood up and tried some tentative stretches. Very tentative. The email popped up, a new subject line this time: DELETE IMMEDIATELY.

– I'll send them from a different email address. Reply to the same address. Delete them immediately. Reply immediately. Do not in any way copy or forward them. If you do, I'll hunt you down, cut off your balls, and shove them down your throat. Understood?

He smiled: even Tedesco's threats had correct

punctuation. So like Gary. Important to remember he wasn't a friend. Might not even be an ally.

An email appeared from *delete.immediately.you.stubborn.bastard@hotmail.com*. So Tedesco had a sense of humour. That was a surprise. He'd obviously spent the last few days putting together the photo line-up. Ten photos of white men between thirty-five and fifty, clear face shots, some posed, others candid. Five Grey-face look-alikes, five Boxer look-alikes. The fourth photo, a visceral reaction: Grey-face. He went through them all again, lingering over the mouths and eyes. No Boxer, but number four was a definite. He hit reply.

– Number 4 is Grey-face.

– *How sure are you?*

– 100% What's his name?

– *You don't need to know that at the moment.*

– Is it Scott?

– *No.*

– Then he's connected to Scott.

– *There is no evidence that Scott even exists.*

– Then why are you worried about your official email being accessed? Why did you react to his name when I first told you about Gary's text?

– *Rumours aren't fact.*

Bingo.

– You can find the facts. If Grey-face and Scott know each other, there'll be a record of it. Scott will be an informant or a witness, an old arrest. If Grey-face is smart, he'll have tried to hide the connection, but you'll find something somewhere.

He stared at the screen for a long time.

– *Give me your phone number in case I need to contact you quickly. I'll call via the relay service. That worked well last time.*

– Better this way. No third person.

– *You're a stubborn bastard.*

– So you keep telling me.

He shut the computer and let out a long breath. Someone on his side. Probably. Maybe.

He made two mugs of tea and carried them outside. The backyard was a sloping hectare of bushland, which Maria had crafted into a surprisingly whimsical garden. Copses of flowering gums and native grasses edged inviting patches of lawn. Gravel paths meandered through them, leading to hidden courtyards. He wound his way towards Kat's favourite nook and stumbled as he turned the corner. A new sculpture guarded the alcove's entrance: a larger-than-life woman hewn from a single tree trunk. She had a warrior's stance, hair of tangled wire and a ball-retracting glare.

He gave her a wide berth and made his way to where Kat was sitting cross-legged on a wooden bench. Despite the ten-degree temperature, she hadn't noticed that her knitted orange throw had slipped from her shoulders, leaving her arms bare. She was bent over a large sketchbook, drawing long, sweeping lines. Preliminary sketches. Next would come the finer details, different angles, calculations for materials. She looked up as his shadow fell across the paper. Her eyes were opaque, still tuned to her inner world.

She'd been drawing trees again – a bare-limbed skeleton and a flourishing gum with sturdy limbs.

He passed her a mug. 'English Breakfast.'

She gripped it in both hands, shivering. He casually lifted the blanket across her shoulders as he sat down.

'Good tea. Thanks.'

'Peace offering.' He hesitated, reaching for the right words. 'I may have overreacted before.'

'May have?'

'Did overreact. Momentary insanity. Is there anything else you need to tell me? Any more phone calls or emails? Smoke signals? No more frothing at the mouth, I promise, just my usual, laid-back self.'

'It's sweet you think you're laid-back, but no, there's nothing else.'

Sweet. Kittens were sweet. Pygmy horses. Still, he'd take what he could get.

'Anything from Tedesco?' she said.

'Nothing on Frankie, but we had a bit of a chat. He's found Grey-face. Won't tell me the guy's name, but he's loosened up a bit. May even be open to the idea I'm not crooked.' He paused. 'The talk we had over the relay service seemed to help.'

For such an expressive person, she had an excellent poker face. 'You must have had an excellent operator.'

'The best.'

She closed her sketchpad, but instead of leaving, sat back and drank her tea. Her breathing was slow and even, hands relaxed: happy to just sit for a while. It was a good place for it; sheltered from the wind, with the brick walls giving back the warmth of the afternoon sun. For some reason he thought of their old claw-foot couch.

A ray of sunlight caught the top of the wild-woman statue, glinting off her hair.

Kat nodded towards her. 'Did you introduce yourself to Bertha?'

'No, I backed away and tried not to make eye contact. I take it she's from your I-am-woman-hear-me-roar phase?'

She held his gaze. 'No, she's from my all-men-are-bastards phase.'

'Right.' He wondered about its autobiographical tendencies. 'And when was that?'

'I'm not entirely sure it's over.'

He smiled, didn't think, just reached down and took her hand. She stilled. The blanket had dropped again, revealing the soft line of her throat. He used to press his lips against that silken skin. The taste of salt and honey and musk. He needed to touch her. To gather her in his arms and inhale her scent until it filled him. Her eyes held his: ocean-dark and endless. And there was nothing but her warmth, the thrum of blood in his veins, her soft lips, parting. His head dipped towards hers.

She stood up.

He reeled for a moment, untethered. She was pulling her phone from her pocket, looking at the screen.

'Hi Ross.' Smiling. Happy to take the call. Delighted. 'No, I'm not busy.'

She started back towards the house. Didn't look back.

12.

The next afternoon, he ventured into town to do the shopping with Kat. It was the first time since the garden that she'd relaxed enough to spend more than a few minutes alone with him. Something to be said for his slow gait: the usually fifteen-minute walk was going to take at least thirty. His legs felt boneless, a little like the way he'd pulled up after his first marathon. Only this time he was well at the back of the pack. Maybe in the St John's ambulance getting his electrolytes back under control. When they reached the primary school on the outskirts of town, he took the opportunity to lean on the low wire fence and gaze at the kitchen garden that had sprung up near the playground. It was his old school, the one he'd gone to in his hearing days. And for a few months of his non-hearing days.

'Kohlrabi,' he read from the little wooden signs. 'Kale, Jerusalem artichokes. Bit different from our vegemite sandwiches.'

'They make their own chutneys, too,' Kat said. 'Date and fennel. I've got the recipe.'

He'd missed the whole autumn term and returned on a windswept day like this. Walking to school that morning, the world had felt new: the larger hand holding his, the longer stride, the smell of Old Spice instead of his mother's White Linen perfume. His father had never taken him to school before. It wasn't until he was sitting at his desk that he realised how wrong everything was. Hands patted his back without warning. Mouths gaped and flapped, but the words travelled through oceans of water. A sour heat churned in his stomach. Then Miss Peterson was there; her face too close, a smudge of lipstick on her front tooth. Her words floated up high, far out of range. She was shaking her head, frowning. He was meant to do something. Say something. Be something. He sat rigid until the heat forced its way up his throat and a burning rush of puke exploded from his mouth.

His father took him back the next day, and the next, and the next, until one day it was his mother holding his hand, taking him to a different school that would 'suit him better'. Failure still smelt of chalk dust and vomit.

Kat's gaze was on him. Wearing a quilted red coat and orange beanie, she was a welcome flash of colour against the leaden sky.

'Are you sure Mum gave you permission to walk this far?'

He released the fence and began walking. 'She said it was up to me.'

'That really doesn't sound like her. What exactly did she say?'

'"Walk if you want to, but if you keel over I'll stick another catheter in you."'

'OK, that sounds like her.' She stopped as they reached the small supermarket on the edge of the shopping strip. 'I'm going to duck in here. How about you pick up some wine for tonight and meet me back here?'

His ears pricked. 'Maria's going to let me drink?'

'No, but that's not going to stop me. Get something that'll go with goulash.'

Soups, risottos, and now Eastern European stews. 'This cooking thing, is it new?'

She thrust her hands into her coat pockets and gave him an unwavering stare, the wind whipping her hair into crazy ribbons. Stunning was the first word that came to mind. Medusa, the second.

'You complaining about the quality?'

'Restaurant quality,' he said quickly. 'Two-hat quality. Just intrigued.'

'Well, I guess it's because my hands feel empty and my brain feels full.'

He felt a pang. 'I'll get you back to your studio soon.'

'It's probably good for me. Gives me a bit of distance from what I was working on.'

He thought about the sketches she'd been doing yesterday, and those in her house, the saplings with leaves of gold-red.

'The trees? I'd love to see more of them.'

A flash of bleakness, then her face smoothed of all expression. Shit. He'd stumbled into one of the wastelands that edged their conversations. He'd caught glimpses of this one before, and it was a vast and desolate place. He searched for a way out.

'So, ah, red wine for goulash?'

'Sure.' She signed it casually, but her shoulders were hunched as she turned away.

What had he done this time? Was it because he'd

mentioned the trees? The cooking? He waited until she walked through the supermarket doors, but she didn't look back. He headed for the grog shop.

The Bay's main street looped in a lazy curve around the beach, the shops turning their salt-speckled gaze out to sea. Its handful of bluestone buildings and wrought-iron balconies featured in all the local tourist brochures, but distance from Melbourne and a wild surf break put off most visitors. There were three new For Lease signs, and judging by the meagre stock in Angelique's Homewares, there'd be another one by the end of the month. His father's old office had been on the market since he died four years ago.

Best Buy Cellars seemed to be the only business doing a good trade. He wandered through its crowded aisles, picking up bottles and putting them down again. He needed something good, something thoughtful, something that would warm icy wastelands and go well with goulash. Too much to ask from a bottle of wine. Then he saw it. It was a grape variety he'd never heard of, from a country he hadn't realised produced wine, but the label featured a sketch of a bird in full flight. He wiped the dust from it and smiled. Yep, a white-bellied sea eagle.

A familiar figure was coming through the doors as he left. One of Kat's cousins, a dark-skinned man with prison ink and eyes a few shades lighter than Kat's. There was a fat-legged baby wearing a pink headband strapped to his front. Eyes the exact shade of Kat's.

'Mick.'

'Cal, mate, long time.'

They thumped each other's backs and went through a

quick, complex handshake. The baby kicked eagerly at the excitement, but Caleb kept his eyes fixed firmly on Mick.

'Didn't realise you and Pauline had had another one. Congratulations.'

'What can I say? I'm a walking fucken sperm factory.' Mick caressed his daughter's soft curls, the tattooed 'Fuck Cops' clearly visible across his knuckles.

When Caleb had first started dating Kat, Mick had taken it upon himself to 'have a little chat' about the consequences of fucking with her. He'd been so convincing, it had taken Caleb months to realise that behind the man's terrifying exterior lay a heart of gooey marshmallow.

Mick's gaze lowered to the bottle in Caleb's hand, lingered on the label. 'You and Kat back on, then?'

'No.'

'Bit of a dickhead buying that then, aren't ya?'

'Lot of one.'

'Good you know, I guess. Listen, that's a bad bit of sorry business with your mate, Gaz. They caught the bastard that done it, yet?'

'No.'

'Let us know when the funeral is, yeah? He was a decent bloke, 'specially for a cop. Helped young Jai out of a bit of shit last year.' He squinted. 'Speaking of fuckwits.'

Caleb braced himself. 'Anton?'

'Yeah. Not to be snooping, but the kitchen window looks right onto his front door, y'know? He's had a couple of visits from the cops this week.'

'They arrest him?'

'Nah, he didn't answer the door.'

Because he didn't want to? Or because he couldn't?

He was probably fine. He probably wasn't slumped on the bathroom floor with a needle in his arm and blue-tinged lips.

'Have you, ah, seen him around? Since then?'

'Yeah mate, I checked on him. Nothing to worry about. Actually looking pretty good these days.'

His heart settled back in his chest. 'OK. Thanks. Appreciate you looking out for him.'

'Family, mate. He came with you.'

'Guess you can dump us both now Kat and I have split.'

Mick slapped his shoulder 'Can't get rid of us that easy. You're a boong-in-law forever, mate. So, bit of cousinly advice, you might want to check on Kat. One of the O'Briens is out there sniffing around her.'

'Shit, really?'

'Yeah. Would've stopped to thump him one, but you know.' He hooked his thumbs under the baby sling's straps.

'You've got the baby.'

'Oh. Yeah. But mainly 'cause Katy gets a bit huffy when I do things like that. Still hasn't forgiven me for that friendly little chat you and I had way back when. Remember that?'

'Fondly. Thanks, I'd better go.' A thought struck him as he turned away. 'The cops, were they locals?'

'Nah, couple of city blokes.'

'You remember what they looked like?'

Mick gave him an assessing look. 'A big guy and a ranga, both in suits. Just down for the day according to Allie at the service station. Could let you know if they come back.'

A seven-hour round trip. Either Tedesco and McFarlane

were very interested in Gary's phone call to Anton, or there was more going on than they'd told him.

'Thanks, Mick. Owe you a couple.'

'We're even as long as you don't tell Katy I sent you.'

He found Kat outside the supermarket, talking to a slope-shouldered man in his late thirties. Not just an O'Brien, but Brad, the floating turd in the toilet bowl that was his family. All four O'Brien brothers liked to joke about boong-bashing, but Brad was the one who followed through with his fists. The prick shouldn't be on the same planet as Kat, let alone talking to her.

He broke into a shambling jog, but Brad was already backing away, shaking his head at something she'd said. By the time Caleb reached her side, the bastard was halfway across the road, walking with an odd, knock-kneed gait.

'Get off your horse,' she said. 'I can handle the Brad O'Briens of this world.'

'Never doubted it,' he said when he could catch his breath. 'What'd you do to him?'

'Put a wogee bogee on him.'

'What's a wogee bogee?'

'Random sounds that came out of my mouth, but he'll be checking his balls a bit for the next few days. Creep. Every time he sees me, he comes up for a nice little chat. Why does he do that? Hasn't he noticed I'm black?'

For a smart woman, Kat was surprisingly blind to her effect on men.

'Because you're gorgeous, Kat. Of course he wants to talk to you – what man wouldn't?'

Silence stretched between them. Stupid thing to have said. A serious misstep.

'Right,' she finally said. 'So dick trumps racism?'

He exhaled. 'Dick trumps everything. We've been through this, Kat – men are a simple sex, driven by simple needs. Don't overestimate us.'

'Believe me, that's not usually a problem.' She looked at the wine bottle. 'What did you get?'

He presented it with a flourish.

'Sri Lankan? Brave choice.' But she was smiling.

He should ask her to have a coffee with him. Maybe not. Yes, he should. Jesus, like being seventeen again. Back then, it had taken some intensive speech therapy and a serious arse-kicking from Gary before he'd managed to ask her out. Not that this would be a date. Just two adults, having a caffeinated beverage.

'So,' Kat said. 'Do you want to grab a coffee before we head back?'

Joe's Cafe was empty apart from an emaciated waitress who ignored them as they made their way to a table by the lace-curtained window. The blue tablecloths and yellow walls hadn't changed since they came here on their first date. It hadn't been much of a date: fish and chips on the beach and a sudden downpour that had sent them scurrying for cover. They'd squeezed into the last two seats left in the place. Faced with half the town's scrutiny and the full wattage of Kat's smile, he'd broken into a flop sweat and completely lost the ability to talk.

'Remember coming here, that first time?' Kat said. 'I was so nervous.'

'You? Nervous?'

'Are you kidding? I couldn't shut up, just rabbited on and on while you sat there, all cool and calm. And that rain – it made my hair go frizzy.'

Lying in bed, he used to run his hands through those molasses-dark curls. They slipped through his fingers like satin.

'So you didn't notice the sweat?' His forehead felt a bit damp now – probably a lingering effect of the illness.

'Sweat? We were soaking wet – who was going to notice a bit of sweat? The frizz, though, God. All those gubba girls staring daggers at me, wondering why you were going out with a golliwog, when you could have been dating someone with smooth, bottle-blonde locks.'

'I love your hair.'

And there it was – that smile. Sudden and blinding. The rest of the room faded, leaving only the curve of her lips. Warmth rose through his belly into his chest. He touched the tip of her finger.

'Kat, I'm...'

A shadow fell across the table. Timing – the secret to good service. The waitress was around twenty, with a fondness for body piercing that had crossed the line from fashionable into ghoulish. He could see through the metal spacers in her earlobes to the specials board: cake of the day and coffee. Judging by her vacant expression and lack of interest in their signing, she'd taken a couple of downers to get her through her busy day.

'Getchewanything?'

He hadn't looked at a menu yet, but the sooner Morticia left, the better.

'Cake of the day and a long black, thanks.'

Morticia scribbled on her notepad and spoke again. A lot of tongue action between the teeth. Did she have a lisp?

'Sorry, what was that?'

She tapped her pencil. 'Thhhhh, thhhh?'

'Sorry, I didn't quite catch…'

'Thhhh, thhhhh?'

Kat was studying the tablecloth with intense concentration. Heat rose up his face. What was that last word – thream? Stream? Cream? Cream.

'Yeah, some cream, thanks.'

Morticia's heavy eyelids opened properly for the first time, a little startled. He'd probably spoken too loudly. Hard to modulate the volume when he was trying to blink away the perspiration running into his eyes.

'Thhhh?'

'Yes,' he said; whispered.

She shrugged and exchanged a few more fricatives with Kat while he melted into a puddle of sweat and oozed away.

'Spanish,' Kat signed when she'd left.

That explained it; he didn't come across too many Spanish speakers. Kat glanced from the waitress to him.

'What?' he asked.

'Did you really want cream in your long black?'

'Oh.' Fuck. 'I thought… No.'

'You want to catch her before she does it?'

'It's OK.'

'Or I could.'

Why was she pushing it? 'It's fine.'

She picked up a teaspoon and flipped it between her

fingers: fast, slow, fast. Kat didn't fidget. Created, sure – tiny people crafted from aluminium foil, origami birds from paper napkins – but never mindless fidgeting. He waited while she decided whether or not to tell him what was bothering her.

She put the spoon down. 'You know what Brad O'Brien said to me once?'

'What?'

'That I could pass.'

The ferret-faced prick; he'd kill him.

'Not for white,' she said. 'Nothing that good. But he reckoned I could pass for something less offensive than an Abo. Indian maybe, or Pakistani.' She rested her chin on her hand. 'Do you think I should? Might be less embarrassing.'

Acid bit his throat. 'I'm not trying to pass.'

'Every time you open your mouth, you're trying to pass.'

'I live in a hearing world, Kat, what do you want me to do? Make everyone learn sign language? My own parents didn't even do that.'

'No, but why not say something like, "I'm deaf, and I'm doing this amazing thing where I watch your mouth and face and body and come up with actual sentences. Could you help me by speaking a little slower?"'

He refilled his water glass, took a good long time doing it. Kat's hands clenched, then reached for the napkin dispenser – looking away in the middle of a conversation was a pretty good way to get something thrown at him. He looked up.

She smoothed out the napkin she'd balled. 'I'm really asking.'

'Why? It's never bothered you before.'

'It's always bothered me.'

Always. Always bothered her.

'Because what I do, and how I do it, is no-one's business except mine.'

'But it isn't.' She was suddenly eager, leaning forward. 'Don't you see? It's...'

She stilled her hands as Morticia slumped her way towards them. The waitress set his coffee in front of him: a cup of greasy brown liquid, topped with a blob of melting cream.

When she'd gone, Kat continued. 'It's the business of waitresses who don't understand why you're looking so angry, of taxi drivers who don't know why you're not answering them. And, more importantly, it's the business of people who love you. You're putting so much effort into pretending you're normal, you can't be anything like your real self with any of them.'

And all these years he'd thought they couldn't have had a worse date than their first one. Not that this was a date – that was pretty fucking obvious. More like an inquisition. Flayed alive: nothing left except raw, weeping flesh.

She touched his hand. 'I'm not attacking you.'

'I know.'

'No you don't, you're wound so tight you're barely breathing. Which is exactly why I've never... Look, I'm doing this all wrong. I think what you've managed to accomplish...'

'... despite being black. Is that how that sentence ends?'

Her eyes were ice-blue slits. 'It's not the same.'

'Some people regard being black as a disability.'

'Are any of them sitting at this table?'

'No.'

'Then why would I care? I like myself. I'm very happy with who I am.'

'I'm happy with myself, too. It's the rest of the world that has a problem. Including you, apparently.'

She lowered her head, but not before he'd caught her whispered 'fuck'.

'Look,' he said. 'I know you're only...'

'No.' She flashed a manufactured smile. 'I overstepped. So, how's the cake? As inedible as it looks?'

Back to polite Kat. It was impressive, really, just how bad he was at life. He went to speak, but her gaze had shifted to something behind him. Two women were coming through the door. His eyes fixed on the youngest one; she was around thirty, but walking with the stooped exhaustion of someone far older. His stomach lifted, then dropped hard and fast – Gary's wife, Sharon.

13.

Sharon felt brittle in his arms as he hugged her.

'You're staying with Michelle?' he asked.

She nodded. She hadn't replied to any of his emails or texts, but he'd guessed she'd be staying with her older sister. That he hadn't confirmed it was cowardice, pure and simple.

'I'm sorry, I should have come to see you.'

His words seemed to take a while to sink in.

'We've had lots of visitors,' she eventually said.

Michelle gestured to them. 'Come and sit down.' An order, not an invitation.

A moment's awkward dance until Kat stepped in and sorted it out: the two of them facing the two sisters, his back to the light. Sharon sat slumped, her brown hair hanging in limp strands over her eyes, but it was her stillness that shook him. She was the organised dervish at the centre of her family: always cooking, sewing, soothing or berating. He'd never seen her sit so still before.

'How are Nell and Cooper doing?' he asked.

Five and six: too young to understand how their lives had been ripped apart, too old to be oblivious.

'They're… confused.'

'Would it help if I dropped round and saw them?'

'Maybe. I don't know.' She slumped into silence.

He checked in with Kat and Michelle. They were deep in conversation: something about plans and dates.

'... the funeral until they release his body,' Michelle said. 'Longer if she decides on a cremation. Maybe a week or so.'

God. He looked around for the waitress: the sooner they ordered, the sooner this ordeal would be over. She'd disappeared again. Give her sixty seconds, then go and hunt for her. Drag her out if he had to.

Kat nudged his leg and made a subtle 'look' sign towards Michelle.

'... Ethical Standards. You'd think Gary was a criminal instead of the victim. He kept saying they knew about the drugs and the money and we should tell them everything. Smug bastard smiled the whole time.'

Bloody McFarlane. What was he up to?

Michelle was looking at him. 'He was asking about you and your brother. Is it true? About the drugs?'

'You know Gaz would never do something like that.'

'All I know is my sister's husband is dead, and it's because of some dumb-arse thing you got him involved in.' Her lips were thin and hard.

Sharon stirred for the first time. 'Gary wasn't doing anything wrong. I told you. It was Scott.'

His breath caught. 'Scott. You know Scott?'

She blinked slowly at him. 'No, Gary told me about him.'

'When? What did he say?'

'I don't know, Cal. I told the police.' Her eyes drifted away.

'Please Sharon, it's important.' He ignored the skin-stripping stare Michelle was giving him. 'Really important. What did Gary tell you?'

'He said he was in trouble and we had to come down here for a while. He rang me at work. He doesn't usually do that.'

'What exactly did he say? Take it from the beginning. You're sitting at your desk, you pick up the phone and Gary says...'

'He said, "I've got us in a mess, babe. Something bad. Get the kids and meet me in Geelong. We've got to go to the Bay for a while." I argued. I told him we weren't going anywhere in the middle of a school week.'

'But he insisted. What did he say?'

Sharon shook her head. 'I dunno, Cal. I can't remember.'

He put his hand on her cold one. 'Close your eyes. Picture the office. Your desk and computer, the feeling of the phone in your hand. You say you're not going and Gaz says...'

'"Please babe, just listen. The kids aren't safe here. Scott will kill them if he finds out."'

Jesus.

Michelle was saying something, spitting it.

'You're worried, you can hear the panic in his voice, and you say...'

'"Jesus, Gary, what's wrong? Who's Scott?" And he says... he says, "Sorry, sweetheart, don't worry, I'll sort it out, I know who to talk to. But you've got to go to the Bay for a while. Just get the kids and meet me in Geelong. I'll explain everything then. Love you." And he hung up.'

She opened her eyes. Tears slipped down her cheeks. 'I waited and waited, but he never came.'

Michelle stood up. 'That's enough. Come on, Sharon, I'll take you back to the kids.'

He went to speak, but Sharon was already struggling to her feet. He went to her and hugged her hard. She limply accepted his embrace.

'I'm so sorry,' he whispered. 'For everything.'

'You're going to look for Scott?' she asked when he'd released her.

'Yes.'

'Good. I'm glad.' Her face held all the emotion of someone commenting on the weather.

He mouthed 'keep her busy' to Kat and received a rigid nod in reply. Catching Michelle's eye, he moved away.

She followed him without hesitation. 'You proud of that little display?'

'I'm trying to work out what happened. You heard the cops – they're trying to prove Gaz was bent.'

'Yeah? I wonder where they got that idea. I don't know what you and Gary were up to, but you'd better not drag his name through the mud to save your own.'

'I want to have a look around the house, see if the cops missed anything. Have you got a spare key?'

She glanced at her handbag. 'No.'

'I could ask Sharon, but I don't want to hassle her.'

'No, you wouldn't want to do that.'

He stayed silent. After a moment, she pulled a bunch of keys from her handbag and thrust them at him.

'You were a sweet little kid, you know. When did you become such a prick?'

There were multiple tools attached to the key ring: a blue pocketknife, a pen, an LED torch. Gary's keys. Caleb had hung a lot of shit on him about them, Gaz responding in his usual, self-deprecating way.

'Mate, there's not much point having a pen in the zombie apocalypse, if you haven't got a torch to see what you're writing.'

He hadn't mounted much of a defense for the off-brand pocketknife, though, just muttered that it contained 'cool stuff'. Probably something embarrassing, like a laser pointer.

Kat came over to them. 'Sharon wants to go.' She looked from the keys to his face. 'Everything OK?'

He nodded. 'Thanks,' he told Michelle. 'I'll be careful with everything.'

'Careful? Now he's dead you'll be careful? Great. I'll tell the kids, shall I? And Sharon and his mum? I'm sure it'll be a huge comfort to them as they lie awake, thinking about him screaming while some bastard cut him open. Sure it'll be a huge fucking relief.' She slung her bag over her shoulder and strode towards Sharon.

A sharp pain in his hand: Gary's keys biting into his palm. Kat slipped her fingers into his other hand and squeezed tight.

14.

He dragged himself back to the house, Kat still gripping his hand.

'*Scott will kill them if he finds out.*'

No wonder Gary's text had been so panicked: not just his life in danger, but his family's.

'*Scott will kill them if he finds out.*'

If. So Scott hadn't known the full extent of Gary's… knowledge? Evidence? Betrayal? McFarlane seemed to be focusing on the drug theory. Or maybe he was still taking stabs in the dark. Well-aimed stabs, if Anton was involved.

Nearly back at the house, thank God. Couldn't make it much further. Except Kat would leave his side once they got there. He should stop walking. He should hold her in his arms and kiss her.

'You should do it.'

He missed a step. 'What?'

'See Anton. You've been avoiding it since you got here, but you need to know why Gary called him. You need to know if he was involved.'

He waited, knowing there was more.

'And he's your brother and you love him. You need to talk to him.'

He didn't answer. Kat had never understood that

brothers were different from sisters. Brothers could safely leave their relationships unexamined for a very long time. Their whole lives, if they were lucky.

They turned in to the driveway and he caught sight of Maria. She was standing on a step stool in order to reach the upper branches of the fruit tree she was pruning. Dressed in a navy silk shirt and black pants, she looked, as always, entirely out of place and supremely in control.

Her dark brows lowered as they drew near.

'She looks cranky,' he said.

'She does, doesn't she?' Kat agreed easily. 'What have you done?'

He looked at the secateurs Maria was holding, and unthreaded his fingers from Kat's.

'You're not moving well,' Maria said, when he reached her. 'Are you in pain?'

'Oh.' It took him a moment to recalibrate. 'I'm just a bit, you know.'

Standing on the stepladder, her head was only a little higher than his. 'No, Caleb, I don't know, that's why I'm asking.'

Kat's head made a jerking movement. Maybe a dry cough.

'I'm a bit stiff,' he admitted.

'Stiff? You're walking as though your spine's fused. Come inside and I'll check you over.'

Kat returned his pleading look with a bland smile.

In the bedroom, Maria ripped the dressing from his side with more force than he thought necessary.

'I thought I said to take it easy this week?'

'It was just a walk.'

'You've been out of bed for one day, Caleb. Doing your superhuman impersonation is going be even less helpful than usual.' She picked up the digital thermometer. 'Hearing aid.'

He hesitated, then removed it. He felt exposed, taking it out in front of her, but it was better than the alternative, threatened, method of taking his temperature.

'Well that's all right, at least.' She checked his pulse. 'You look tired. Are you still having trouble sleeping?'

Surely she was almost finished; she had gardening to do, a strict schedule of activities to keep.

'I'm fine.'

'You're a long way from being fine, Caleb.' She released his wrist and wrote on the clipboard she kept by the bed. 'Have you put any more thought into getting some counselling? I can recommend some good therapists.'

'I appreciate the thought, but I really am all right, thank you, Maria.' The words felt stiff in his mouth, too formal. He probably sounded like the BBC news presenters his father had listened to. '*And in other news, Caleb is intensely uncomfortable when discussing his psyche with his mother-in-law.*'

'Is this conversation making you uncomfortable?' she asked.

'Deeply.'

A hint of a smile. She took a breath, but released it without speaking. Maria hesitating? This was going to be bad. Cancer. End of Days. Relationship advice.

'Sometimes the truth can hurt people,' she said, then stopped.

Cancer.

'Rip off the bandaid, Maria.'

'Kathryn told me you're looking into Gary's death.'

'Oh. Yeah.'

'You're a very determined person. I'm sure you'll be as focused on the investigation as you are on everything else you do. More so. But you need to remember that you're dealing with other people's lives.'

Her urge for an impromptu consult suddenly made sense.

'Maria, do you know something about Gary's murder?'

'Only what Kathryn's told me. But one of the things about being a GP in a small town is that you know things. You know that the young couple down the road are worried they're going to be evicted and that they're right to be worried. You know that the woman serving you in the supermarket is going to divorce her husband and that he has no idea it's coming. You know all that, but can never speak about it.'

Her words were as clear as always, but her meaning took a little while to sink in. 'So what can you tell me?'

'That the police have spoken to Honey Kovac and are happy she had nothing to do with Gary's death.'

Honey Kovac. Married to Vince Kovac, the man McFarlane had quizzed him about.

'Honey? You mean Vince – the guy Gary called the day he died?'

'Vince travels a lot for work. He was out of the country when Gary called.'

'So what's Honey got to do with it?'

'Nothing. That's what I'm telling you. She's had a hard couple of years, you should respect her privacy.'

He scrubbed his face. 'Let me get this straight. You're telling me that I don't need to speak to Honey Kovac because the police have already interviewed her and established she's not involved in Gary's murder.'

'Exactly. I'm glad you understand.' She gave him a brisk smile and left.

He stared after her. What the hell had that been about? He went over the conversation, but only ended up more confused. Too tired, synapses misfiring. His bones were aching, too. This was what old age must feel like. He sat down on the bed, but resisted the urge to curl up and sleep for a week. Facts first: Gary called Vince, Vince was away, Honey picked up the phone. End of story. Except it clearly wasn't. What did he know about Honey Kovac? Not a lot: bright, sweet, mid-twenties, a kid or two. Koori, so there was a good chance Kat would know more about her. The Bay's Koori community was linked by a complex web of connections he could barely grasp, but which Kat knew intimately. She'd taken pity on him once and drawn a diagram: an enormous swathe of paper filled with multi-coloured lines and arrows. None of the details remained, but her social ordering had stayed with him: family, friend, outsider. Which label would she assign him these days? Focus. Honey Kovac. Ask Kat about her. And if she mentioned the conversation to her mother? Awkward. If by awkward he meant terrifying.

He hauled himself to his feet. Time for a discreet chat with Honey.

Honey Kovac's address was easy to track down, and her house even easier to find: it was diagonally opposite Maria's clinic. Not hard to work out how Maria had known about the police visit. The house was one of the Bay's simple bluestone cottages. The local quarry had built dozens of them for its workers in the late 1890s. Most of them still stood, but the quarry had shut twenty years ago, leaving a hundred people out of work and a raw wound in the earth where nothing would grow. The last time he'd been in town, there'd been talk of making it into a tourist attraction. It seemed like a flawed plan. A little like standing here, in full view of the street, waiting for someone to answer the door.

A tap on his shoulder.

He jumped.

Not Maria; an ancient man with a face like a bleached raisin. A lot of brown clothing, all of it three sizes too big. Name. Name. Heraldson. Hanson. Henderson. Yes, Henderson.

'Hi, Mr Henderson.'

'It's young Caleb, isn't it? I've been yelling away. No wonder you didn't hear me.' Mr Henderson laughed. Or coughed up a lung. He pressed a dubious-looking handkerchief to his mouth and hawked.

Caleb averted his eyes for a moment. 'I was just looking for Honey Kovac. Is she around, do you know?'

'That's what I was yelling about. I said to myself, "My God, he must be deaf or something."' Another bout of chest heaving.

'Honey?' Caleb prompted.

Mr Henderson fished a packet of Benson and Hedges

from his coat pocket and offered the packet. Caleb shook his head.

'Wise man. Very wise.' He paused for another hawk and spit, then lit the cigarette. 'Just saw her. I'm out for my daily constitutional. Your mother-in-law checks to make sure I'm doing it, you know. Terrifying woman.'

Caleb glanced towards the clinic. 'Where did you see Honey?'

'In the playground. She was…'

'Thanks, Mr Henderson.' He fled.

He found Honey in the little park at the end of the street. She had a pram parked by her side and was pushing a young boy on the swings. Her short hair was scraped into a ponytail and she was wearing a long mauve skirt and blue woollen jumper. A bit of a change from the skin-tight jeans and midriff tops she used to wear. The hard couple of years Maria had mentioned were written in the lines around her mouth and eyes, and she was too thin to be the mother of what looked like a nine-month-old baby. She still had the same shy smile, though.

'Honey?' he said as he approached her.

'That's right.' A faint frown. Worried she was being rude in not recognising him.

'I'm Caleb. I think my brother Anton was a couple of years ahead of you at high school.'

The frown smoothed as she darted a quick look at his ear. 'Right. I thought you looked familiar. Hi.'

'Is it OK if I ask you a few questions?'

'Questions? Like a survey?'

'No. It's about the phone call Gary made to you before he died. I know the police have already asked you about it, but would you mind going over it with me?'

The swing she was pushing slowed in its arc. 'Why? It was just a wrong number.'

'A wrong number?'

She glanced towards the pram and draped a blanket across the opening. 'Don't wake up yet, sweetie. Yeah, Gary rang by accident. He misdialled the number.'

'Who was he after?'

'His mum.'

'Oh. Did you talk at all?'

She started rocking the pram. 'Not really, just "Hi, how's the family", that sort of thing. I didn't know him that well, just from work parties and things.'

'Work parties?'

'Yeah, Sharon and I used to work together before they moved to Melbourne.'

'Did he...'

'Look, I have to feed the baby. Once he starts crying like that there's no stopping him.'

'Just a couple more questions.'

'If they're quick.' She unclipped her eldest son from the swing. 'Let's go home for dinner, hey?'

'Did Gary ask to speak to Vince?'

'No. I told you, he was just trying to get onto his mum. OK, seriously, I can't bear it when he cries like that. Sorry, I've got to go.' She swung the pram around.

'One last question – is Vince friends with Anton?'

She shook her head. 'Anton? What's he got to do with it?'

'Just wondering.'

'I don't think Vince... I mean, don't get me wrong, but

I don't think he'd approve of your brother. Sorry, I've gotta go.' She grabbed her oldest son's hand and strode away.

Caleb watched her go. She was walking so quickly the boy had to run to keep up. Just a frazzled mum going home to feed a screaming baby. A baby that had been soundly asleep when she'd pulled the blanket over the pram.

15.

He wrenched himself from sleep, heart pounding, the darkness pressing down – 2.43 a.m. Long, long hours to go before dawn. Images lurked behind his eyelids, ready to pounce: blood-splashed tiles, Gary's blank eyes, Frankie's dirt-covered face. He pulled on his jeans and went to the kitchen. He needed a run. Maybe he could try a short one tomorrow, just a light jog. It was that, or start smacking his head against something solid. He lit the gas under the kettle and scrounged for a teabag. Slumming it. Kat would tell him that only loose-leaf tea held calming properties, but he was probably beyond its powers at the moment. His brain kept looping back to Gary's last hours. Panicking, packing his bags, and he stopped to make two phone calls: one to the Kovacs, one to Anton. The Kovacs might have been a mistake, but calling Anton didn't make sense. Not entirely true – there was one scenario in which it made perfect sense. And he was going to have to face up to that sooner or later. Later.

The overhead light flicked off and on. Kat was in the doorway, hair cascading to her shoulders in wild curls. She was wearing a long T-shirt decorated with a cartoon of an incredibly ugly cow, and, by the looks of it, nothing else. He remembered to breathe. She went to the stove and turned off the steaming kettle. It had probably been whistling madly for a while; an out-of-range pitch, even when he had his aids in.

'Shit, sorry.'

'We've really got to get you sleeping better,' she said.

With her tousled hair and long, bare legs she looked as though she'd stepped from the pages of a travel brochure. Somewhere warm and volcanic, with the promise of sultry afternoons and exotic fruit. The air felt a little tropical now; thick and perfumed. Probably humidity from the over-boiled kettle. She yawned and her breasts swelled against the T-shirt. Focus on the blue cow. No, bad idea. He lifted his gaze to her face.

'Sorry. Have I been disturbing you?'

She gave him a heavy-lidded look that raked the coals in his blood. 'Yes, you have.'

Was that what he thought it was? No, just hormones running his brain.

'Tea?' she asked.

'I'll get it.'

They moved at the same time and he brushed against her sleep-warm skin. He breathed in her familiar, heady scent; it travelled through him, nestling low and tight in his groin. She paused. A heartbeat, two, three, then she reached up for the mugs. His heart stopped. Definitely not wearing anything under the T-shirt. Look away. Look at the floor, or the wall. Don't look at her lean, brown legs. Don't remember how they felt wrapped around him. Or the smoothness of her skin, the soft weight of her breasts.

She turned and caught the direction of his gaze. She was going to rip off his head. Or some other part of his anatomy.

She passed him his tea. 'Exercise usually helps you sleep.'

Good, a safe subject. Boring. Impersonal. 'I might try for a run tomorrow.'

Her lips formed a soft pucker as she blew across the surface of her tea. His jeans got a little tighter.

'I meant tonight,' she said.

A night-time walk to the beach with Kat. The moonlight skimming her body...

'I'll just...' He put the mug down. 'I think I'll go back to bed.'

She placed her cup on the bench and closed the distance between them.

'Good idea.' And she draped her hands around his neck and kissed him.

The taste of tea and something wild and sweet. A fierce need stoked inside.

He pulled away. 'We shouldn't...'

'Stop talking.'

'I'm...'

'Can't usually get you to talk. Now I can't get you to shut up.'

She kissed him again and all of his words, and most of his blood, left his brain. He pulled her to him. Soft skin, heat, salt. A distant voice told him they'd better move now, because pretty soon he wasn't going to be able to. He grasped her to him and managed to direct them into the bedroom without once releasing her.

'Well that shut you up.'

His body was made of a warm jelly-like substance, not a muscle or bone in it.

'Is that a common thing for you these days? Using your sexual wiles to get your way?'

'Mmmm. Gets me great service in shops.'

'I can imagine.'

She smiled sleepily. 'I'll give you a demonstration tomorrow.'

She curled against him, resting her head on his shoulder. Within seconds, her breathing slowed and her heartbeat settled. He pressed his lips to her forehead as heat gathered in his eyes and slipped down his cheeks. Home.

16.

The next morning, they returned to Kat's bedroom for an encore performance. Performances. A definite improvement in his stamina. He made a mental note to include sex in his cross-training.

'Excellent,' Kat announced. 'Just the way to start the day.' She was lying with her legs kicked up behind her, tracing a lazy pattern on his chest with one finger.

Excellent, yes. It was amazing the way sex with someone you loved could put an entirely different slant on life. Joy to the world and goodwill to all men. He propped the pillow beneath his head to gaze at her. The morning sun lay gently on her face, lighting the planes of her cheekbones and threading amber through her hair.

'God, you're beautiful.'

She flashed him a smile. 'Indeed I am. And what else?'

'Modest.'

She twisted his nipple.

'Funny,' he said. 'Smart, talented.'

'And?'

Loved.

'Insatiable.'

Her chuckle vibrated through him, had him reconsidering his energy levels.

'Is it serious with that guy?' The words were out before he realised he'd signed them. No. Bad move.

'What guy?'

'The guy on the phone the other day. In the garden. Just a yes or no answer, no need for details.'

'Oh, that guy. You want to know his name?'

He wanted to know where he lived. 'Sure.'

She held a crooked finger to her palm – R. Then an O and an S. He'd been right, the bastard's name was Ross. Then she tapped her index finger – E. Rose.

A sudden easing of pain, like a vice had been loosened.

Spoken names should be banned. Rose looked like Ross, Matt looked like Pat, Ian looked like nothing at all. Everyone should have a sign name. It was easy to remember his own CZ, or work out who Black Hair was, or find the guy called Scar Face. And then there were names so right you wanted to sign them just to feel their perfection. Names like Kat's. Her face had lit up when he'd told her the name his Deaf friends had given her.

'Do it again,' she'd said. So he had. Two soft strokes to mime cat's whiskers: the sign for panther. Every time he'd done it, her smile had grown.

She was smiling now. 'What are you smirking about?'

'You.'

'Good. So, your brother…' She pressed a finger to the furrow between his eyebrows. 'If the wind changes, you'll be stuck like that. Anyway, Anton – love him to death, but he's not exactly reliable.'

'Your point?'

'Gary was a smart guy. Let's imagine for a moment he was leading a mysterious double life as a crook – why would he choose to work with someone as flighty as Anton?'

He wouldn't. Of course he wouldn't. Anton would be the last person Gary would work with.

'He wouldn't,' he said. 'Then why call him?'

'Crazy idea, but you could always try asking Anton.'

Put the puzzle of the Kovacs to one side and think about who Gary called that day: family, him and Frankie. He's scared, needs to tell someone about Scott, but he'll be on the road soon. Or dead. Frankie misses his call, Caleb can't speak on the phone. But Anton can. He's the perfect messenger: close enough to trust, far enough away to be safe.

And stoned enough to have forgotten to pass on the damn message.

A weight lifted from his chest. A message, not some dodgy scheme.

He sat up and kissed Kat. 'You're a genius. I'm going to see Ant.' He began pulling on clothes.

'Then do you want to run away somewhere? Somewhere warm.'

'Not Melbourne, then?'

'Western Australia,' she said. 'Or Queensland. I've got a new bikini I'd like to try out.'

He paused with his T-shirt half on: Kat in a bikini against white sand. 'Either. Both.'

'If we leave now, we could catch an evening flight.'

We: such a beautiful word. It lifted from her lips like a blessing.

'I can't,' he said.

She pulled her laptop from the bedside table. 'I'm

thinking the Whitsundays. One of the little islands. Just the two of us.'

No people, no death, no knives, just Kat by his side, always within reach.

'I can't.'

Her fingers flew across the keyboard. 'There's a flight leaving at nine tonight. Looks like there are seats available.'

'Kat.' He put a hand over hers to stop her frantic typing. 'I can't leave. Not until I've found Frankie.'

'The police are looking for her, Caleb. What can you do that they can't?'

'Care.'

'Caring isn't going to find her; it's just going to get you killed. And you won't even know why.'

'I'm not going to get…'

'Don't,' she said. 'Don't you dare promise that.'

Which left nothing but empty words. He knelt on the bed and pulled her to him. There was no softness now, just rigid muscle.

He coaxed the Beetle the few kilometres to his old family home and pulled up in a cloud of black smoke. The house looked as though it was holding up well under Anton's benign neglect. The eaves needed painting, and four years' worth of weeds strangled the lawn, but there was no obvious damage to the place. It was a two-storey box with far too many rooms for a family of four. Ivan Zelic had laid most of those bricks himself, commandeering his sons to help every weekend and after school. Caleb had dreamed of climbing ladders for months. Up and down, up and down, painting and repainting every inch Ivan hadn't deemed perfect.

'*If your best isn't good enough, try harder.*'

As he climbed from the car, the next-door neighbour's front door opened and Mrs Naylor shuffled out; five foot nothing, with sparse white hair. Too late to pretend he hadn't seen her. Too weak to make a run for it.

'Young Caleb. My goodness, it's been the longest time. I said, IT'S BEEN A LONG TIME.'

He crossed to her front gate. She'd shrunk since he'd last seen her, but her garden was the same unyielding square of lawn it had always been. In its centre lay the concrete pond he and Anton had used to dare each other to piss in. Points awarded for duration and aim.

'How are you, Mrs Naylor?'

'Oh well, I can't complain. I said, I CAN'T COMPLAIN.'

Her yelling was accompanied by the exaggerated mouthing she'd always used with him. It was a study in perpetual motion; the worse she spoke, the less he understood, the worse she spoke, the less he understood. As a child, he'd gone to a lot of effort to avoid her. Except when playing Anton's translation game.

'*Tell her she looks like a gorilla*,' he'd sign to Anton. '*And farts like a cow*.'

'*Mrs Naylor, Caleb says you look beautiful today*.'

Points awarded for duration and outrageousness.

'. . . and the tablets, but she's got it worse. I said, SHE'S GOT IT WORSE.'

'That doesn't sound too good.'

'Mavis Harrington said she saw you in town with

Kathryn yesterday. Are the two of you back together again? I said, ARE YOU AND KATHRYN BACK TOGETHER?'

'No.'

'That's a shame. I said, THAT'S A SHAME. I hate to see you young ones give up on marriage so easily. My Harold and I were together forty years. FORTY YEARS. But I suppose a mixed marriage has its own troubles. I said, IT MUST BE DIFFICULT.'

Hard to argue with that. Living with him had definitely been hard on Kat. A whole new language to learn, no concerts or large groups, no uncaptioned movies, no... Maybe he should stop before he drowned himself in the piss-filled pond.

'... maybe it's for the best. After all, your children would have been half-castes and that never works out well.'

'What?'

'I said, IT NEVER WORKS OUT WELL FOR THE CHILDR–'

Fuck that. He walked away, leaving her mid-screech.

The front door opened before he reached it and Anton peered out through his long, brown hair. Normal pupils, shaved, clean. A little weight on his skeletal frame.

The knot in his stomach loosened. 'Hi, Ant.'

'Cal. Fuck me. Well, that explains all the yelling.' He waved over Caleb's shoulder. 'Hi, Mrs Naylor. Cal says you're looking quite lovely. Oh, she's gone. You in town long? You want to stay here? Hey, cool car. You in the porn business now?'

He weeded out the real question and answered it. 'I'm not staying, I just need to ask you something.'

'You? Ask me?' Anton's face went through a parody of

emotions: shock, surprise, humility. 'And so the student becomes the master.' He bowed and swung the door wider; always the clown, even when he was rotting inside.

Caleb paused on the threshold. Under the recent smell of cigarettes lay hints of other things: furniture polish and eucalyptus oil, lavender and White Linen perfume. The house still exhaling the aromas of long-gone family life. He followed Anton down the wide hallway, their footsteps reverberating dully on the terracotta tiles. Empty room to each side, a fine layer of undisturbed dust. It couldn't be good for Ant, rattling around this mausoleum on his own.

'You ever think about getting some boarders in?'

Anton stopped in front of him. 'You want some rent? I'm doing OK, I can give you some now – I've got a job down the bottling factory.'

The bottling factory. An IQ double Caleb's and he was working in a fucking factory.

'No. I was just wondering.'

The living room was a lot cleaner than when he'd last been here three years ago. And a lot emptier. The dining table was gone, the grandfather clock. Looked like all of their school awards were still in the trophy cabinet, though. Probably not worth enough to bother selling. A little ironic considering the blood he'd sweated over them. The piano was there too; squat and warm, its keys yellowed by age. Not that it meant anything to him, but it was good that Ant was still playing. Did a house soak up music the way it did scents? All those Chopin Études their mother used to play. He ran a hand along the wall as he passed, but felt nothing.

Anton led him to the small sunroom at the back of the house. It looked as though he spent most of his time in here. There was a small pine bookshelf and MDF coffee table, a couple of brown beanbags that looked like dead sea lions. Thrift-shop decor. But clean. No syringes or burnt spoons, no twisted joint ends floating in half-drunk cups of coffee. He wasn't about to crack out the bubbly, though: they'd been here before.

'Take a load off,' Ant said, folding himself into a beanbag.

Caleb tried to copy his easy descent, but ended up looking at the ceiling with his knees around his ears.

Anton smirked. 'And it's a 3.2 from the Russian judge.'

Still speaking, not signing. Growing up, he'd only used his voice with Caleb when their father was in the room.

'*Silly monkey business, speak properly.*'

'I'm really sorry about Gaz,' Anton said. 'I was going to write, but an email seemed so impersonal, then I thought maybe a letter, but that seemed too formal. Anyway, I'm sorry.'

'Yeah. It's Gary I want to talk to you about. I'm trying to work out why he was killed. The cops are saying he was bent.'

'Gaz? No way. Straight down the line. It always surprised me that he became a cop, you know? I never could imagine him squaring it up with the big boys. I used to think you might, though, particularly after you scared off Jasper Halloway for me. And Ben Jardin. Steve O'Brien.'

He was used to Anton's narrative meanderings, but this was a new road to wander down. 'Me a cop? You didn't think there might be a problem there?'

'Well, this was back when I thought you had superpowers.'

He'd forgotten about the superhero phase. Anton had been four, heavily into comic books, and convinced that because Caleb went to a special school, he must have special powers. It was possible Caleb hadn't discouraged the idea.

'I was hoping you'd teach me how to fly,' Anton said. 'But I was OK with you being a cop, too. I figured you'd let me use your gun.'

'Yeah, that definitely would've happened. Listen, when Gary called you last week, did he give you a message to pass on to me?'

'Gaz?' Anton looked around the room as though expecting him to appear. 'Call me?'

'Ant, seriously, this is important. What did he say?'

'He didn't call me.'

The weight that had lifted settled again, heavier than ever. 'The cops have got his phone records, Ant. He rang you a couple of hours before he was killed. You talked for over a minute.'

'Oh.' Nothing but open puzzlement on his face. But Anton was an expert at bewildered innocence: he hadn't touched the money, the pills were just headache tablets, he was minding the grass for a friend.

'Were the two of you doing something together? Selling something?'

'Is this about the furniture? Sorry, I know I should have asked first, but I didn't think you'd mind. Well, not too much, anyway. And it was a couple of years ago now. I tried to buy the clock back, but the shop'd already sold it.'

'No, Ant, I'm asking if you were dealing drugs with him.'

'Dealing? With Gaz?' Anton's face creased in a doubtful smile. 'Is this a joke?'

'Just tell me straight, were you dealing drugs with Gary?'

'No. Of course not. I don't deal.'

'You went to jail for dealing, Anton.'

'Jesus, Cal, that was eight years ago, I was nineteen. And it was knocked down to possession.'

He didn't reply.

'I'm clean. I've been clean for fourteen months. Don't look like that, Cally, I am.' He hunched forward in the beanbag. 'I've been going to those meetings, the ones I emailed you about. I'm over the hard part, I wouldn't stuff that up by dealing.'

'The cops think you're up to something.'

'Oh shit, really? Fuck. They came round a few days ago, but I just sort of... ignored them.'

'Why?'

'Why do you think? Because they never stop hassling me. Every time someone knocks over a house or sells a bag of weed they're around here. But shit, they really think I'm involved in Gaz's death?' Anton's hands kneaded his thighs. 'I can't go back inside, Cal.'

He had a flash of the emaciated, twitchy wreck his brother had been after his six-month sentence.

'It won't come to that. Just tell them what you've told me. Outside, though, don't let them in the house. If they want you to go to the station, call Dad's old lawyer. Don't say anything until he gets there. Anything. Don't even ask for a glass of water. Understand?'

'Keep my mouth shut.' The kneading continued. 'But

you believe me, right, Cal? I mean, even if you think I'm a piece of shit, you know Gaz wasn't.'

'I don't think you're a piece of shit, Ant. Just a dickhead.'

Anton smiled, but without much conviction. 'Fair enough.'

'Listen, Gary also called Vince Kovac that night. Do you have any idea why? Did they know each other well?'

'Vince?' Anton screwed up his face. 'I would've thought Gary had better taste in friends. Then again...' He flicked a flinger towards Caleb.

'Why? What's wrong with Vince?'

'I guess you haven't see him lately. He got Born Again a few years ago. Changed him from being a wet stick-up-the-arse to a total stick-up-the-arse.'

'Ah. I guess you're not friends then.'

Anton gave a thin smile. 'The only reason he'd talk to me would be to cast out Satan.'

'OK, thanks.' He struggled from the beanbag's clutches.

Anton shot to his feet. 'Why don't you stay for a bit? I could ring for pizza and...' He stopped. 'Phone. Hey, hang on.' He grabbed the phone from the bookshelf. It was a cordless one, with a base station that looked as though it could fly a Boeing jet.

'I don't want pizza, Ant.'

'Hang on.' Anton had the phone to his ear, frowning in concentration as he listened to something.

Caleb's heart thumped – a message.

'Is it from Gaz?'

Anton lowered the phone, eyes shining. 'Shit, I never check for messages. I mean, who leaves messages? Who even rings landlines anymore? I don't even known why

I've still got one. Shit… It's a bit weird hearing his voice like that.'

'Anton, for fuck's sake.'

'Yeah, sorry, it's Gaz. He's asking… He was asking if he could bring Sharon and the kids here to stay. Something about not wanting to go somewhere obvious. Does that make sense?'

Total sense. But not something he'd thought of. No, he'd gone for the my-best-friend-and-brother-are-trafficking-drugs scenario. Not a huge stretch in Anton's case, but Gaz was the kid who never nicked stuff from the milk bar, the one who'd watch your back while you snuck into the cinema, but would always pay his own way.

'Yeah, it does. Listen, you have to go straight to the cops with that. They'll leave you alone once they hear it.'

'Good idea.' But Anton's face had gone blank.

'What's wrong? You can play it remotely, can't you?'

'Yeah, easy.' Still no expression.

'So what's the problem?'

'No problem, I'm just not a big fan of cop shops.'

'It's not like they're going to lock you up or anything. They'll say "thanks very much" and send you on your way. Ring the solicitor if you're worried.'

'Yeah, good idea. I'll give him a ring in the morning.'

Shit, Ant was going to do his usual ostrich impersonation. He was going to have to drag the idiot down there himself. Into a building full of cops. Fuck. Still, what were the odds any of them would have a connection to Grey-face?

'It's important, Ant. Let's go now. I'll take y–'

'It's fine, I'll go tomorrow.'

Or he could let the dickhead work it out for himself.

'Up to you.'

They walked to the front door in silence. Anton stopped in front of it, his eyes not quite meeting Caleb's.

'Cal...' He tapped his chest, then brushed his palm down and away – *I want*.

Now he decided to sign.

'How much?' Caleb said.

'What? No. No, I don't need money. Just, you sure you don't want to stay for a drink or something? It's been a while.'

'Maybe next time.' He paused halfway out the door. 'I almost forgot, have you got Scott's phone number?'

'Scott? Scott who?'

Good eye contact, no change in breathing.

'You know – the guy Gary was working with. He said you knew him.'

'Sorry, no, don't think so.' Anton's face brightened. 'Want me to ask around? I could make some calls, see if anyone's got his number.'

'No, it's right. Thanks.' He hunted for the right words. 'Sorry to have, ah...'

'Accused me of being a murdering drug dealer?' Anton shrugged. 'I'm the one who stacked the BMX you got for your eleventh birthday, so I guess we're even.'

'That was you? You little shit. Mum said it was stolen.'

'Like I said – even.'

'Let me know if you change your mind about the cops,' he said as Anton closed the door. 'I'm at Maria's.'

There was an odd lightness to his feet as he walked to the car.

17.

Kat ran out to meet him as he pulled up in front of the house. Shoeless on the gravel driveway, breathless, clutching his phone. He was out of the car before the engine stopped shuddering.

'What's wrong?'

'It's Frankie. She's all right.'

She hadn't said it. He was just seeing what he wanted to see.

'Frankie,' she said again, then finger-spelled the word: F. R. A. N. K. I. E.

He reached for her arm. 'She's OK? She isn't in hospital?'

'She sounds fine. I've still got her on the line.'

'Did she...? No, wait, give her your Skype name, I want to talk to her.'

Kat nodded, but looked like she remembered his previous attempts at video calls. He ran into the house and hunted for the laptop. Not on the bedside table, not under the bed. An entire week. Why hadn't she called before now? What could have happened? Not in the kitchen. Try the living room. Had she been concussed? Held hostage? There it was, on the couch.

Kat wandered into the room, deep in conversation. 'Yeah, I'm a bit surprised, too.'

'Did you give her your Skype name?' Caleb said.

She nodded as she curled onto an armchair. 'I know, but there's this crazy hope that he's changed.'

'Kat, will you hang up?'

'Hang on, he's getting snotty. Ha, yeah, you're right, a little vein on his forehead.'

He plucked the phone from her hand. 'I'm hanging up. Skype me straight away.'

Frankie must have been near her computer, because the little blue sign began to flash almost immediately. Her pale face filled the screen; hair flat against her skull, skin like over-washed material. A fading bruise yellowed one eye.

His throat tightened. 'Fuck, Frankie. Are you all right? You look like shit.'

She raised a grim smile and launched into speech.

'A bit slower, Frankie.'

She spoke again. Something about a kettle and a pot. Was she cooking? Still drunk? And then he got it – pot calling the kettle black. This was going to be slow.

'Yeah,' he said. 'I've been a bit crook. I'll catch you up in a minute. What about you? What happened?'

'... fucker... arsehole... the fucking prick...'

'Sorry, could you say that again, Frankie? A bit slower.'

'... kitchen... fucker... arsehole... on the head... the fucking prick...'

He could feel the tension radiating from Kat. Her hands were clasped to prevent them from flying to his aid.

'*It's always bothered me.*'

He turned to her. 'I'm just missing the odd word. Could you...?' His face was as stiff as her back.

'Sure.'

'Once more, Frankie. Kat's going to help me.'

'I'm fine,' Kat translated. 'Just a bit bruised. Some prick snuck up behind me in my fucking kitchen. Unfortunately for him, I've picked up a few of your ninja tricks – felt the breeze as he moved. Didn't even think, just turned around and whacked him on the head with a bottle. Followed it up with a knee to the balls on his way down.'

He had the same fighting style as a 57-year-old woman. Excellent.

'But you're all right? There was blood.'

'Yeah, he didn't stay down the first time, so he got in a couple of jabs, gave me a blood nose. He was a bit wobbly by then, though, so Mr Bottle and I finished him off without too many problems.'

'He didn't have a knife?'

'Knife? Fuck no. Why would you put that image in my head? Jesus.'

'You get a good look at him?'

'Yeah, wiry little fucker, bit sick looking.'

'I think we might have met. I call him Grey-face.'

'Yeah? I call him Cunt-face.'

He blinked, a little impressed with Kat's translation skills. 'Where have you been? I've been going crazy. Even the cops have been looking for you.'

'Shit, really? I've been staying with an old mate from my drinking… well, an old mate.'

'Why the hell didn't you ring me?'

'I did. I'd forgotten you'd lost your phone. Only remembered this morning when I snuck back home for mine and found about twenty messages from your new number.'

'And you didn't think to call again when I didn't answer? Jesus, Frankie, I've been shitting myself.'

'I just assumed you were pissed off. Not that I blamed you, I'm pretty pissed off with myself, too. Six fucking years. But enough about me, what's been happening with you? Why are you in the Bay? Apart from the obvious, that is?'

He gave her a quick rundown of the past week. When he'd finished, she ran a hand through her hair, but didn't manage to return it to its usual spikiness. 'Jesus. I'll jump on the train and come down.'

'No. Stay in Melbourne.'

'Give me a fucking break, Caleb. I stuffed up, but I'm back on track now. I haven't had a drink in forty-eight hours.' Her expression was uncomfortably close to pleading.

'There's no point coming down, I'm coming back up.' Eventually. 'Take a bit of time to sort yourself out and we'll work out what to do next.' He scanned the room behind her. Bad print of a bush landscape, beige curtains, beige bedspread. Budget motel.

'You pay cash for that room?'

'Cash? No.'

'You'd better move, then.'

'Mate, don't you think that's getting a bit paranoid?'

'I think Gary's dead and the only reason we aren't is down to blind luck and some over-confidence on their part. Text me the address. We'll talk soon.' He reached out to disconnect.

'Cal. Mate.' Her mouth moved slowly enough for him to catch the words. 'I'm sorry.'

He should say something forgiving. Something healing.

'Yeah. See you soon.' He pressed end.

Frankie was alive, that was the main thing. Alive and relatively unscathed. But could she stay sober? Maybe he should go it alone for now. They worked well together, but it wasn't like he needed her. Sure, he'd miss the odd thing, but he could use technology to cover that. Tape everything and use voice-recognition software to transcribe it. And bouncing ideas off a well-matched mind? Was there a computer program that could replace that?

Kat was watching him. 'OK?'

Relieved, furious, overjoyed. Furious.

'Relieved.'

She waited, then said, 'And Anton? How did that go?'

'Pretty good. Gaz just called him to ask if the kids and Sharon could stay there.'

'Oh, that's great. We need to celebrate. I've got a beautiful Earl Grey that's crying out to be drunk.'

Earl Grey – Kat's choice for lazy afternoon sex.

'Sounds perfect.' He pulled her into his arms and kissed her.

She melted into him for a moment, then wriggled free. 'Work first. Let's see if there are still seats available on that evening flight.'

The Whitsundays. Yes.

'Is it a small bikini?'

'Outrageously. I'll make tea, you book the seats. I've got the page open on the computer.' She disappeared into the kitchen, a hint of tango in the sway of her hips.

One-way tickets were the way to go. Hide away with Kat until everything was over. Maybe longer: they had eighteen lost months to make up for. He pulled the computer onto his lap. Which page? She had fifty of them open in different tabs: travel agents, airlines, telephone directory. Telephone directory. Honey claimed Gary had rung her by accident. Plausible, particularly for someone in a state of panic. Still, it was always good to check the details. He searched for Honey's number, then Gary's mother's – the only similarity was the area code.

Kat appeared in the kitchen doorway. 'Any luck?'

'I haven't looked yet.'

Her grin faded. 'Just so we're clear – now would be the time to tell me if you're having second thoughts.' Her eyes held his. 'About anything.'

'God no. You're my first, second and third thoughts. Something's just bugging me about the case. Do you know Honey Kovac?'

'Sure. She's Aunty Vicky's youngest. You know – Uncle Fred's cousin's wife.'

His eyelid twitched. 'Sure. How well do you know her?'

'Not that well, but we've seen each other a bit since I lost... since I was in hospital. She was the one who brought me all those flowers.'

'Oh.' Hospital meant after the miscarriages. He hadn't realised that had been Honey.

Kat's eyes were fixed on him. Waiting for something. Probably for him to get to the point.

'What's Vince like?'

'He's a bible-thumper. Those poor kids aren't allowed to put a foot wrong. Or Honey. She lost a string of pregnancies after her first and Vince's idea of support was to quote the Old Testament at her. Apparently it was her fault. She's had another baby now, though, so that's great.' There was an artificial brightness to her smile.

He steered the conversation in a safer direction. 'Has he ever been involved in anything dodgy?'

'Vince? Not even before his re-birth. Why all the questions?'

'Gary called their house the day he died. Honey said he'd misdialled.'

'So why all the intrigue?'

Good question: why?

He stood up. 'I need to check something. I'll be back in a sec.'

'Now?'

He kissed her forehead. 'The tea won't even get cold.'

Honey answered the door holding the baby on one hip. She was dressed in grey tracksuit bottoms and food-stained T-shirt that had lost all its shape.

'What are you doing here?' She glanced over his shoulder towards the empty street. 'You can't be here. You have to go.' She swung the door shut and he put his hand out to stop it.

'I know you're scared, but I'm not here to cause you trouble.'

'Well you are.'

'Is it Scott you're scared of?'

'Scott? Who's Scott?'

Not the expected response. And from what he'd seen of Honey so far, acting wasn't her forte.

She was scanning the street again. 'Look, just come in, will you.'

She scraped the back of his heels as she closed the door. From the hallway he could see into both bedrooms and the rear family room. It was eerily neat for a home with two small children. Honey didn't invite him further into the house, but some of the stiffness had left her.

'Make it quick,' she said. 'Things are bad enough without you hanging around.'

'Because of Scott?'

'I don't know who Scott is, but Vince doesn't like me talking to people while he's out. So tell me what you want and go.'

'Just one question – why did Gary call you?'

Her eyes flicked away. 'I told you, he rang a wrong number.'

'The only way he could have mistaken your number for his mother's is if he had his eyes closed when he dialled. So please, will you tell me why he rang?'

She started jiggling the baby, but couldn't pretend he was crying this time.

He kept his voice low. 'Whatever it was, you can trust me.'

A sharp laugh. 'Trust you? I barely know you, why the hell would I... Look, I've told you what happened, just go, will you?'

'You might not know me, but you know Kat, don't you? She's my wife. Ex-wife.'

Her mouth twisted. 'So you fucked a black woman and left. That doesn't make you special, any gubba can do that. Fuck and leave, that's what your lot does.'

She spat each word with a venom that could only come from pain. A thought seeped into his brain, as sour as vomit.

'Is that what happened to you? You had an affair with someone who left?'

Her head jerked back. 'No!'

'With Gary?'

'Youcan'ttellanyone.'

It was true.

She grabbed his sleeve. 'You can't tell anyone. Promise. Promise you won't tell. It only happened once. We were drunk and sad and in shitty marriages...'

'Gary wasn't in a shitty marriage.'

The harshness returned to her face. 'Well, then maybe he just wanted a fuck.'

'And the...' He tried to get his thoughts straight. 'The phone call. What was that? Were you still seeing each other?'

'No! He just wanted to warn me that they were all coming down. I think he wanted to make sure I wouldn't make a fuss. Please, don't tell anyone, Vince'll throw me out.' She hugged her baby to her chest. 'It was after a Christmas party and we were drunk and we... Please don't tell Vince.'

'I won't.'

Tears spilled down her cheeks. 'I think he really hated himself afterwards. I think he hated me.'

He shook his head. 'No, Gaz didn't hate anyone.'

But the Gary he knew would never have slept with another woman. A married woman. He fumbled for the door handle and walked blindly outside. How else had he been wrong about his friend?

18.

He could see Kat through the window, her head bent in concentration as she sketched at the kitchen table. There were two cups of tea cooling by her elbow. She would look up as soon as he opened the door, see his face, and immediately know something was wrong. He paused, then turned towards the garden. So Gary had cheated on Sharon. It happened. A drunken mistake, a lapse of judgement. He would have regretted it immediately. So much so, he'd never so much as hinted at it.

He caught a flash of dull red through the trees. Something metallic towards the bottom of the garden. Had to be one of Kat's sculptures. He stepped off the path and made his way towards it. A bit of art therapy would be good right now. He rounded a garden bed and stopped. Not a single sculpture, but a pair: two hip-high saplings crafted from rusted steel and red gum. The leaves were grey-green ceramic, topped by a fiery crown of new growth. Bronze. So that's how she'd done it. He could kiss her, she was so clever. But why were they hidden away down here? They should be in a public park somewhere, giving joy to thousands. Then it hit him: two saplings that would never become trees.

She'd seemed to cope so well after the first miscarriage,

a little less well after the second. But then... Then what? He still didn't know. Time to back quietly away, and not let her know he'd seen them.

Kat opened the back door as he strode across the lawn.

'Sorry,' he said when he reached her. 'All done now. I'll make a fresh pot.'

But she was looking past him, towards the saplings. Her expression slipped, revealing something so vulnerable it hurt to witness.

'You saw the saplings.'

'Yes. They're beautiful.'

They stood for a moment, but she didn't move from the doorway.

'And?' she said.

'I like the way you've done the leaves.'

'That's it? You're really not going to say anything else?'

'I... They're... What do you want me to say, Kat?'

She stepped back and the wasteland he'd been glimpsing all week opened between them. He'd been wrong about its size: it wasn't vast; it was tiny. Small enough to cradle in his hands.

'You're fluent in two languages, Caleb. You go to speech therapy once a month to make sure of that. You've fought, begged and battled to be able to say anything you could possibly want to say. So talk to me.'

He lifted his hands, but they were empty of words.

'What was this?' she asked. 'Just a fuck for old time's sake?'

'No! God, no.'

'Then what? I thought you'd changed, I really thought... But you won't talk to me about Gary or Anton, or what's obviously upset you at Honey's. You won't talk to me about you. About us.' She reached a hand towards him, palm up. Wanting something. For him to apologise? Beg? Grovel?

'I'm sorry.'

Her hand fell to her side. 'You know, all this time I've been missing you, wondering if I did the right thing leaving, but I'd forgotten just how fucking lonely our marriage was. Because I never had you, did I? Not the real you. Just whatever small part you could bear to reveal to me.'

'You've always had me, Kat.'

She was motionless, but he could feel her slipping away.

'All of me. Ever since we met.'

'I can't do this again. You need to go.' She was turning from him.

'Kat, please. I love you. I've never stopped loving you.'

'I know. But it's not enough.'

He took the Beetle. Just for a drive. If it was over, he wanted it to end better than that.

It couldn't be over.

He stopped at the intersection to the highway: right towards town, left towards Melbourne. He could do it if he had to, go back to that bright and soulless flat. He'd done it before. Right or left? Neither. There had to be an option C: turn around, gather Kat in his arms, and somehow make amends for everything.

It's not enough.

A black SUV appeared over the crest and did a screaming

left-hand turn towards him. Gravel spat against the Beetle as it flew past. He watched it recede in the rear-view mirror. A BMW. City car, city driver, not used to country roads.

It's not enough.

She'd given him plenty of warnings; he'd just chosen to ignore them. Not hard to see how he'd failed, just how he'd succeeded at all.

The plume of dust was growing in the rear-view mirror. Had the BMW run off the road? No, it was heading back towards him. Still going too fast, the idiot. At that rate it was going to – Shit. He shoved the car into gear. Too late. The Beetle slammed forward. His jaw snapped shut. Fuck. How could the guy not have seen him? He was sitting in a porn-mobile in broad daylight. A glimpse of the driver's face through the settling dust. Broad, with a flattened nose, a dark bruise visible on his pale forehead – Boxer.

He was opening the BMW's door.

Caleb floored the car. Left onto the highway. Boxer was already back in the car, coming after him. It'd take the BMW seconds to overtake him on the open road. Make a U-turn towards town? No, too slow. Take one of the turn-offs towards the beach, try to lose the bigger car in winding tracks. One up ahead in thirty metres. The BMW was pulling alongside. Some witnesses would be great about now. Five metres from the track. Four. Three. He hauled the wheel around, barely made the turn. Boxer followed him. Loop around to the left? No, that would lead him back towards Maria's. Had Boxer been heading there? The nightmare of Kat opening the door to him.

A jarring shudder. Blood in his mouth. The Beetle surged forward, then slowed. Shit – the engine was in the rear, couldn't cope with too much more of that. Another turn-off up ahead. Little more than a sandy track, might be too narrow for the BMW. Might be too narrow for the Beetle. Do it. He spun the wheel, over-steered into the bushes, then wrestled the car back onto the track. Had the black car slowed? Stopped? It was twenty metres back. Looked like it was wedged between two...

Crystals of glass falling into his lap. Wind in his face. The Beetle skewed into the bushes and stopped. What the hell? Something thudded against the car. A bullet. Boxer had a gun. A fucking gun.

He turned the ignition key. Nothing. Boxer was out of the car, walking towards him. A dark shape in his hand. Another go at the ignition, one hand on the dash to feel for the engine's rumble. Start. Fucking start. Nothing. He flung open the door and ran. Sprinting through the scrub, ti-tree branches whipping his face. Get down to the beach. If the tide was out, he'd be able to get around the cliff to the next bay. Nearly there. The sand plumed in front of him. He threw himself down. Jesus, fuck. Don't stop, keep moving. He commando-crawled across the sand, muscles braced against the expected slam of a bullet. Over the edge of the dune. Get a weapon. Seaweed, shells, not even a fucking stick. He'd use a handful of sand if he had to. He wasn't going to lie here and die like a dog. There – a piece of driftwood, a good metre in length. Footsteps reverberated against his chest. He lunged for the stick. A shadow loomed over him and he swung the branch low and hard. A jarring thud and Boxer fell past him down the dune.

Down after him, sand pulling at his legs. Boxer was struggling to his feet. Don't think, just hit. Boxer flung up an arm. A sickening jolt and the gun flew from the man's hand. Both of them lunged for it, slipping further down the dune. Boxer whipped towards him, the gun held awkwardly in his left hand. Caleb threw himself to one side. A bang. Sand pluming to his left. Onto his back, a hard kick at Boxer's knee. The man fell, crashing down on top of him. Gun, where was the gun?

A sharp blow under his ribs. Then Boxer was standing; kicking him, stomping. Felt his own raw scream as a foot ploughed into his scarred side. He curled into a ball, arms instinctively protecting his head. Hands going through his pockets. The sharp grunt of a question then a foot slammed into his ribs. Another kick, and another. His knees jerked to his chest; pain everywhere, no breath for screaming now. He tried to roll away and caught a blow to his spine. The brief touch of something hard against his chest. The gun. A sudden weight on his back pinned his arms beneath him. The ashen smell of cigarettes, more angry questions. A pause, then a sharp smack on his temple. Brain spinning. Wouldn't get up if he caught another knock like that. The weight lifted – Boxer standing, getting ready for another kick. Gun. Get the gun. He hunted blindly for it. There. He gripped it. Rolled onto his back. Fired.

Noise. Punching recoil.

He opened eyes he hadn't realised he'd shut. A bright sky. Sand clinging to his lashes. Boxer was sprawled on the sand, his hands scrabbling desperately at his throat. Blood spurted between his fingers in bright spouts. Caleb somehow made it to his knees, air wheezing in his lungs. He pressed his hands to the pulpy mess of Boxer's neck. The man's hooded eyes held his, wild and panicked. The pulse ebbed beneath his fingers, fluttered, and stopped. A long, slow shudder shook Boxer's body and everything was still.

Caleb's hands still gripped, unable to loosen. Blood on them. Bright red, still flushed with oxygen. The warmth of it was on his face and neck. In his mouth. He turned and vomited violently. The taste of blood and bile. Of fear. He got to his feet and stumbled towards the sea. The lapping waves were like the sucking of Boxer's throat. He waded in, ripping at his T-shirt. Rivulets of red ran down his skin. His blood, Boxer's. Heaving sobs shook his body. He collapsed to his knees and wept.

19.

It was the cold that finally made him move. His body was shuddering, teeth chattering so hard they cut his lip. He went to stand, legs buckling. Tried again and made it to his feet and out of the water. The waves had deposited his T-shirt onto the sand. It would be clean; the salt water would have washed the blood away. He made himself pull it on and it stuck to his skin in dank folds. Pain in every movement as he started up the dune, each breath tearing at his lungs. Up to the top. One step, then another. Get to Boxer's car, drive. Go somewhere a long way from here. There it was, nose hard up against the ti-trees that had blocked its passage. He opened the driver's door and climbed in.

No key in the ignition.

He sat.

Cold. So cold. Tired.

Go back down and get the key from Boxer's body. Do it.

He retraced his footsteps and slid back down the dune, his foot kicking something as he went – the gun. He didn't want a gun. Never wanted to see another gun again in his life, but couldn't leave it around here for kids or the police to find. The police. Christ, he'd killed a man. No. Later. Deal with it all later. He picked up the gun, the heft of it surprising. He knew nothing about guns. Was there a safety? Nothing obvious. He fumbled and managed to release the clip, shoved the separate parts into the back pockets of his jeans.

Boxer's body was sprawled at the bottom of the dune, the nightmare spray of his blood staining the sand black. Don't look at his face, the ruin of his throat. Stomach roiling, he dug his hand into the man's pockets. A wallet. He hesitated, then pulled out the driver's licence and shoved it, unexamined, into his jeans. No key in Boxer's other pockets. He checked again, then sifted through the sand. Nothing but shells and grit.

Hard, bone-shaking shivers now. Joke of a way to die – dodge a bullet but get killed by the weather. Boxer's jeans and jacket were dry. No, nothing could get him to wear the bloodied clothes of a man he'd just killed. He made his way back to the car. When he was fourteen, he'd made a brief and unconvincing attempt at being a bad boy. He'd failed miserably, but he'd learned the basics of car stealing: jam a screwdriver in the ignition, or strip the wires under the dash. How much harder could a modern BMW be than an old Ford? He opened the door. Much harder. No exposed wires, no idea where they might be. He poked around until his brain finally kicked in; modern cars had immobilisers. No point in starting the thing if you couldn't steer it. Fuck.

He slammed the door as he got out. Stopped. Shouldn't he have heard something then? Yes, a soft thud. He swung the door shut again. Silence. Like he didn't have his aids in. Had the sea water got into them? A cold trickle of fear: or was it hearing damage from the gun blast? Life would be hard if he'd lost the remnants of his hearing. Harder. No hints of words, no snatches of tone. God – speaking without any feedback. If Kat thought people were pissed off with him now, imagine how they'd feel when he started yelling at them in a monotone.

Stupid thing to be worrying about now. Blood on his clothes, a dead man on the beach. Anton's place was closest, only a kilometre or two. Shouldn't be too hard.

He began to walk.

He stumbled up the front steps and banged on the door. Many parts of him hurting now. Not the sharp pain of the assault, but deep, with gripping fingers. It came with the fear that it might not end, but just keep building. If Anton was out, or, more likely, off his face, he was going to have to break in.

The door swung open.

'Well, you look like shit,' Anton said. 'Why are you wet?'

'I need you to make a call for me.'

'Hang on.' Anton patted his pockets. 'I want to write this down. A seminal moment: July the second, my big brother asks me for help. A young Cary Grant will play me in the film.'

Caleb pushed past him into the house. 'Now.'

'You going to explain why you've been swimming in the middle of winter?' Anton asked as he dialled Kat's mobile.

'In a minute.'

'And you and Kat, huh? You think you're in with a chance again?'

He wrapped his arms around himself. 'Later. Is it ringing?'

'Yep.' Anton pulled off his jumper and shoved it at him. 'Put this on, you're making me feel cold.'

He pulled it over his wet T-shirt. His teeth were still chattering. 'Are you sure it's ringing?'

Anton frowned. 'Well, not totally. Do you think a ringing sound means that it's ringing? Kat, hey, it's Anton. I know, ages. How's it going?'

'Anton, for fuck's sake.'

'Hang on, I've got Cal here, freaking out about something.'

'Tell her Boxer knew, that Boxer knows I'm in the Bay.'

Anton repeated his words. 'OK, she's pretty worried about that. She wants to know what happened. That makes two of us. Hey Cal, what's going on?'

'Tell her I'm fine, but I'm worried he might have known I was staying at Maria's. They need to leave until I can get the word out that I'm not there any more.'

Anton relayed the message. No joking now. 'She says OK. What else do you want me to tell her?'

'That's all she said? OK?'

'She said, "Oh, shit. OK." Then added, "Does he want to tell me anything else?"'

'Tell her, tell her that I'm sorry and that I'll... Tell her that when this is over I'll try to...' He looked away from the pity in Anton's eyes. 'Tell her that I love her and I'm sorry.' God.

A tap on his shoulder. 'She wants to know where you're going.'

Was that a polite question, or an invitation to go to her? Would it be safe? How long before someone realised Boxer wasn't coming back? A three-hour drive to Melbourne, so they'd have a few hours before any of his mates raised the alarm.

Unless one of them was already in the Bay.

He grabbed Anton's arm. 'Tell her to get out now.'

'I've told her, Cal. Calm down.'

'No. I mean right now, straight away. Tell her Grey-face might be here. Tell her to get in Maria's car and go.'

'Are you meeting her?'

'God, no, I'm fucking toxic. Just tell her to get out.' He watched to make sure Anton didn't soften the message.

Anton lowered the phone. 'Mate, I think she's crying. Maybe I should run you over there so you can talk in person.'

'Hang up. She has to get out of the house.'

'I'm not going to hang up on her. That'd be a totally arsehole move. If you guys are trying to work things out together…'

Caleb took the phone from him. The red button winked its message at him: end, end, end. He pressed it.

He stood under the hot water until the shaking stopped, then dressed in some of Anton's clothes: a long-sleeved T-shirt, thick jumper and black jeans. A bit of a worry that they fitted him. He'd dropped more weight than he'd realised.

Anton was in the kitchen, hunting through a cupboard. He turned around as Caleb sat down.

'... the... on?'

'Sorry, what?'

'...?'

No. He couldn't do it any more. He closed his eyes. Something hit him in the chest and landed in his lap: a packet of tomato soup mix.

Anton was standing by the cupboard, gripping another packet. 'What's your...?'

'What?'

'What's. Your. Fucking. Problem?'

'My aids are on the blink.'

'So? It's not like you get much from them anyway.'

'And it's hard, Ant. It's always hard, but this is... I just can't do it right now.'

Anton looked from his face to his battered hands. 'You want something to drink?' he signed.

'Have you got tea?'

'Tea? Jesus. Well I can look.'

Anton drifted around the kitchen in his usual, aimless style, but there was something different about him. What was it? The usual jeans and battered Volleys, plain navy T-shirt. Then it struck him – short sleeves. It was years since he'd seen Anton's bare arms. They were pale and wiry. And smooth. No fresh needle tracks. Nothing on the backs of his hands or in between his fingers, nothing on his neck. Still, there were veins in other parts of the body. Feet, maybe. Anton was standing in the middle of the room, an I've-asked-you-a-question look on his face.

'You want to see?' he signed.

'See what?'

'My feet. You can check my legs while you're at it.'

'No need.'

But Anton was already pulling off his socks. He wriggled his toes like thin, white worms.

'Fourteen and a half months,' he said. His smile was tight, with no teeth showing – the same expression he used to wear when presenting schoolwork to their father.

'That's great, Ant.' No, it needed something more than that: fourteen and a half months broke the record by exactly six. 'I'm proud of you.'

'Awesome. Now I can die happy.' But his smile had loosened into a grin. He poured near-boiling water onto two tea bags and brought them to the table. 'Tea, good sir.'

Caleb cupped his hands around the mug. It took a couple of tries before he managed to raise it to his lips. Being upright hurt. Being awake hurt.

Anton watched his efforts and lit up a cigarette. He inhaled deeply. 'OK, spill.'

'You going to give up the fags, too?'

He exhaled a plume of smoke in Caleb's face. 'You going to stop avoiding questions?'

Impressive that he could sign and smoke at the same time. Not too many people could achieve that level of dickishness.

'I'm in some shit with some scary guys. Something to do with Gary's death. You can't tell anyone I was here, OK?'

'Sure.'

'I mean it, Ant. No-one. Not the cops, not friends, not some guy down the pub.'

'Got it – keep my mouth shut. Are you OK? You don't look too good.'

'Yeah, just a bit bruised.'

'How's the other guy? Boxer, right?'

Slack-faced and empty-eyed. Already beginning to rot.

'He's... a bit bruised, too.'

He'd been so careful. Who knew he was here? Sharon, her sister, Mrs Naylor, Mick... Who was he kidding? Everyone in town had known he was here the minute he'd walked down Bay Road with Kat. But for someone to have rung Scott, they'd have to know Scott. Maybe it had been some form of electronic trace he hadn't considered. His new phone? He'd had it less than a week, and been careful not to call Tedesco on it, but he'd had to use ID to buy it. He pulled it from his pocket and turned it off, took the battery out for good measure. Water seeped from its inner workings. Another phone gone – it was beginning to feel like a habit.

He looked up to see Anton watching him.

'What are you doing?'

'Being paranoid. Listen, have you still got Dad's old Toyota?'

'What's wrong with your porn wagon?'

'It's Kat's. And it's dead.'

Anton laughed. 'You must be rapt with her driving around in that. But yeah, the Toyota's still out the back. It's yours if you want it. It might not be roadworthy, though. Actually, it might not be registered, now I think about it.'

'As long as it goes.' He levered himself to his feet.

'What, you're going now? You don't look up to much driving. Why don't you stay here and leave in the morning?'

Choose one of the empty rooms and curl into a sobbing ball. But if he stopped now, he might never get up again.

'No. I've got to get going.'

Anton stubbed out his cigarette. 'Text me so I know you haven't wrapped yourself around a pole, OK?'

'Phone's dead.'

'Then buy another one.'

'OK.'

'Seriously. Buy one tonight and let me know.'

Anton grasped him in his sinewy arms. A strange moment, years since they'd hugged. Ant thumped him on the back, then released him, leaving behind a pall of cigarette breath.

He waved his hand. 'You stink like a fucking ashtray, Ant.'

Anton's eyebrows waggled. 'I don't get any complaints from the ladies.'

Boxer had stunk of fresh smoke, too. He'd probably stopped for a fag in town before coming to kill him. Town. That needed examining: why had Boxer been coming from Resurrection Bay, not Melbourne? What had he been doing in town? Looking for him? Talking to someone?

'Did you tell anyone I was down here?'

Anton shrugged. 'Don't think so, why?'

'Or mentioned Kat's car?'

'Why would I mention her…? Oh, yeah, that's a car worth mentioning, but no, I haven't had a chance. I only saw it this morning.'

'I'm not mad, just be good to know.'

'Why would you be mad? Ah.' Anton's face shuttered. 'You still think I had something to do with Gary's death.'

'No, I'm just trying to work out what happened. If you mentioned to someone that I was here, they might have talked to Scott.'

'Scott? The guy whose number you asked me for?' Anton's frown was replaced by a dull-eyed smile. 'Oh, I get it – asking me for his number was a little test. Nicely done, I'd forgotten how smooth you are. So Scott's the guy who killed Gaz? And you think I was dealing with him? That I told him how to find you? Nice.'

'I'm just trying to . . .'

'. . . work out if I'm helping someone who wants to kill you. Yeah, got it.' He sat down and pulled a cigarette from the packet. It took him a few tries to light it. 'Car key's by the front door. Pretty sure you know your way out.'

'Ant, come on. I'm not accusing you of anything.'

'Sure.' He blew smoke at the ceiling. 'See you in another three years.'

20.

He lay with his eyes screwed shut until the need for a piss forced him from bed. A short pause for his body to adapt to an upright position. The motel room looked worse than it had last night: a sagging ceiling and mildewed walls, something that had once been carpet on the floor. He shuffled to the bathroom. Not looking too pretty himself. Unshaven, red-eyed, bruised. Great dark patches marked his limbs and stomach, his back too, by the feel of it. Even his internal organs felt bruised. Was that possible? Trying to piss, he decided it was. No blood in the urine, though. That had to be a good sign.

He splashed water on his face, then stood for a moment. Before stumbling to bed last night, he'd cleaned his hearing aids and left the batteries out to dry. Time to try them. He gave them another clean, adjusted them, re-adjusted them, turned up the volume, and, when he couldn't think of any other way to procrastinate, clapped his hands. Nothing. OK, a handclap probably wasn't very loud. What would it be, seventy, eighty decibels? Maybe less. What he needed was something with a bit of heft. He hunted through the cupboard under the sink and found a spanner. He weighed it in his hand. Good and solid, but no cause for alarm if he couldn't hear its thump. Any number of things could have stopped his aids from working: salt water, low batteries, something else he couldn't think of at the moment. So just fucking do it. He slammed the spanner against the basin and chips flew into his face. Silence. He blinked hard: just the debris making his eyes water.

Frankie screwed up her eyes as she opened her motel door. 'Christ, what time is it?'

She was wearing thick woollen socks, a black cardigan, and pink pyjamas with kittens on them.

He tore his eyes away from them. 'Can I come in?'

She yawned and gestured him inside, switching on lights as she went. No empty bottles, and only the smell of pine air-freshener and last night's pizza. She'd obviously been using one of the beds as an office. The other one looked as though she'd been practising her wrestling on it: the bedclothes were in a heap on the floor and the bottom sheet was bunched halfway down the mattress.

'Not sleeping well?' he asked.

'Not with you hammering on the door.' She slumped onto it and yawned again. 'What… big… anyway?'

'Sorry, what?'

'What's the big emergency?'

'No emergency, I was just awake.'

'I… text me… way?'

'Sorry?'

She shook her head. 'Is your brain working?'

'I need new batteries for my aids. You'll have to slow

down a bit until I get them.' He avoided her eye by shifting a stack of papers from the office-bed. He glanced at the top page as he sat down. 'You've been looking into the warehouse employees?'

'Yep. Nothing of interest. So, what's up? You look like crap. Did you find out Gary was bent or something?'

He winced before he could stop himself.

She raised her eyebrows. 'You're kidding? Saint Gary?'

'No. Nothing like that, but he may have been... I found out he had an affair.'

'So now you're wondering how well you knew him.' She examined his face. 'Where'd you get the bruises?'

He told her. Slowly at first, then in a garbled stream: the gun, the fight, Boxer's gruesome death. When he finished, she stared at him without speaking.

'OK, that's...' She scrubbed her hands through her hair. 'Fuck. Are you OK?'

'Dandy.'

'Yeah, I'd imagine. Jesus. Did you report it to anyone?'

'No. Do you think I should?'

'God, no, last thing you should do. Although maybe you should get in contact with your mate, Tedesco. Not to give him any details, just to let him know that one of Scott's guys found you.'

'Why?'

'Because we need friends in high places and he's the closest thing we've got to it at the moment. Is the, ah, body, still there?'

He pushed away the image of the blood-soaked sand. 'Yeah.'

'OK, I'll phone in an anonymous report. We don't want

any ten-year-old boys finding it. No, scratch that, I don't want my voice on tape – I'll email it from an internet cafe.'

Frankie in full practical mode: it was both reassuring and unsettling. He had a flash of her as a cop. She would have made it to the top ranks if she could have controlled her weakness.

'Do you know how they tracked you down?' she asked.

'No.'

She held up a hand. 'Back up. Something very shifty just happened with your eyes. Let's try that again – do you *think* you know how they tracked you?'

'Sure. I've got a dozen theories. They could've traced my phone, or the prescriptions Maria wrote for me. I might have let something slip to Tedesco, someone in town could have told Scott.'

'By someone, you mean your brother?'

Straight to the heart of it.

'I don't think so. He's got a job, he's clean. It's the longest he's ever been clean. And the phone call Gaz made to him checked out – he was asking if he could bring the family down to stay.'

'How do you know?'

'What?'

'How do you know that's why Gary rang him?'

'Because he left Anton a voice message.'

'And you heard this message?'

'No, I didn't fucking hear it. Look, if it ends up that Ant's involved in something stupid, I won't be too shocked, but he wouldn't do anything to deliberately hurt me. It's all about unintended consequences with him.'

'Guess you know him better than me.' She smothered

another yawn. 'I can't think like this. Make yourself at home while I have a shower.'

He sat on the bed and read through her notes while she had the longest shower in the history of Western civilisation. She'd done a lot in just one day, but it smacked of busy-work: research into people who were obviously unconnected, records of similar cigarette heists and warehouse robberies. He got the strong feeling it had all been done for his benefit.

She finally emerged looking a lot more like herself with freshly gelled hair, and dressed in jeans and a leather jacket.

'No more pink kittens?' he asked.

'Piss off, it was all I could get from Target.' She looked at the pages in his hand. 'Anything strike you as interesting?'

'No. Good that you've done it all, though.'

'You going to give me a gold star, too?' She took the pages from him and stuffed them in her suitcase. He watched as she gathered her clothes from around the room. Steady hands, perspiration-free. A little washed out, but overall looking a lot better than the day she'd disappeared.

Her eyes raised to his as she zipped up her backpack. 'I'm dry.'

'I know.'

'Then fuck off.' She grabbed her bags and headed outside.

She was leaning against the car by the time he shuffled out to her. 'Jesus, Cal, have you seen a doctor? Sorry, stupid question, I mean, should I take you to a doctor?'

'No.'

'Why not?'

He pulled his keys from his pocket. 'Because I'm not wasting my time being told something I already know.'

'That you're an idiot?'

'That I've got a bit of bruising and it will heal. Let's take Ant's car – if they can track me to the Bay, they can trace your rego.'

'It's fine, no-one even knows I'm alive.'

'Until you run a red light.'

She considered that. 'Fine, but I'm driving. I'm not putting my life in your… hands.'

'In my what hands?'

'Palsied,' she said clearly.

'Right.' He threw her the keys. 'Thanks for the sympathy.'

'You want sympathy? See a fucking doctor. You… the…?'

'What?'

She squinted at him. 'You got spare batteries for those things at your flat?'

'Yeah.'

'Think that might be our first stop.'

His apartment door was closed and, for a crazy moment, he thought Boxer and Grey-face had locked up when they'd left. They hadn't. The local junkies had gone through the place like locusts. The shitty television was gone, the good computer, every electrical device, including the lamps. He wandered through the living room, stepping over the slashed couch cushions and ripped papers. It was going to take days to clear up. Why hadn't the pricks just taken his belongings instead of smashing them? Maybe it had been frustration – there'd been nothing of any value in the place except for his laptop.

The chaos continued in the bedroom. The mattress had been thrown to the floor and sliced open, the bedside table upended. Frankie helped him search through the mess and found the container of batteries under the wardrobe. She threw them to him without comment and left the room. For that alone, it was worth putting up with all her shit.

He took one of the broken bed slats into the bathroom and locked the door. Steady hands as he slotted the new batteries into his aids. He turned the volume to full and gripped the slat. A last run through of the litany of reasons his test might not work: corroded wiring, dud batteries, sand in his aids. Destroyed hearing. Hands not quite so steady now. He closed his eyes and brought the wood down on the basin. A thud. A definite thud. He rested his forehead against the mirror. Thank Christ.

He found Frankie in the kitchen, half-heartedly shoving food back into cupboards.

'Leave it,' he said.

She turned around. 'You get the feeling they were looking for something?'

'Jewellery, money.'

'No, this wasn't smack-heads. At least, it wasn't just smack-heads. It was searched before the locals got to it. Look around: freezer emptied, cushions slashed. Our mates don't think we know something – they think we've *got* something.'

He had a flash of Boxer's hands on him. That brief moment before the kicking began.

'Boxer searched me. And he was shouting. I think he was shouting questions. Really put the boot in when I didn't answer.'

Frankie was very still. 'What did he want?'

'I don't know, I didn't catch anything.'

'I know they weren't ideal conditions, but you would have caught the odd word. Think back, you're on the sand, Boxer's face is...'

'You don't need to go through all that – I'm telling you I didn't get anything. I couldn't see Boxer's face because mine was in the sand.'

'Nothing at all?'

'It's not a fucking superpower, Frankie. I've got two eyes like the rest of you.'

'I'm not criticising, I'm clarifying. OK, Boxer thought you might have it on you, so it's something small. A key, a letter.' She waited for him to speak. 'A CD, a...' She gestured.

'Photo, USB stick, credit card, diamond ring.'

'Good boy. See how well we do when you play nicely?'

'It doesn't get us anywhere. All we know is that they're looking for something and we haven't got it.' His words struck him. 'Gary didn't have it, either. Whatever Scott's after, he didn't have it.'

All the torment his friend had suffered – the broken bones, the knife wounds – all for nothing.

He looked at Frankie. 'If Gaz didn't have it, where is it?'

She shook her head. 'No, the question is, what is it? We won't be able to find it unless we know that.'

21.

Frankie's sixth sense for finding cholesterol led them to a nearby greasy-spoon. Eighteen months living in the area and he'd never noticed the place. The smell of burnt bacon grease assailed him as he opened the door. The owners needed to get a new extractor fan. Maybe a new cook while they were at it. The handful of solo diners looked a little more frayed around the edges than him and Frankie, but not by much. He chose a table as far away from the kitchen as possible while Frankie caught a waitress and ordered them both coffees and a cooked breakfast.

Something dug into his hip as he sat down. He pulled it out and found himself staring into Boxer's hooded eyes. His driver's licence. Michael Petronin, thirty-eight years old. Not going to see thirty-nine. He'd killed this man, felt the heat of his blood pump into his hands.

Frankie tapped a spoon on the table. 'Something interesting?'

He showed it to her.

'Petronin,' she said. 'Russian name. You don't think it's a Russian Mafia thing, do you?'

'Hope not. I've got his gun, too, by the way. It's in the boot.'

'"By the way?" You've got his gun "by the way"? And

you're just mentioning it now? Jesus fucking Christ. What if the cops pull us over?'

'I forgot I had it.'

'You forgot? You forgot you had a dead man's gun on you?'

A few of their fellow customers' heads turned their way.

'Yes, I forgot. I've been a bit busy while you were on the piss – a few things might have slipped my mind.'

The waitress appeared with their coffees, setting them down with a thump that sloshed brown liquid into the saucers. Frankie dropped her glare to the table. He gulped his coffee. It was thin and bitter, but hopefully contained caffeine.

They sat without speaking, until Frankie stirred. 'What next? Gary's house?'

He tried for an even tone. 'Eventually, but it's pretty unlikely there'll be anything there – Scott and his guys tore the place apart. Let's check out Petronin's place first.'

She didn't say anything, but there were calculations going on in her head. He stayed silent while she went through them.

'High risk,' she finally said. 'Neighbours, flatmates, dogs. An apartment, so only one door in and out. And fourth floor, going by the number. No, too risky.'

The waitress reappeared with two loaded plates. A layer of charcoal coated everything: bacon, eggs, toast, sausages. Had to give the cook points for consistency.

'We can walk away if it doesn't feel right,' he said when the waitress had left. 'But it's our best lead. Our only lead.'

'What do you think you're going to find? A teledex with

the name Scott written in it in big red letters?'

'Any colour will do.' He tried the sausage. It held none of the usual mystery associated with sausages; this was clearly a product composed of sinew, sawdust and offal. He picked up a piece of toast. Frankie was ploughing her way through her meal like it was her first one in days.

'Petronin's flat is the next obvious step,' he said.

She shook her head and attacked the bacon.

'We have to be more aggressive than usual. Scott's guys have attacked us both. They broke into your house and my flat, they found me in the Bay. If we don't work out what's going on, we'll be running for the rest of our very short lives.'

Frankie started in on the sausage without replying.

'But I'm happy to go there by myself if you want to sit this one out.'

'For fuck's sake.' She lay her cutlery on the plate. 'You do everything I say. Everything. If I say we get out, we get out. Understood?'

'Yes, Sergeant.'

'I'm fucking serious. I'm not getting cornered by some hit man in a flat. Or worse, by my ex-colleagues.' She pushed back her chair and signalled for the bill. 'And while we're on the subject of exes…'

'I don't want to talk about it.'

'Like that, is it? You fucked that up pretty quickly, well done. But I was thinking about her car. Is it still at the beach?'

The bottom dropped out of his stomach. Sitting there, metres from Boxer's body. The cops would think Kat was involved once they found it. And Boxer's mates.

'Fuck. I mean, fuck. I didn't even think about it.'

'Or the fact that your trace evidence is all over it, and Boxer's car. But don't worry, I'm onto it.'

Trace evidence? What a joke – his fingerprints were all over it.

She patted his hand. 'Don't stress, I've got the brains part covered, you're just here to provide the looks. Or something.' She stood up. 'You get the bill while I make a couple of calls.'

The owner being as good at padding bills as he was sausages, paying took a bit of negotiation. By the time he got outside, Frankie was pocketing her phone.

'Sorted. It'll be moved this morning.'

'That was quick. Who'd you call?'

'Your brother.'

'Shit. He's got a record, Frankie. He can't be anywhere near a crime scene. Not to mention his total lack of... Christ.'

'Don't get your knickers in a twist, he's not doing anything. I just got a name and number from him.' She opened the driver's door.

He got in the car. 'Was he...?'

'What?'

Coherent? Breathing? Off his face?

'Nothing. Whose name did he give you?'

'Some guy called O'Brien.'

'Brad O'Brien? Neo-Nazi Brad? Kat just put the fear of God into him, he'll go straight to the cops!'

'Stop yelling. It wasn't Brad, it was Jeremy.'

He did a catalogue of the O'Brien brothers. 'There isn't a Jeremy.'

'Old guy with a walking stick and an eye-patch?'

'The grandfather?'

'Great-grandfather, I think. And he's more than happy to help Kat out. Thrilled even.'

'What. Why?'

'Because he's got the hots for her. Apparently it runs in the family.'

'He's a hundred, for fuck's sake.'

'Ninety-two and Anton says everything works just fine.' She was grinning. The shit, she was really enjoying this. 'Apparently Jeremy was telling Anton just the other day how wonderful the Viagra's been.'

He'd never be able to scrub that image from his mind. 'Didn't he go to prison for killing puppies or something?'

'Don't exaggerate. He fire-bombed a neighbour's kennels sixty years ago. Which happens to be a good thing for you. He said he'd quite enjoy torching Boxer's car while he was at it. Hasn't had a good bonfire in a while.'

Petronin's apartment was in a large blond-brick building, in a street full of other large blond-brick buildings, all built some time in the 1950s. The garden of quartz pebbles and straggling yucca plants looked as though it hadn't been touched since. The grimed lobby smelt of stale piss, hopefully from a cat.

'Not as much money in the murder business as I would have thought,' Frankie said as she checked the flat numbers. 'Looks like I was right – fourth floor.'

He tried to pretend it wasn't killing him for the first

flight, then gave in and wheezed his way up the remaining stairs, holding grimly on to the handrail.

Frankie waited for him at the top. 'You still sure I shouldn't take you to a doctor?'

He shook his head.

'Yeah? Give me one good reason.'

'It's getting better.'

'Jesus, you sound like a chain smoker kidding himself he's just got a bit of a cough. Come on, I think it's this way.'

The flat was at the end of a long corridor.

'What d'you reckon?' Frankie said. 'Knock? If someone opens it, we can pretend we're Mormons or something.'

He looked at her jeans and battered Doc Martens. 'And if that doesn't work?'

'Then I'll run away. You'll have to come up with your own plan.' She rapped hard, but the door stayed closed. 'Next idea?'

No CCTV in the corridor, a cheap plywood door, and an even cheaper-looking lock. Odds were there wouldn't be an alarm, either. He lifted the hallway fire extinguisher from its bracket.

'When in doubt, use brute force.'

The plywood might have been cheap, but the extinguisher barely dented it when he took a swing. He dropped it and staggered back, clutching his ribs. Jesus Christ.

'Let me try, Rocky.' She held the canister like a battering ram and slammed it against the lock. The wood splintered.

He scanned the surrounding doors, but no-one appeared to investigate.

'There's a lot of background noise,' Frankie said. 'Traffic, music.'

She set the extinguisher on the floor and kicked. The door flew open and smacked against the wall. A narrow hallway, rooms to either side. Carpet the exact shade of baby-shit. They ventured in. There was a kitchen to the left, a small living room to the right, one or two bedrooms at the rear.

'Really shit security for a bad guy,' Frankie said.

'Really shit security for anyone. I'll do the living room and bathroom, you take the rest.'

The living room was strangely bare, containing only an oversized television and a cream couch with worrying stains. No armchairs or knick-knacks, no curtains. He dug through a pile of magazines on the couch and found the expected tits and clits and a TV guide. Nothing under the cushions except crumbs and an empty condom packet. There were no shelves or boxes, no tricky hiding places, no hollowed-out books. No books at all.

He stepped into the small hallway as Frankie exited the bedroom. 'Only one bedroom,' she said. 'Nothing much in it.'

'Yeah. Doesn't feel like he's been here long. Found a phone book or anything?'

'No. Let's wrap it up quickly, I'm getting jumpy.'

The bathroom was as sparse as the rest of the flat. Nothing in the vanity to get excited about other than a tube of antifungal cream. The cabinet under the sink was empty of everything, including cleaning products. A quick check of the toilet told him Petronin hadn't just run out of them. He lifted the cistern. Nothing.

Frankie turned quickly away from the fridge as he entered the kitchen. 'Let's go. There's nothing here.' A strange intensity to her expression.

'What's wrong?'

'The fridge – I'm going to have nightmares about that cheese. At least, I think it was cheese, could've been bread. Let's go.' She stepped forward, crowding him.

He held his place. 'Move.'

She squared her shoulders, then sighed and stepped aside. He instantly saw what she'd been trying to hide: photos on the fridge door. Petronin, his face alive with laughter. A girl, maybe six years old, front teeth not yet grown. She was laughing up at Petronin. A clear family resemblance in their eyes and broad cheekbones. Caleb pulled a photo from the door. It was a casual family snap at the gaping-mouthed entrance to Luna Park: Petronin and the girl with a woman. The child was holding an oversized lollipop, her grin nearly as large as the lolly.

There was an intense pressure in the centre of his chest.

Frankie pulled him around to face her. 'Just because he's got a kid, doesn't mean he was a good guy. He tried to kill you. Remember the gun? The kicking? That was this guy.'

Caleb nodded, but his eyes went back to the photo.

The woman had her arms around Petronin and the girl. Dark-blonde hair and a slightly crooked smile. She came sharply into focus. A memory. Something about the face.

'The woman,' he said. 'I've seen her before.'

22.

Frankie drove sedately away, made good use of the indicators, came to a complete halt at stop signs.

When they were a few blocks away, she signed, 'Remember who she is yet?'

'No, just that I've seen her.'

Not someone he knew – a passing face. Someone he'd seen in the supermarket? A friend of a friend of a friend at a party? No, too big a coincidence; she had to be connected with the case. So where could he have seen her, but not taken note? A delivery person at the warehouse, someone on the street outside Arnie's house. A friend of Gary's.

'Where?' Frankie asked. 'In Melbourne or the Bay?'

'I don't know.'

He studied the photo. Petronin's wife. A recent divorce, maybe. The man obviously hadn't been living in that desolate flat very long; the lack of detritus collected in day-to-day life spelt that out. Not a total deadbeat dad, though – the pictures of his child were the only decoration in the place. But there was nothing to show she was in his life, not a single My Little Pony or glittery sticker. So, probably not a happy split. If they could find the ex, she might be bitter enough to tell all.

Frankie pulled over and swivelled around in her seat. 'Someone at the warehouse?'

'I don't know.'

'Arnie's?'

'I don't know.'

'You can remember the face of every person you've seen since you were born, how can you not know?'

'Maybe it's the fucking pressure, Frankie.'

She began tapping the wheel.

He resisted the urge to rap her over the knuckles. 'Relax, it'll come to me.'

'Well while it's coming, let's set up a meeting with your mate, Tedesco. We're so far out of our depth here I can't see the fucking shore.'

He thought it through. The idea of presenting himself to a member of the Victorian police was a little uncomfortable, but Frankie was right, they needed help.

'OK, I'll text from a phone booth and give him a time and place. If he can make it, great. If he can't, you and I can have a picnic.'

'Just use my phone,' she said. 'I don't care if he gets the number.'

'No. Everyone thinks you're gone. It'd be great to keep it that way.'

She patted his cheek. 'Aren't you adorable, trying to protect me like the big, strong man you are.'

'Well, yeah, but it's mainly strategic. You're my secret weapon.'

He chose the park from Google Maps, but when they arrived, he realised he'd been there before. It was by a lake, with an old locomotive engine that now served as play equipment. A dusty childhood memory of a picnic, some sort of family reunion.

'Look,' he said. 'I don't want to have an argument about this, but...'

'I'm the secret weapon blah, blah, blah. I'll stay in the car, OK?'

It'd be better if she took herself off for a drive. What were the odds? 'Or you could go for a drive.'

She reclined her chair. 'Or I could stay in the car.'

He got out and headed for the train. He must have come here soon after he got sick: a memory – off-kilter balance – an underwater feeling in his head. He'd climbed to the top of the engine and not wanted to come down; it had been so peaceful up there. A couple of dog owners were out power-walking, carrying little plastic bags of shit in their hands. Despite the chill, there were young children out with their mothers. One exhausted-looking father watching a hyperactive three-year-old run up and down the steps to the driver's compartment.

He was beginning to think Tedesco wasn't coming, when a late-model white Ford Falcon pulled into the parking lot, six cars down from Frankie. He caught Caleb's eye as he climbed from the car and jerked his head towards a nearby park bench.

'Mr Zelic,' he said when Caleb reached him.

'Detective.'

'Tell me your story.' He was looking a little more scuffed than the last time they'd met: drooping skin on his lower eyelids, dark smudges under his eyes.

Caleb went through Boxer's attack on him, skirting skilfully around the gun, Boxer's death.

'They trashed my flat, too. The same way they trashed Gary's place. I think Scott's looking for something.'

Tedesco's grey eyes examined him. 'Something you've got?'

'I wish. I'd give it to him.'

'Did you report any of this to the local police?'

'No.'

'Why not?'

'You know why not.'

'Ah, the conspiracy. You see my problem, Caleb? All these accusations and no proof.' Tedesco sat back.

Caleb took in his splayed legs and crossed arms. 'What's happened?'

'Happened?'

'Something's happened to make your defences go up.'

'What makes you say that?' The detective's face was impassive.

'You're sitting there, thinking you were stupid to start trusting me, wondering how I managed to convince you I was legit when you're usually so good at spotting bullshitters.'

Tedesco nodded slowly. 'There are persistent and detailed rumours that Senior Constable Marsden was involved in something he shouldn't have been.'

'Are we really back to this? Gary and I weren't doing anything illegal together. He wasn't mixed up in anything.' Hold on to those words, believe them. 'He was just a good guy, trying to make a life with his family.'

'Detective McFarlane from Ethical Standards doesn't seem to think so. Neither do the guys from IBAC.'

He shook his head. 'What's IBAC?'

'You really are a babe in the woods, aren't you? They're the old Office of Police Integrity. They're the serious guys, Caleb, the ones with all the money and the power.' He paused. 'We had an anonymous tip that there was ice involved.'

'This is getting ridiculous, it'll be fucking bank heists next. Is there any evidence, any evidence at all, that Gary was crooked? Because I've been to his house, I've seen his family. His wife drives a fifteen-year-old Astra and runs herself ragged working part-time while caring for two young kids. They don't go on holidays, and a big night out is pizza at the local shops. So where's all the fucking money? Did you find an extra bank account? Did you find thousands stashed away in his shed?'

'No.'

But there had been a slight hesitation before Tedesco's admission. No extra money, but something hadn't added up.

'Was there money missing?'

Tedesco's dark eyebrows rose. 'You knew?'

'No. How much?'

'Two hundred dollars in cash every fortnight for the last ten months. Marsden kept a fairly detailed spreadsheet for the family budget, but this was labelled as miscellaneous. Any idea what extra expenses he might have incurred lately?'

Ten months. Honey's baby was nine or ten months old. The way she'd clutched it to her when he'd gone to her house, Maria's insistence he didn't talk to her.

'... *you need to remember that you're dealing with other people's lives.*'

Fuck.

He shrugged. 'A few hundred? Maybe he'd taken up a hobby.'

Tedesco got to his feet. 'Email if you decide to give me the real story.'

A white heat shot through him. He stood up and Tedesco stiffened, instantly on the alert.

'You're looking in the wrong direction. Stop fucking around with Gary and start looking for Scott. Start with Boxer, he'll have a record.' He pulled Petronin's licence from his pocket and shoved it at Tedesco.

'He gave this to you?'

'He dropped it.'

The detective looked at him for a long moment. 'What do you know about Gary's missing money?'

'It's not relevant.'

'This is a murder investigation, Mr Zelic; everything's relevant.' When Caleb didn't answer, he turned away.

Shit, shit, shit.

'Gary had an affair with Honey Kovac. I think her youngest child is his. He would have given her child support.'

The detective turned back. 'What else have you neglected to tell me?'

He passed the detective the photo from Petronin's flat. 'This woman is involved somehow.'

'Petronin again.' Tedesco settled on the bench and tilted his head for Caleb to join him. 'Who's the woman?'

'I don't know, but I've seen her somewhere.'

'Uh-huh.'

'She's important. Petronin lives on the other side of town from me, but I've seen the woman with him in this photo. I can usually slot people in, but I can't do it with her. I think I've just seen her, not met her.'

'You're projecting. It can happen on a case. You want…'

'No, I've seen her somewhere in the last few months. I remember people.'

Tedesco's eyes narrowed: interested now. 'Because you're deaf?'

Time to change the subject. Except he needed Tedesco to believe him and start looking for her.

'I don't know, it's just something I do. I don't think she's served me in a shop – I'd remember if she'd spoken to me.'

'Why? I'm an expert witness, but I don't think I'd remember the woman who served me fish and chips three months after the fact.'

'Everyone has their own cadences and rhythms when they speak.'

Tedesco made a small 'go on' motion with his hand.

'I pay attention to them.' He shifted on the bench. 'People are easier to understand when I know their patterns.'

Tedesco's eyes drifted towards the playground. Not distracted, just aware of his discomfort. That was good, very subtle.

'You remember people's words, too, don't you? You've quoted me back to myself a couple of times.'

He had? 'I guess so.'

'What did Gary's message say?'

'"Scott after me. Come my house. Urgent. Don't talk anyone. Anyone."' When Tedesco didn't move, he added, 'Why are we back to this?'

'Who did Gary not want you to talk to?'

'Oh.' Stupid that had never occurred to him. He'd been so focused on Scott, he'd forgotten to look further. 'It could have just been a figure of speech, something to emphasise his words.'

'Does that sound like Gary? Was he an emphasiser of words?'

'No, but none of it sounds like him. He was scared.'

'With good reason.' Tedesco pulled his phone from his pocket and snapped a picture of the woman. 'I'll ask around.'

A good outcome: he hadn't spontaneously combusted and Tedesco was on side. Maybe Kat was right and he should be more open. He rolled the stiff muscles in his shoulders. Maybe not.

'Who's in the white Toyota?'

Shit.

The almost-smile crept back into the detective's eyes. 'He's been sitting there looking at us the entire time, hasn't moved an inch.'

Not a clear view, then. 'Just a friend. Listen, I've been trying to work out how Boxer found me. Could someone have traced me through prescriptions, or a new phone, one I'd only had a few days?'

'They could,' Tedesco said slowly. 'If they're very well connected.'

'So,' Frankie said when he was back in the car. 'No knives, no guns, I'm thinking he isn't out to kill you.'

'Looking that way.' He watched the white Falcon pull out and drive away.

'What do you think? Do you trust him?'

'He's really hard to read, but, yeah, I think he's OK.'

'Thank God for that.' She started the engine. 'Someone on our side.'

'Not actively against us, anyway. He's still unsure about Gary.'

'Mate, we're all unsure about Gary.'

'No we're not.'

'Come on, Cal. You would have sworn a couple of weeks ago that he wouldn't root around on his wife. Tell me you're not wondering what else you didn't know about him.'

'I'm wondering that about everyone.' Including himself. Gaz must have found out Honey was pregnant right around the time Kat and he had split. Which explained why his friend hadn't confided in him, but didn't explain his own blindness.

He clipped his seat belt as Frankie pulled into a non-existent gap in the traffic.

She turned to him. 'Let's go to Arnie next, I could do with some flirting.'

'Eyes front. Let's go to City Sentry first, I want to catch the receptionist on her lunch break.'

He angled the mirror towards himself to watch for white Ford Falcons. The detective had played him beautifully, shadowing his every move and emotion. And managed to get more personal information out of him in five minutes than most people got in five years. That was impressive. Worrying.

23.

Frankie circled the block twice and ended up parking in a no-standing zone twenty metres from City Sentry.

She caught his glance at the fire hydrant and shrugged. 'What are the odds of them actually needing it while we're here?'

Lower than the odds of the car being towed, but with any luck Elle would be out on the early side of lunchtime. Not the type to eat lunch at her desk; she'd be bored and wanting to fluff her feathers in the winter sun.

'Idea bad me,' Frankie signed.

They were back to this again. She'd lost the argument about whether to meet with Elle, but couldn't seem to let it go.

'Idea good me,' he signed back.

She narrowed her eyes, suspecting he was taking the piss, but not sure enough of her syntax to take issue.

'Love with man and woman dangerous.'

Truer words had never been signed.

'Love?' He switched to English. 'Who said anything about love?'

'Is that what that sign is? I thought it meant sex.'

'You think sex between a man and a woman is dangerous?'

'Piss off, you know what I was trying to say.'

'I really don't.'

'That if there's something between the receptionist and Sean, it's a dumb idea to talk to her.'

He thought back to Sean's aggressive posturing, Elle's brilliant smile. She hadn't been unaware of her effect on the manager, but hadn't been taking it too seriously.

'I don't think there's anything actually there. It's more in Sean's mind. Or his pants.'

'He's a man, it's the same thing. But even if you're right, it's a risk.'

'She's five foot nothing and doesn't like chipping her nail polish.' He looked at Frankie's gnawed and stubby nails. 'I think you could take her.'

'And if she goes blabbing to Sean? He might tell someone you're back in Melbourne.'

'He already knows I'm looking into him. But it's a good point about you – you should stay in the car again.'

'Fuck that, I'll just use a different name. Something Shakespearean maybe. I've always liked the name Cordelia.'

A flash of red caught his eye: Elle, dressed in a shimmery silver coat, a flame of hair showing beneath a purple beret.

'That's her.' He got out and caught her as she stepped onto the footpath. 'Elle.'

A moment's hesitation, then her eyes cleared. 'Caleb from Trust Works.'

'Can we talk? About work,' he added quickly as her face settled into an I've-got-a-boyfriend expression. 'This is my partner, Goneril.'

Frankie stepped on his foot as she leaned forward to shake Elle's hand.

'Nice hair,' Elle said.

'Yours too. Goes well with the hat.'

Elle beamed. 'You want to talk to Sean? I can pop up and see if he's still in.'

'No, we want to talk to you. How about we buy you lunch?'

Elle picked at the sandwich she'd ordered. They were sitting in a laneway cafe that served excellent coffee and shit tea. Caleb gave his soggy teabag another poke and wondered what had made him order an English Breakfast in the coffee capital of Australia.

'You want me to spy?' Elle said.

Her nails were silver today, with tiny purple spots. Had she chosen the clothes to go with the polish, or the polish to go with the clothes? He re-evaluated her importance to City Sentry; anyone that organised had to be a boon in any office.

'No,' Frankie said. 'Nothing like that. We're trying to clear City Sentry's name. It's obvious the company had nothing to do with the robberies, but we're having trouble getting the evidence to prove it. Sean's being a bit close-mouthed about everything.'

Literally, Caleb thought, remembering Sean's miserly lip movements.

'Yeah, I don't know. I don't really like the idea of talking behind his back.' She studied Frankie for a moment. 'You ever think about adding a bit of pink? It'd go well with your colouring.'

'No.'

'Yeah, maybe you're not a pink type of girl. Orange'd work, too. Be a good contrast with the purple. I can recommend some hairdressers.'

'I usually just do it in the bathroom sink.'

Elle's mouth opened in shock.

Caleb jumped in before she could start listing salons. 'If the insurance company takes legal action against City Sentry it'll be ugly. I'd hate to see people losing their jobs just because Sean and I didn't hit it off.'

A blush rose up Elle's cheeks. 'He's not usually like that, he's a bit of a joker, you know? I've never seen him...' She chewed her lip. 'I thought he was going to hit you.'

He ignored Frankie's raised eyebrows. 'He was just worried. He's got a lot of people working for him. It's a big responsibility.'

'It is. He's been so stressed with all the redundancies. And he says the new owners keep threatening more.' She began picking at her sandwich again.

Frankie caught his eye and an unspoken 'stay silent' passed between them.

When she'd pulled all the crusts from the bread, Elle looked up. 'Just information?'

'Just information,' he said. 'Sean said that the guards don't have the keys to the actual warehouse, just the gates. Is that right?'

'Sure, they only ever have the keys to the gates. No need for them to have the building keys. If they find anything unlocked, they have to call in anyway.'

'How closely monitored are the keys to the warehouse?'

'Monitored?'

'Can anyone take them, are they left in an unlocked cupboard or drawer?'

'No. Everything goes through Mrs Hitchens. She keeps them in the safe and changes the code every week.' Her expression morphed into one of po-faced severity. 'There's a "strict operating procedure for the benefit of our company and clients".'

'So when Sean gets the keys out...'

'Sean doesn't get the keys out, that's Mrs Hitchens' job.'

'And if Mrs Hitchens is away?'

'She's never away.' She leaned forward, eyes wide. 'She's worked for City Sentry for thirty years. Some of the guys joke that she's a vampire.' She didn't look convinced that it was a joke.

'What about the codes to the warehouse alarm? Who has them?' Caleb asked.

'Oh, that's not one of ours.'

'So no-one at City Sentry knew the alarm code?'

'No.'

Damn, there went that theory. 'Can you get us a list of everyone who's had the keys to the warehouse doors in the last year? We'd usually go through Sean, but...'

Elle picked up her sandwich, then lowered it again. 'Do you really think the insurance company will sue us?'

'They lost two million dollars, Elle. What would you do?'

'Just a list of people? That's all?'

'That's all.' Frankie slipped her a business card. 'Email it from a private account, don't use your work one. And don't make photocopies or anything, Sean might be offended that you're trying to help. Men, you know.' She jerked her head towards Caleb. 'They've got such fragile egos.'

Elle's cheek dimpled. 'I'd better go. But hey, listen.' She looked at Caleb. 'I've been practising – *hvordan har du det*.'

Not a single identifiable word. 'Sorry, what?'

Her face fell. 'Oh, didn't I get it right? *Hvordan har du det*.'

She looked like she was holding marbles in her mouth. Fuck it, he was going to have to ask Frankie for help. No, she was looking equally blank.

'*Hvordan har du det*,' Elle said again.

She was usually so easy to read, but that didn't look like English at all. Ah. He remembered his supposed background as a Danish immigrant.

'That's great,' he said. 'Really clear.'

'So I did it right?'

'Couldn't have said it better myself.'

'*Hvordan har du det*,' Frankie said when they were outside. 'Does that mean, "I've got a crush on you" in Danish?'

'No, Goneril, it means you should dye your hair pink.'

She patted its spiky tips. 'I might just do that. What was the Danish all about, anyway?'

'Bit of a misunderstanding.'

'Yeah? You seem to be having a few of those lately. What happened between you and Sean?'

'Nothing much. He just assumed I'd scare off easily and gave it a go.'

She examined him. 'Ah. Did the nasty man hurt your feelings?'

Two seconds to imagine the testosterone-fuelled interview, work out the reason for Sean's assumption, and calculate his own reaction to it. She was terrifying, really.

'So, Giannopoulos now?' she asked.

'You're awfully keen to see him. Do you really think he's going to be of any use?'

'No, I just want to see if you're going to yell at him again. Particularly now I know about you and Sean. I'll be ready to video it this time. Be a useful training tool for my next partner – how not to talk to witnesses.' She pulled out her phone and frowned at the number. 'Hello?' A look of almost comical surprise crossed her face.

She held it to her chest. 'It's Detective Tedesco. He says hello.'

He stumbled. 'What? How the hell did he work out I was with you? Or that you're even alive?'

'Guess the man's good at his job. Kind of nice to know.'

He couldn't summon the same amount of enthusiasm.

'Well done, Detective,' she said. 'Yes, I'm very well, thank you. Sorry to have inconvenienced you all. So, did you ring just to show off your detecting skills?' She winced and covered the phone with her hand. 'He said Detective McFarlane found out that he's been speaking to you privately. And because McFarlane bawled him out about it in the middle of the Broadmeadows cop shop canteen, we should assume that pretty much everyone else in Melbourne knows about it, too.'

Shit. 'I guess it was bound to happen sooner or later.'

She turned her attention back to the phone. 'Is that it, or did you just ring for a chat?'

A lot of nodding, not many words. Unease stirred: Frankie's expression remained carefully neutral, but her shoulders had stiffened.

'What's up?' he said as she hung up.

'Look, don't panic, but he was asking about Kat.'

'He knows...' He took a breath. 'He knows about Kat?'

'Him and McFarlane.'

'He told fucking McFarlane?'

'Other way round. McFarlane went to Tedesco because there's a tap on Kat's phone in Collingwood, another one at Maria's house.'

'The fucking arsehole. He's going after every member of my family, isn't he? What now? Kat's the leader of a bikie gang? Or is she supposed to be cooking up meth in her studio while Anton stands guard?'

'No, you don't understand. McFarlane didn't order the tap, he just found out about it. Apparently... Look, this is the bit I don't want you to freak out about, OK? But apparently neither of them asked for the tap. Someone else did. Someone with a lot of pull, because McFarlane hasn't been able to find out who.'

Ice in his veins. 'Scott. Scott knows about Kat.'

'He's probably just trying to find out where you are.'

'He's not that subtle. If he's interested in Kat, it's because he's after her.'

She didn't disagree. 'I'm ringing her now.'

Scott will kill them if he finds out.

Frankie was talking to Kat, thank God. No, leaving a message. A fucking message.

Scott will kill her if he finds out.

He had to get to her. Resurrection Bay was hours away. Or would she have gone back to Collingwood? No, she knew it wasn't safe there. Fuck, fuck, no idea where she was. What was he going to do?

Frankie touched his arm. '... fine.'

'What?'

'I've left messages on her mobile and at Maria's house and clinic. She'll get them, she'll be fine.'

'The clinic closes at four.'

'Which is why I left a message on her mobile,' she said slowly.

'If Scott... Frankie, I just left her there. I thought she'd be safe out of the house. I thought he was just after me. No, I didn't think. I didn't fucking think.'

Half the town's mouths flapping, gossip flying from their lips. The conversation would have taken less than a minute. '*Excuse me, local person, do you know Caleb Zelic? Staying with Dr Anderson? His ex-mother-in-law? You don't say. And her daughter's name?*'

It was hard to breathe.

24.

There was a forthcoming auction sign staked in the middle of Arnie's dandelion-specked front lawn.

'Misjudged him,' Frankie said. 'Didn't strike me as the type who liked change. What was your impression?'

'Same. Can you ring Anton? She might still be in the Bay somewhere. He'll find her if she's there, he knows everyone.'

'Sure, but give her a chance, it's only been twenty minutes. She's probably just got her phone on silent.'

He followed her from the car. 'I don't want to wait. Ring him now.'

'Give it an hour, then I'll call.' She nodded at the real estate sign. 'So what do you think that means?'

'That Arnie's selling his house. Why are you trying to deflect me?'

'You want to do this? OK.' She stood still. 'What would you do to keep Kat safe?'

'What?'

'Throw yourself in front of a train? Give yourself up to Scott?'

'Yes.'

'So Scott's pretty clever to go after her then, isn't he?'

'Are you trying to make me feel worse?'

'No, I'm walking you somewhere you don't want to go. Scott does two things: he goes after people, and he goes after their families. Anton's your family, but Scott isn't going after him, he's going after your ex-wife. Why? If someone came after my ex I'd say have at him. So how does Scott know that Kat's your vulnerable spot?'

It started to rain, but neither of them moved.

'She's Maria's daughter. Maria was treating me.'

'Are you being deliberately obtuse?'

Yes. Yes, he was. Because following that line of thought made him want to scratch out his brain.

'You're wrong,' he said. 'Ant loves Kat, he wouldn't do anything to hurt her.'

'Come on, Cal, you've been worried all along that Anton's involved in this somehow. Three names keep coming up in this investigation – Gary's, Scott's, and Anton's.'

'There's no way he'd set Scott onto Kat.' He started up Arnie's front path.

Frankie kept pace, talking quickly, but he didn't look at her.

She grabbed his arm just before he reached the house. Droplets were clinging to her eyebrows and lashes.

'Na-ah, you don't get to break your own rules – you watch me while I say, very clearly, that you're kidding yourself if you think Anton has loyalty towards anything except his habit.'

He wrenched his arm free. 'Back off, Frankie.'

'He's a junkie. You can trust him as far as you can kick him.'

'Seriously – back the fuck off.' Rain was running down the back of his neck and soaking his shirt.

'I'm not saying this for fun. I know all about addiction, I know exactly what Anton...' She drew in a sharp breath. 'Oh shit.'

He followed her gaze. A scrap of something blue and white was fluttering from Arnie's front door. Police tape. He felt dizzy. Killed? Or just attacked again? Something horrendous, either way: they didn't bother stringing up police tape for a break-and-enter.

Frankie wiped the rain from her eyes. 'Neighbours might know what happened.'

He surveyed the surrounding houses. The one diagonally opposite was the best bet: pram on the front porch, fairy stickers on the front window. Young mum at home with the kids. Young mums were even better than old ducks: very observant, very vigilant, very bored.

'House with the kids,' he said.

She nodded but didn't move. 'And Anton?'

He unclenched his jaw. 'Don't call him.'

He turned for the road before she could tell him he'd made the right decision.

A man answered their knock, a baby thrown over his shoulder, a three-day old beard and the smell of sour milk on his clothes. Young dad at home with the kids.

'Sorry to disturb you,' Caleb began.

'Hang on. It's cooking.'

Context was half the trick of comprehension. Maybe the word had been 'looking'. No, that didn't work, either.

'Sorry, I...'

'It's still cooking,' the man said. 'It takes three minutes. Watch the little hand on the clock.'

Right. Another child in the house, an egg boiling. Or well-done two-minute noodles.

'Look, what is it? I don't want to buy anything. Or donate anything.' He looked at the squirming baby. 'Unless you want one of the kids. Could give you a couple of those.'

'Do you know what happened in the house across the road? Arnie Giannopoulos?'

'Oh.' He grimaced. 'You're not friends of his, are you?'

'Business acquaintances.'

'Oh. Oh good.'

'The police tape – can you tell us what happened? Was he killed?'

'Yeah, last week. I'm surprised you didn't see it on the news. Nice old bloke like that, hard to believe. Bloody family couldn't wait to get that auction sign up. Don't think he was even buried yet.'

'Do the police have any theories?'

The dad glanced at his wrist. 'Another twenty seconds – watch the clock. They said it was someone on meth or something. Arnie was a little paranoid, had these bars on the window, but the guy just smashed the back door in. Shocking stuff, meth. Turns people into animals.'

'So the house was wrecked?'

'No, that's the tragedy of it. The bastard didn't take a thing, just went straight to Arnie's bedroom and cut his throat. OK, time's up.'

He wasn't hungry, but he drove to a souvlaki joint on Sydney Road so they could dry off and think. Frankie had been silent for the past ten minutes, eating her way through her souvlaki with mechanical disinterest. She finally screwed her paper bag into a ball and looked up.

'Maybe we're looking at this the wrong way. What if Scott had nothing to do with the cigarettes being stolen? What if he was smuggling something through the warehouse, through lots of warehouses? He's got a nice little set-up until Arnie comes along and steals the cigarettes and, along with them, whatever Scott's smuggling. So he beats Arnie up to get his goods back, then comes back a week or so later to kill him because there's too much interest in the case.'

As a theory it had everything going for it. Except for the part where Arnie organised two major robberies.

'Arnie couldn't organise his life, let alone two warehouse raids involving heavy machinery and an alarm system. The only thing he'd changed in that house were the bars on the windows and he didn't even think to replace the shitty back door. He's a follower.'

'Followers need someone to follow,' she said. 'Maybe he knew someone with connections.'

Good point. And Arnie had mentioned a friend when they'd interviewed him. Mentioned him more than once, the way people do when they're trying hard not to think of someone.

'His mate,' he said. 'That's who we need to find.'

'What mate?'

'The guy he mentioned in that story about falling over on the way back from the pub.'

'It was a story, Caleb – he didn't fall over, he was bashed. By Scott.'

'And, like all good stories, it had an element of truth to it – the friend's real. Had some weird name, think it started with P.' He thought back to Arnie's chapped lips and staccato sentences. What had he said?

'*Had a few drinks down the pub with me mate...*' Pierre? Pytor? Percy?

'Got it: Pearose. The mate's name is Pearose.'

'Pearose? That doesn't sound right. You sure?'

His neck was hot. 'No.'

'Pearose, Pearose, Pearose.' She slapped the table. 'Got it: Pearose.'

He didn't know what his face told her, but her grin dropped. She typed on her phone and turned the screen towards him – Spiros. Well, fuck, how the hell was he supposed to know that?

'All right,' she said. 'So all we need to do is find an ageing Greek guy in Melbourne called Spiros. Like looking for a leaf of parsley in the tabouli.'

'Tabouli's Middle Eastern.'

'Greek, Middle Eastern, how do you propose we find him? We don't even know his surname.'

'Start with Arnie's death notices.'

'Yeah, all right.' She wiped her mouth. 'If you're just going to sit there and not eat that, let's get started.'

They found an internet cafe squeezed between a bridal boutique and a sex shop at the end of the block. There was a worrying stickiness to the computer keyboard: if there was any crossover custom between the three businesses, he didn't want to know which ones. A search through the last week's death notices found Arnie's: much-loved father of Toula, grandfather to Zoe and Oskar. No message from a friend named Spiros, conveniently giving his surname and address. He googled the name Toula Giannopoulos and got a few results, all of them in Greek, from Greece. Looked like Arnie's daughter had either emigrated or taken her husband's surname.

'I'll ring the funeral parlour,' Frankie said. 'They might give me the daughter's contact details.'

He nodded and scrolled through the notices again: there was a chance they could trace Spiros through one of Arnie's other friends if they'd posted a message of condolence. Nothing from the same day, or the next, or the next. Wait. He went back. There was a message, but not for Arnie.

Our dearest Pop Pop

We'll always love you.

Gone too soon.

Spiros Galto

'Fuck.'

Frankie lowered the phone. 'What?

He stabbed a finger at the screen. 'He's killed Spiros, too.'

'Jesus. I guess that's that, then.' She went to put her phone away, but he stopped her.

'Ring Kat again.'

Only fifteen minutes had passed since her last call, but she went through the motions without arguing.

'It's only been an hour,' she said as she hung up. 'Still no reason to worry.'

'Yeah.' He pushed back his chair and walked outside.

A churning heat in his stomach. Two options: drive to the Bay, or keep dicking around here. Both felt useless. No leads here, no idea if Kat was there. He pulled the car keys from his pocket as he went to cross the road. They felt too heavy: Gary's keys, not his. He swallowed. How many more people were going to die before this was over?

A sudden rush of air.

The smell of disc brakes and diesel.

Hands yanking him back.

Frankie was gripping his arm, her face white. 'Fuck. Cal.'

Shit, he'd just stepped out in front of a truck. 'Sorry, wasn't concentrating.'

'I mean, right out in front of it. Like a toddler.' She pointed to the road. 'That could have been you.'

Gary's keys were lying in a tangled bunch on the asphalt, surrounded by shards of plastic. He waited for a break in the traffic, then fetched them. The torch was broken, and the pen. The keys looked all right, but Gary's 'cool stuff' pocketknife was cracked down the middle. He tried to push the casing into place and the entire back fell off.

'Fuck.'

He tried again, feeling a ridiculous need to make it whole. It took him a couple of attempts before he recognised what was lying in his hand: a USB stick. A clever design; it must have been hidden in the middle of the pocketknife. Trust Gaz to carry a memory stick around for emergency backup situations.

He looked at Frankie. 'He always saved everything.'

'It's OK, we can probably replace all the parts.'

'No, I mean Gaz. Scott took his computer.' He held up the USB. 'But he always backed up.'

She stared at the stick. 'The small thing they're looking for?'

'Could be.'

'Pity you just threw it under the wheels of a fucking truck then, isn't it?'

He examined the stick: the circuitry was exposed and the head was pinched closed. 'We could take it to someone. A computer hardware specialist.'

'Computer medium, more like. It's fucked.' She pulled out her phone and glanced at the screen. 'Not Kat,' she told him before answering. 'Detective, hello. Sure, what's up?' Her face wiped blank.

'What's wrong?' he asked.

'But why...' She turned from him and he was left scrabbling to catch her words. '... you... photo... Fuck, OK.'

He grabbed her shoulders to hold her in place.

'Half an hour. I will.' She hung up.

'Don't you fucking dare do that to me! Give me the fucking courtesy of...'

'Cal.' Tears started in her eyes.

The air left his lungs. He suddenly didn't want to know what the phone call had been about.

'Tedesco wants us to look at a photo. They found... They found the body of a woman. Cal, he thinks...'

He looked away so he couldn't see the rest of her words.

Not Kat. No.

25.

A hand on his shoulder.

'We're here,' Frankie said.

He nodded and got out. They were at a large park. A lake, children, ducks. Tedesco was sitting at a picnic table near a small wooden kiosk. Caleb walked towards him; one step, then another, across the wet grass. There was a children's playground here. A pool too, grey-blue under the clouded sky. One lone swimmer was ploughing through its frigid waters. Cold getting changed, walking to the water's edge. Colder still in the water, the blood congealing in your veins.

Tedesco looked his way and stood up. He was holding a large envelope.

Caleb's feet stopped moving.

'They broke Gary's fingers.' The words came from nowhere.

Frankie rocked back. 'I know.'

'Cut him.'

She nodded.

'If they… I can't… If Kat…'

Frankie lifted her hand, then lowered it. 'It might not be her,' she eventually said.

He started walking again. His feet didn't seem to be

working properly, or the ground wasn't where it was supposed to be. Tedesco gave a quick nod when they reached him and launched into a slow and methodical speech. Something about formal identification and coroners. Caleb's eyes went to the envelope. It was plain, buff-coloured, nothing to show the horror it contained. His chest was tight, no air getting through to his brain.

Frankie tapped his arm. 'Let me look.'

He shook his head and Tedesco slid a photo from the envelope. Had to blink a few times to get his eyes to focus. She was lying on a stainless steel slab, looking straight at him, a dull sheen to her blue eyes. Dead. So obviously dead. Drained of anything that had made her sparkle in life. Her hair straggled over her face, unbrushed. For some reason that seemed like the final indignity.

He thrust the photo at Tedesco. 'It isn't Kat.'

The detective's mouth was moving, but he turned away and stumbled to the toilet block. Just made it into the cubicle before throwing up. Felt like he was being turned inside out. Everything out. Everything except the fear; that stayed in. An overreaction. It wasn't Kat. It had never been Kat. Some other woman was lying dead with her hair in tangles, not Kat. But he was unable to leave that alternate world, the one where he turned the photo over and saw Kat lying there. He got to his feet and rinsed his mouth at the basin, splashed his face. Slow, slow breathing. Air in, air out. Air in, air out. Not Kat. It had never been Kat.

Frankie was waiting a discreet distance away, tapping her fingers against her thighs. She turned as he approached and pulled him into a tight hug, leaning her forehead against his shoulder. He stood for a moment, then broke away. The sunlight felt hot against the back of his eyes.

'Sit down come,' she signed. 'Coffee big man butterfly.'

He laughed. There was a strong chance she'd done that on purpose, but he appreciated it either way.

They sat side by side at a picnic table and watched Tedesco head across the playground towards them; he was carrying numerous cups and bottles and wrapped foods. The envelope was tucked under his arm.

His heart skipped. 'What if I... What if I was wrong? I should look again.'

'I checked – it isn't Kat. I promise.' Her eyes flicked to Tedesco. 'Back in a tick.'

She strode towards the detective. Tedesco passed her the coffee cups and they stood talking, the top of Frankie's head not quite reaching the detective's chin. Caleb had the strong sense she was telling him off and Tedesco wasn't taking it lying down. She finally snapped something that made the big man shut up, and they walked back to the table in an apparent truce.

They sat opposite him, Tedesco sliding a coffee and sodden-looking lamington across the table.

'Carbohydrates. Good for shock.'

'Thanks,' he said, but didn't pick it up. It was going to be a while before he trusted his stomach enough to put anything solid into it.

Frankie and Tedesco made small talk while they drank; two strangers trying to find common ground until the world could return to its normal axis. They were discussing coffee. Tedesco liked his weak, with lots of milk and sugar. Frankie was looking at him with an expression akin to disgust. Possibly not the safe subject they'd assumed it was. He watched their mouths, but wasn't really concentrating. His body felt heavy, adrenaline ebbing. A sleep would be good now. Maybe right here on the picnic table. He could zone out for a few hours while Frankie and Tedesco argued about whether a cappuccino was a respectable thing for a police detective to drink.

'That's great,' Frankie said.

They'd moved on from caffeine.

'What's great?' Caleb said.

'I've found out a bit about Michael Petronin,' Tedesco said. 'He's known to the police. No great surprise there. A few assaults, served some time in his twenties for it, but since then we've never been able to prosecute. No-one's been willing to testify against him.'

Caleb had a vision of that soulless smile: not hard to imagine why. 'Did you find his ex-wife?'

'He's never been married.'

Damn. 'So you don't know who the woman in the photo with him is?'

'No.'

'Do you know anything else about him?'

Tedesco consulted some internal code before answering. 'No known loyalties, but there are rumours he's done standover work for a couple of the local kingpins. Apparently he's quite persuasive.' He paused. '*Was* quite persuasive. He was found dead yesterday, near a little town called Resurrection Bay. Homicide.'

They sat for a moment without speaking.

'Do you have any leads in his murder?' Frankie asked.

The detective's face was as unreadable as ever. 'Possibly

gangland related. He was killed by the same gun that killed a policeman last week.'

Caleb sat up. 'Another cop? Who? When?'

'Senior Constable Anthony Hobbs. He was killed in the early hours of June the twenty-fourth.'

The same day as Gary. 'So his death is connected to Gary's.'

'That hasn't been ascertained.'

'Did Constable Hobbs have a connection with Petronin?'

'Not that I'm aware of.'

'Or Scott?'

'Not that I'm aware of.'

'Or Gary?'

The slightest of hesitations. 'Not that I'm aware of.'

Caleb glanced at Frankie – she'd caught it, too. Not a certain link, but a possible one. Why would Tedesco suspect Gary and Hobbs might know each other?

'Where was Hobbs stationed?' he asked.

'Craigieburn.'

Not Gary's current station, but he'd worked there four years ago. A mid-sized station, in an outer suburb, two senior constables; there was a good chance they'd have known each other. The real question was the nature of their relationship.

'What was Hobbs like?' he asked.

'I didn't know him.'

Like pulling teeth. Big, stone teeth from an Easter Island head.

'What was his service record like?'

'Exemplary.' Tedesco drank his coffee and waited silently for the next question.

Frankie squinted at him. 'You're a chatty bastard, aren't you?'

A glint in Tedesco's eye. 'That hasn't been ascertained.'

She nodded in appreciation and tapped the envelope by his elbow. 'In more than three words, explain to us the connection between the dead woman and the case.'

'I doubt she's connected. That was a matter of me seeing her photo and jumping to conclusions.' He met Caleb's eyes; a moment of openness. 'Sorry to have put you through that.'

Caleb shook his head.

Frankie was frowning. 'How do you know what Kat looks like?'

'I've got a photo-board. Helps me see connections.'

'In the middle of Broadmeadows fucking police station? With Scott running around, paying off cops?'

His expression didn't change. 'It's at home, *Ms* Reynolds. This isn't exactly official business.'

She took a minute, then said through stiff lips, 'Sorry. Guess I'm a bit jumpy.'

Caleb looked at them both bristling. This he could do without. 'Detective...'

'Uri,' Tedesco said.

'Sorry?'

'So am I, mate.' The detective cracked a smile for the first time, a transforming expression. 'It's my name.'

'Uri, we had a theory that Scott might have been smuggling something through the warehouse. Something Arnie may have accidentally stolen.'

'Good theory. Do you have any evidence to support it?'

'No, but we've found a USB that belonged to Gary. There

might be something on it.' He reached into his pocket for the memory stick and Frankie kicked his shin. He froze.

'I keep telling you we won't get anything off that.' She looked at Tedesco. 'He threw it under the wheels of a semi. It's fucked.'

Caleb slowly withdrew his hand and reached for his water bottle.

'You'd be surprised what the computer whizzes can do these days. Where is it?'

'With our computer guy,' Frankie said without hesitation.

'It's potential evidence, it should be in a police lab. What's the address? I'll send someone for it.'

She shook her head. 'I'm not too happy about giving it to some probationary constable who may or may not be working with Grey-face. Unless you've got time to drive down to Frankston yourself, how about we pick it up and give it to you?'

Tedesco was silent for a long time. 'All right.'

The muscles around Frankie's eyes relaxed. 'I'll give you a ring when we've got it.'

Caleb took her cue and shook the detective's hand. 'Thanks, Uri. It's a relief to have someone in the know on our side.'

Tedesco gave him a grim smile. 'Sorry to burst your bubble, but I've been in this position for five whole weeks. Barely know my way around Melbourne yet.'

Those dust-bowl cadences that still showed through his cop-speak. Maybe he hadn't been fast-tracked; maybe he'd been mouldering away in a one-pub country town until now. Which could mean he was either very stupid, or very bright.

'You're from the country?'

Tedesco looked at him for a beat. 'Originally. But don't worry, I trained with the big kids.'

Very bright.

They watched him stride across the park. Agile for such a big man.

26.

'What was that all about?' Caleb asked as they walked back to the car.

'That didn't ring any alarm bells?'

'Which part?'

'The part where Tedesco just happens to know about Kat. Just happens to have her photo. Just happens to find a picture of a dead woman who looks like her.'

'She wasn't that similar.' Similar enough to give him nightmares for a long time.

'Similar enough to draw you out into the open. And all that "call me Uri" stuff?' She shook her head. 'Not sitting well.'

He thought through the conversation as they got in the car. Tedesco obviously didn't like breaking the rules, but he'd answered every question they'd put to him. The touch of humour had seemed genuine, too.

'I don't get that vibe from him – it feels like he's trying to help. And I met with him this morning. Out in the open, plenty of opportunity to attack me.'

'I don't want to dis your Spidey sense, but he met you at short notice, at the venue of your choice. If I was going to get to someone, you know what I'd do? I'd make sure they were tired and distressed, then I'd chat to them for a little while to show them what a great gal I am. Then, when they started to relax, I'd walk away and let the heavyweights take over.'

She was right: Tedesco was smart, subtle and ambitious. And the I'm-just-an-outsider line could have been a ruse. He could be best mates with every cop in Melbourne and they wouldn't know it.

'So we're agreed?' she said. 'We go for a long and very scenic drive in a well-populated area right now, and not meet with Tedesco again in person?'

'Yeah. And you need to get rid of your phone.'

She clutched it to her. 'My iPhone? Fuck that.'

'If Tedesco's working for Scott, it'll lead him straight to us.'

'Shit.' She switched it off, swearing fluently as she struggled to get the sim card out. 'Happy?' she said as she gently laid the parts in the glove box. 'I'll leave it off except to check messages.'

'Do you need a hug?'

She gave him the finger, glanced in the rear-view mirror, and pulled out in front of a bus. When he could look again, he angled the mirror towards himself and watched the road. After twenty minutes of one-way streets, sudden stops and unexpected right-hand turns, he relaxed. No-one could be following them.

He pointed towards a multi-storey car park. 'Pull in here for a sec.'

She drove in and parked. 'What's up?'

'If we're going to be paranoid, we may as well do it properly and change the plates.'

He grabbed two screwdrivers from the tool kit in the

boot. Anton couldn't have known it was there or it would have been long gone. He handed one to Frankie.

'Get ours off and I'll find some replacements.'

He wandered down the aisle. Nothing too new, nothing too special. A car that was just a car, one where the owners might not notice the changed plates right away. There – an old Renault with a wire coathanger in the shape of Australia serving as its aerial.

'Once a crim, always a crim,' Frankie said when he returned with the plates.

'One car, Frankie. And I was twelve.' Five cars and he was fourteen, but who was counting?

She kicked the balding tyres. 'Driving around in an unroadworthy car isn't too smart for a master criminal like you. Any cop could pull us over for these.'

She was right. It was time to stop trying to avoid the unavoidable.

'Let's check out Gary's place in the morning. I can get my car while we're there.'

'I was more hoping you'd steal me that Merc over there, but that sounds like a plan, too.'

The rest of the drive passed with only minimal road rage, and, half an hour later Frankie pulled in to a motel. Neither of them made a move to get out.

'Bad day at the office, huh?'

'Yeah.' He wasn't sure he could handle too many more like it.

She clipped the pieces of her phone back together and checked messages. His heart lurched at her sudden stillness, but she was grinning as she handed him the phone.

'Think this one's for you.'

– Safe. Not in the Bay or Melb. Kat

The weight of a thousand fears lifted from his shoulders and somehow lodged in his throat.

Safe. She was safe.

'Pity that didn't come in a bit earlier,' Frankie mused. 'Could have saved us all a bit of grief.'

Safe.

Heat pricked his eyes. Think about the message. It sounded like Kat was taking sensible precautions, like she was organised. Not too happy with him, though – no customary 'x' before her name. Had she ever texted him without signing off with a kiss before? Had she ever texted anyone without one? Text – shit.

'She's still using her phone. I thought you told her to leave it behind?'

'Ah. You didn't read the second one.'

'Second what?'

'There's a second message.'

He swiped the screen.

– its a public phone u idiot. give me some fucking credit.

Frankie thumped his arm. 'Calls for a bit of a celebration, don't you think?'

'God. Yes. Dinner's on me.' He dug in his pockets. 'Think it'll cost more than three dollars?'

Frankie paid for his beer and two plates of steak and chips at the nearest pub. She ate a few chips and sat nursing a mineral water; he sculled his beer so she didn't have to look at it.

'Solid food, that's a step up,' she commented, watching him mop gravy with his chips. 'You'll be sleeping next.'

She was right; as soon as the last mouthful hit his stomach, he was ready to lie down on the stinking floor and sleep.

'At least you're a cheap date.' She got to her feet. 'Come on, Princess, off to bed with you.'

They walked back to the motel, the three blocks feeling a lot further than on the way to the pub. As they passed a public phone, a thought that had been tickling the back of his brain since getting Kat's message finally formed. He'd been so focused on the calls Gary had made, he'd forgotten about the one he'd received. Detective McFarlane had grilled him about it in his interview. He could still see the red-headed man's disbelieving smile.

'*Come on, Caleb, you managed to call emergency services yesterday. You can handle a phone.*'

He stopped walking. 'Why would someone use a public phone?'

Frankie's lip curled. 'To piss in, judging by the smell.'

'Or to keep your number from appearing in someone's phone records.'

'Sure. Why? Are you thinking of stalking someone?'

'Gaz received a call from one the day he died. The cops kept going on about it, particularly the guy from Ethical Standards. I'm wondering if it was someone who knew the cops were going to be crawling all over Gary's phone records, someone who knew he was about to be killed.'

'Or someone with a flat battery, or no credit, but OK, let's go with your idea. So, what? It's a public phone, we've got no way of identifying who was using it.'

'No, but it might be interesting to get the number and find out where the phone is. I'll ask Sharon.'

There was a good chance she wouldn't read his text, an even better chance she wouldn't have the energy to check her phone records, but it was worth a try. He backtracked to the phone, but caught Frankie's expression as he lifted the receiver.

'You don't think it's a good idea?'

She shrugged. 'As long as you realise that there's a second reason someone might not have wanted their number showing up on Gary's records. The reason Ethical Affairs is so interested in the call.'

'Because the caller was involved in something dodgy with Gaz? Yeah, I'm not telling Sharon that part.' Or his niggling fear that the call might have come from the Bay.

They walked the rest of the way to the motel in silence. A shower, a little bottle of whisky from the mini bar, and he'd be ready to fall into a coma. He paused at his door. Frankie alone with a mini bar all night. Maybe he should clear it out for her.

'I'll come and clear out your mi–'

She turned away, giving him a little wave as she walked down the corridor. He waited until she'd disappeared, then opened his door. He locked it and just stood in the middle of the room. Safe. Kat was safe. A lifetime since he'd held that photo in his hands; he could feel every second of it weighing on his eyelids. Eight o'clock: too early for grown-ups to be thinking about sleep. Maybe just a nap. He lay down, fully clothed, and closed his eyes.

27.

The bed was shaking. Must have forgotten to turn off the alarm again. He reached for Kat to apologise, but his hand encountered only cold sheet. He peeled open his eyes. Frankie was standing over him, holding a takeaway coffee cup and kicking the bed.

'And he's awake,' she said. 'Refreshed from his beauty sleep.'

'How'd you get in?'

'Popped the lock. Lucky I'm not Scott – took two seconds.'

He sat up, blinking. His neck felt stiff, as though he'd slept in the one position for the past…

'Wow,' he said, looking at the bedside clock.

'Yeah, impressive. Don't think I've ever witnessed a thirteen-hour sleep marathon before. Had to resist the urge to check you were still breathing.'

He scrubbed his face. 'I think I left some of my brain on the pillow.'

She shoved the coffee into his hand. 'Well, get it back with this, we've got things to do.'

He took the coffee into the bathroom and drank it while he showered, even managed to piss while he was in there. Who said men couldn't multi-task? He pulled on a random selection of the clothes Anton had lent him – black jeans and a deep-red jumper – and checked out his reflection. Almost human.

Frankie eyed the ensemble as he entered the room. She was sitting crossed-legged on his bed, making short work of a sandwich.

'Almost fashionable. Didn't the shop stock out-of-date Midnight Oil T-shirts?' She threw something to him, underhand. A bundle of cash secured by a rubber band.

'Bit early in the day for bank robbery, isn't it?'

'We're going cardless. That's the maximum I could get out.' She lobbed him another package.

He examined it. 'A salad sandwich for breakfast? Are you on a health kick or something?' He regretted the words as soon as he'd said them, but she just shrugged.

'It was that or chocolate cake.'

He gave her a surreptitious once-over as he ate the roll. She was looking good this morning. No twitching or tapping, no bags under her eyes. And she was happily eating a salad sandwich. Excellent. With both of them fully functional, they might actually get somewhere today.

'Little email from Elle this morning,' she said, passing him her phone.

It was the promised list of people who'd had access to the warehouse. A lot longer than he'd been hoping for. She had arranged the names in alphabetical order, with most of the letters covered from A: Alston Electrics, through to L: Light Solutions. No, there was another page – P: Premium Occasions.

'Oh, come on.'

Frankie handed him something heavy in a brown paper bag. 'This might cheer you up – I went for the chocolate cake, too.'

He ate the cake on the way to the car, another bit of multi-tasking he wouldn't have been capable of yesterday. Food, sleep, relief: all a man needed to function properly. Well, nearly all. He had a vision of Kat's long limbs wrapped around him. He dragged his mind from the image and got in the car.

'Where to?' Frankie asked.

He took a deep breath. 'Gary's.'

Even from the street the house looked empty. No car in the driveway, no skateboards or bikes on the front porch. The grass in the front yard was longer than usual. If Gaz were here, he'd be out with the mower and whipper snipper, cutting it back into submission.

'Take yourself off for a coffee or something,' Frankie said. 'I'll have a quick poke around.'

Tempting, but he was the one who knew the house, knew the family.

'Be quicker with both of us.'

He walked to the front door and opened it before he could change his mind. The air was still. He stood just inside the hallway, trying not to remember the last time he'd been here. Trying even harder not to remember all the times before that. The hall table was gone, and the photos that had lined the walls. He made his way down the hallway, aware of Frankie close behind him. The family room had been cleared of furniture and books. A smell of bleach and pine.

A shadow marked the tiles where Gary had died.

He jumped as Frankie touched his shoulder.

'You do upstairs,' she said. 'I'll do here.'

He took the stairs without looking back. The bathroom and master bedroom were empty. No furniture, no toiletries. He opened the wardrobe. Nothing. He ran his hand along the architraves and pulled at the door panels, but there were no hidden recesses or secret messages. The carpet was tacked firmly to the floorboards and showed no signs of having been disturbed. He checked the kids' room. Pointless; Gaz wouldn't have kept anything dangerous near them. Which was worth examining. If Gary had had something he didn't want near his family, but needed to keep close, where would he have put it? Maybe the garage.

He averted his eyes from the stained floor as he descended the stairs. Out through the connecting laundry door, to the garage. It had been stripped clean. Not a single screw or nail left in the place.

The light switched on and off. Frankie was in the doorway.

'If it was here, it's gone,' she said. 'Where's all their stuff?'

'I don't know. But I don't think it was ever here – Gaz wouldn't have brought anything dangerous into the house.'

'I might just give Sharon a ring anyway, find out where their belongings are. What's her number?'

He hesitated.

'Cal, come on, you know I won't harass her. Just a quick couple of questions.'

'It's not you, it's just that I can't... She's pretty fragile at the moment and she's never met you.'

'Yeah I know, it's a shit, but I'll be as gentle with her as you would. Promise.'

She made the call while he transferred their belongings to his car. She finished while he was still changing the numberplates.

'Well Sharon's sister hates your guts,' she said.

'Yeah.' He lowered the screwdriver. 'How's Sharon?'

'Didn't get to speak to her. Didn't need to as it turns out. Michelle hired a professional crew to clean out the house. Sounds like most of it went to the tip. She's sending you the bill, by the way.'

Seemed fair. 'Another dead end, then.'

'Not entirely. She did pass on a message from Sharon: the number of the phone booth Gary received a call from.'

'Have you...'

'Doing it now.' She entered the number in a reverse directory: Queens Parade, Clifton Hill.

Nowhere near the Bay. Nowhere near anything connected to the case. He knew the street, he'd driven down it coming back from the warehouse the other day. What was there? Shops, cafes, more cafes.

'Any ideas?' he asked.

'No, but we can hunt down everyone's home address and see if anyone lives in Clifton Hill. You never know, we might get lucky.'

There was a first time for everything. He finished attaching the rear numberplate and returned the screwdriver to the boot. Frankie was watching him, tapping the phone against her leg.

'What?' he asked.

'Sharon's sister – what's with the aggression? She bit my head off when I pushed back about wanting to speak to Sharon.'

'She's protective. You know how older sisters are.' Too late, he remembered Frankie's estrangement from her own younger sister. 'I mean some older sisters. Over-protective ones.' Shut up now.

'Over-protective as in mamma bear? Or over-protective as in she knows something that's worrying her?'

'For fuck's sake Frankie, Michelle was not involved in Gary's death.'

'I'm not saying she was. But how d'you reckon she'd respond if she knew something that would endanger Sharon and the kids?'

Exactly the way she was now, with bluster and acidity. But what could Michelle know? Something Sharon had told her.

'You think Sharon knows more than she told me?'

She lifted a shoulder. 'Probably not, but if I can get her on the phone...'

'No.'

'I wouldn't...'

'No.' He thought back to the scene in the cafe: ripping the details about Gary's last phone call from a quietly weeping Sharon. He couldn't put her through that again on a whim.

'If it has to happen, I'll do it in person, but it's option D right now.'

She stood for a moment, then slipped the phone in her pocket.

'OK, option D.'

He drove without looking back. At the Alexandra Parade lights Frankie tapped the wheel and pointed straight ahead.

'Let's go to Richmond. We can drop off the USB and start in on that list of names Elle gave us.'

'Has Geekmate moved?'

'No, I thought we'd give someone new a try. They once mentioned a guy in Richmond who'd be good for a rush job – Sammy somebody. Ng, I think.'

He looked at her for a moment. Geekmate had always been their go-to computer guys. Fast, reliable, and trusted by numerous security companies. Including those run by ex-cops.

'You want to change because Tedesco knows about the USB?'

'Yeah, the paranoia's setting in nicely.'

The address Frankie had for Sammy Ng turned out to be an internet cafe of the upmarket kind. A lot of exposed brick and stainless steel, with Apple Macs interspersed among original artwork. Most of the clientele wore heavy-framed glasses and architecturally styled clothing.

'Fate,' Frankie said. 'I needed coffee and a computer

without sticky keys and the gods gave them to me.'

Caleb caught a waitress as she approached, lattes brimming.

'I'm looking for Sammy, the computer...'

'By the window,' she said, edging past.

'By the window' meant either a schoolgirl elbow-deep in homework or an elderly man with scraggy dreadlocks. He made his way towards the girl, Frankie close behind.

The girl looked up and gave them an open smile as they reached her. She had very white teeth and the unblemished skin of a ten-year-old raised on a macrobiotic diet.

'Sammy?'

'Sammi with an "i".' She stuck out her hand. 'Pleased to meet you.'

'*You're* Sammi?' Frankie said.

The girl sent a frown in Caleb's direction. 'She always this slow?'

Frankie's mouth closed with a snap.

'I'm Caleb,' he said, pulling out a chair. 'The slow one is Frankie. The guys from Geekmate gave us your name.' He paused. How old was she, anyway?

'Yeah I know, I look about twelve,' she said, apparently reading his mind. 'I'm sixteen.'

'Why aren't you in school?'

She squinted at him. 'What are you – my fricken mother? D'you wanna know if I've cleaned my room too, or d'you want my help?'

'Help.' He pulled the USB from his pocket and handed it to her. 'Can you see if you can get anything off this?'

'Old school.' She turned it over in her hand. 'Seven ninety-five at Officeworks.'

'Yes, but…'

'You need what's on it.'

'Yeah.'

She sat back and looked them both over. 'What are you? Private eyes or something?' Her eyes widened. 'Are there state secrets on it?'

'Nothing that exciting. Think you can get anything off it?'

'Well, I dunno,' she said. 'You try sticking it in a computer?'

He blinked.

'Jesus – men. Is it plugged in? Is it switched on? How do you all manage to find your dicks when you piss?' She sent a look in Frankie's direction. 'I expect better from a sister.'

Frankie choked out a laugh. 'How old are you again?'

'Old enough to know more about computers than you're ever gunna.' She stood up. 'Come up to the workshop and I'll have a look.'

'It won't make you late for school?' Caleb asked.

'Seriously? You're playing Mummy again?'

He gave her a level stare and, to his surprise, her eyes lowered.

'It's just Sport,' she said.

The workshop was at the top of a narrow flight of stairs; a wide room crammed with computers, routers, printers and hard drives. Sammi settled herself in front of a computer and set to work on the USB with a pair of needle-nose pliers. She pried the metal edges apart, blew on it a couple of times, and stuck it in the hard drive. Her fingers skipped across the keyboard and text appeared on the screen.

'You're kidding me,' Frankie said.

Sammi chatted away, facing the monitor. He edged closer, but it was impossible to catch anything.

Frankie tapped his arm. 'Some of it's corrupted, but she might be able to rescue it.' She paused. 'It'll take a while so we should wait in the cafe.'

The girl swivelled around. Her smile had gone. 'Don't I speak well enough for ya?' Her face was flushed.

It was about now that Kat would usually look, very deliberately, at the floor.

He took a breath. 'You're fine, I just don't hear too well.'

He ignored Frankie's turned head.

'Oh, right.' Sammi's scowl dropped, but the redness stayed. 'Fair enough.' She grabbed a handful of pages from a printer and shoved them at him. 'Fifty bucks should do it for this lot.'

'You stuck it in a computer and printed it out. I could've done that myself.'

'Yeah, but you didn't. Manage to piss yet today?'

He pulled twenty dollars from his pocket and handed it to her. 'You can have the other thirty if you get anything else off the stick.'

Her grin flashed. 'Done.'

Damn it, he should have said ten.

They retreated to the cafe and settled in a corner table. He divided the printed pages between them and started reading. After thirty seconds, Frankie looked up.

'Not the small thing Scott's looking for.'

'No.' Definitely not. There were no photocopied state secrets or maps to buried treasure, just page after page of Gary's interviews.

'Still,' she said. 'We might learn something.'

'Yeah.'

'Probably heaps of stuff.'

'Yeah.' But he got up and ordered them both coffee. Damning evidence could be examined on adrenaline alone; thousands of words of annotated interviews needed caffeine.

Their coffees came quickly: thick, dark and fragrant. He could see why the place was busy, even at the extortionate prices they charged. He turned off his aids and sat back to read. Gary had recorded the results of his interviews with a meticulous attention to detail that had him feeling a little guilty about his own cursory written reports. After an hour's solid reading, Frankie got up to order more coffee.

He looked up as a shadow fell across the page. Sammi was standing in front of him, grinning, a sheath of papers in her hand. He flicked his aids back on and caught the end of her sentence.

'. . . owe me big time.'

'You got the rest of the files?'

'About half. But that's fantastic, you should have seen the mess they were in. I had to do some pretty frigging awesome data-recovery stuff to get it.'

'You're over-egging the pudding – I'm going to pay you anyway.' He pulled out thirty dollars and gave it to her. 'You were pretty quick, maybe you can still make it to Sport.'

'Nah. I've safely missed that. Thanks.' She walked away, a bounce to her ponytail.

He flicked through the pages: a lot of nonsensical symbols and blank space, along with a handful of names. All people he knew: the warehouse owners, Sean Fleming, Elle. He stopped halfway down the third page – Premium Occasions. A name he'd seen very recently.

Frankie set two coffees and a danish on the table and flopped into her seat. 'Fair trade fucking organic coffee. Have to get a second mortgage if we stay here much longer.' She paused with the danish halfway to her mouth. 'Something interesting?'

'Got the stuff back from Sammi. Have a look at the names – Premium Occasions are on Elle's list, too, aren't they?'

'Dunno.' She pulled out her phone. 'You're right. Premium Occasions had access to the warehouse six weeks ago. Interesting that Gary was looking into them. What did he say?'

He scanned the page. 'Nothing. At least not that Sammi's managed to recover.' He flipped to the next page. 'The odd bit about the... Fuck me.' He read the name again, but he hadn't imagined it: Petronin. But not Michael; Margaret. A break at last, maybe even the break that would crack this whole mess open.

He looked at Frankie. 'The woman in the photo. We've got her name.'

'What?'

'It's Margaret Petronin.'

'Petronin. So Michael's sister? Or was Tedesco lying about Petronin not having been married?'

He stood up. 'Let's find out. Grab that computer.'

His excitement settled after the first Google search: there were no hits on Margaret Petronin.

'Not a sister then,' Frankie said. 'Maybe a de facto and she didn't legally take Petronin's surname.'

Fuck it, there wasn't much they could do with just a first name.

'Try Premium Occasions,' he told her. 'At least we know that's the right name.'

A popular one, too; a Google search got them over 200,000 hits.

Frankie scrolled down the page. 'Wedding organisers, photographers. Oh look, a massage place. They do full release. Could help with your tension. Want to read their client recommendations?'

He grabbed the mouse and clicked on the next listing: *Premium Occasions: parties for the discerning and daring.* A page of mood-lit photographs. Beautiful people in beautiful clothes, sipping champagne and smiling.

'No good,' Frankie said, trying to pull the mouse from his hand.

'Wait.' There wasn't a chandelier-lit ballroom in any of the photos. Every party looked as though it had been staged in an unusual place: a sheep shed, an aquarium, a warehouse... He clicked on the 'contact us' button and a name popped up.

CEO, Vanessa Galto.

A frisson ran through him.

Galto – a name he'd read only yesterday.

He looked at Frankie. 'Do you think Vanessa Galto might be related to the late Spiros Galto?'

28.

They made the trek to St Kilda and the sleek glass offices of Premium Occasions. It was only a kilometre from Petronin's flat, but miles away in terms of comfort and price.

Frankie looked around the light-filled atrium, her mouth forming an 'o': either whistling or spitting. 'What exactly does Vanessa Galto do? And how do I get into it?'

Whistling.

'She's an event and project facilitator.'

'I reckon I could do that. Once I work out what it is.'

She pushed open the opaque glass doors. More glass and polished concrete greeted them: if Vanessa's rent was calculated using the same algorithm as their own office, she was paying a dizzying amount each month. The receptionist was a thin young man with a shaved head and probable anaemia. He greeted them indifferently, called through to Vanessa, and returned to his phone. After a short wait, a woman appeared from a doorway on the far side of the foyer. She was immaculately dressed in a figure-hugging black skirt and cream blouse, with long, dark hair that fell to her shoulders in a rigid sheet.

Her face formed something like a smile as she reached

them. Her red lipstick had recently been reapplied. She did a quick, dismissive scan of Frankie and turned to Caleb. Not a woman's woman.

'I'm Vanessa Galto, how can I help?'

He felt Frankie stiffen. Even money on whether she'd get in Vanessa's face, or go with it.

He made quick introductions before she could speak. 'We understand you did some work at an old warehouse in Coburg?'

'Our Bianchi Fashion Ball, yes. That was a great success. I imagine you saw the photo spread in the *Age*? Come into the office and we can chat.'

Caleb smiled; sometimes the ducks just lined themselves up.

He caught Frankie's eye as they followed Vanessa across the foyer. She made an 'all yours' gesture towards the woman's rigid back. The office was pure white and furnished with perspex furniture, including an enormous suspended chair with fat white cushions. The only sign any work went on in the place was a very thin white Apple Mac sitting on the perspex desk. The view was even more expensive than the furniture: a clear expanse of Port Phillip Bay, and a glimpse of Luna Park.

'Please.' Vanessa gestured towards two spindly looking chairs. 'Have a seat.'

They both remained standing.

Vanessa glanced from Frankie to him. 'Are you... um... Are you interested in organising a large function or um, or something more intimate?'

'You work with your father sometimes, don't you? Spiros Galto? Or you did, I suppose I should say.'

'My... What's this all about?'

'Your father was murdered.'

Her hand went to her throat. 'Who are you? What do you want?'

'And his best friend, too, Arnie Giannopoulos.'

'It's been a... difficult few weeks.' She tried for a wan smile, but ended up with something rictus-like.

'They were killed because they robbed the warehouse.'

'What warehouse?' But there was no conviction in her expression.

'We couldn't work out how the thieves got in – everyone kept insisting that the guards didn't have the warehouse keys or the alarm code. But I guess it would have been a bit hard to throw a party without them.'

'I don't know what you're talking about.'

He moved closer and stood just inside her personal space. 'You didn't know that your father ripped off the warehouse twice? Using the keys you had copied?'

'He only did...' She clamped her mouth shut.

That was unexpected. 'He only robbed it once? Which time? The first time, or the second?'

'I don't know, I don't know anything, just that he...' Her hand fluttered from her mouth to her stomach. 'I didn't have anything to do with it.'

'Vanessa, you had the keys, you had the alarm code, you're the daughter of the man who robbed the place. You know what happened.' He lowered his voice. 'Aren't you scared that you'll be next?'

Her face crumpled. 'I don't know what happened. They did the job and everything was fine. They even pretended that Arnie got hit on the head, but then he really did get hurt and then someone killed him and Daddy wouldn't tell me what… And then, and then, Daddy was…' She wiped her eyes, streaking mascara across her face.

'What about the cops? Why were Gary Marsden and Anthony Hobbs killed?'

'Policemen?' She put a hand out to steady herself on her desk. 'They killed policemen, too?'

Shit, that looked genuine. A glance at Frankie's face told him she was thinking the same thing.

'Why the surprise?' he asked. 'You know what Scott's capable of.'

'Scott? Who's Scott?' No flicker in her expression, just blank confusion.

'What did Arnie and your father find in the shipment?'

'Just… It was cigarettes.'

'What else? What did they find that they shouldn't have? What did they have that Scott wants?'

'I don't know who Scott is, but they stole cigarettes. Just cigarettes.'

'Was anything taken from your father's house when it was ransacked?'

She shook her head. 'I don't know what… His house wasn't ransacked.'

One last chance. He pulled Margaret Petronin's photo from his pocket.

'Tell me about this woman.'

Vanessa clutched the picture; it fluttered in her hands as she stared at it. She finally raised her reddened eyes to his.

'I don't know. Really. I've never seen her before. I'd tell you if I had.'

He took the photo from her and looked at Frankie. 'Let's go.'

Vanessa grabbed his sleeve as he turned. 'Wait. Who's Scott?'

'He's the guy you should be hiding from.'

Out on the wind-whipped street, he turned to Frankie. 'Arnie and Spiros didn't have what Scott was after.'

'Then why beat Arnie up? Brand him? Kill them both?'

'I don't know. But Scott didn't search either of their houses, so either he's found what he was looking for and we can relax and go home, or he knew they didn't have it.'

'Let's assume he's still looking for it. What now?'

'Throw the name Margaret Petronin around and see what happens.' Caleb said.

'Throw it where?' Frankie said. 'We've hit a dead end.'

'City Sentry and Tedesco, then everyone Gary interviewed.'

'That's a long list.'

It was. Too long, surely, to have just been a smokescreen.

'What's with the smile?' Frankie asked.

'Gaz was working the case. Really working it. It wasn't just for show.'

She considered his words. 'Looks like it.'

Frankie somehow convinced him to let her drive again, claiming ease of communication, but she waited until they were almost at City Sentry before speaking.

'Eyes front,' he said as they approached a pedestrian crossing.

She kept talking, but he stared at the road. Positive modelling, that's what he should have been doing all this time. She smacked his arm.

'Ow.' He rubbed it. 'What?'

'Get my phone – it's ringing. I must've forgotten to turn it off.'

He pulled it from the glove box, but the screen was black. 'It's off.'

'It's not. It's ringing.'

It wasn't vibrating. He prodded the dark screen: dead. Which meant...

'It's mine,' he said. 'Pull over.'

She looked blankly at him.

'My mobile's in the car somewhere.'

She pulled into a loading zone. He felt between the seats, then got out and peered under both of them. There, in the rear footwell, black against the black carpet. It must have slid under the driver's seat. Three per cent battery, four missed calls, twenty-six texts.

'Have you got a car charger?' he said.

'The cord's fucked. Bloody Apple, you'd think they could make a charger that lasted as long as the fucking phone. Shits me up the wall.'

That was a lot of anger directed towards a fairly unimportant thing. He lowered the phone and looked at her properly: her body was vibrating with a rigid energy. She'd been unusually quiet during the car trip. And she'd capitulated very easily at Vanessa's office.

How to distract an alcoholic itching for a drink?

'You want to get something to eat before we hit City Sentry?' he asked.

'No.'

OK, now he was really worried. 'Well I'm hungry. Let's go to Melbourne Central. I can pick up a charger there, too.'

'Right. OK.' She strode down La Trobe Street so quickly he had to jog to catch up.

She thumped the pedestrian signal, tapping her thighs as she waited.

'You know what,' she said. 'You go eat and while I check our post box. Never know – Gary might have sent us a nice surprise.'

'Good idea, but let's go together.'

'Quicker if we separate.'

'Safer if we stay together.'

'We're in the middle of the city,' she said. 'I think we'll be OK. I'll meet you back at the car.' She set off across the road.

Shit, he was going to have to call her on it. He caught up to her.

'I know you want to drink.'

Her mouth worked for a moment. 'Yes Caleb, I'm an alcoholic, I always want to drink. Glad you understand. See you in an hour.'

He grabbed her arm. 'I'm not leaving you alone while you're like this.'

She shrugged him off, fists clenched. 'I don't need a fucking babysitter. I've been doing this by myself for a long time. A very long time.'

'And look where it's got you: divorced, out of the force, estranged from your family.'

Her face was a white mask. 'Looked in the fucking mirror lately?'

'If you flake out on me again, we're through.'

'Fuck you, Caleb Zelic. I have one fucking slip and you watch me all the time. Every time I move, every time I turn around, you're there, watching me. So great, maybe I'll be better off without you.' She flicked her hand. 'See ya.'

Fuck, fuck. How had he got here? Another awful, stomach-twisting failure.

'Frankie, please.' He switched to signing. 'I need you.'

She stood still.

'I can't do it without you. Any of it.'

'Oh, for fuck's sake.' She blinked rapidly. 'Now you go getting all... OK, I'm going to tell you something. Afterwards, you're going to nod your head, walk away, and leave me with a tiny shred of dignity, OK?'

'I'm not going to...'

'Just listen. Please.'

'OK.'

'I feel like shit. More than shit – I'm really struggling. It's always hard getting clean, but it's harder when you're stressed. And mate, I am fucking stressed. I need a bit of privacy so I can have a little cry and call someone who can help. You reckon you can give me that?'

He opened his mouth.

'No. Do not fucking ask me anything. Just nod your head and leave me the fuck alone, OK?'

He nodded.

'Great. See you back at the car in an hour.'

He watched her go; head down, fists clenched. Shit.

29.

He bought a charger and returned to the car before remembering that Frankie had the keys. He leaned against it and watched for her loping figure, even though he was half an hour early.

Have a little cry.

What were the odds she could make it back sober and functioning? What were the odds he could make it through this nightmare without her? He shivered and checked his watch. Twenty-eight minutes to go. He could stand here, freezing his arse off and worrying, or he could get something done. It was 5.48 – there was a chance he could still catch someone at City Sentry. He texted Frankie and headed down the hill.

Elle was coming through the reception doors as he got there, handbag over her shoulder, a bright-green hat perched on her head. She looked like a manic elf.

Her hand flew to her mouth: beetle-green nails today. 'What are you doing here?'

'Hi, I was wondering if Sean was in. It's Caleb Zelic from Trust Works.'

'Oh.' She gave him a pantomime-worthy wink. 'Of course, Mr Zelic, I'll just check.'

He checked to see there was no-one in the open-plan office and slipped Margaret's photo from his pocket.

'Do you know this woman?' he said quietly.

'Um, is she on TV? On that hospital show?'

He paused. An actress. That possibility hadn't occurred to him.

'Margaret?' he said. 'Margaret Petronin?'

'Nah, I think it's Janelle or something.' She jerked her head towards a door off the reception area. 'I'd better…'

'Yeah, thanks.'

She disappeared and returned a moment later with Sean in tow. She gave Caleb another wink and left.

'Caleb, good to see you again.' Sean attempted an aren't-we-good-mates grin. 'I'm just finishing up on the phone. You OK to wait for a couple of minutes?'

Caleb went with the script. 'Sure. Take your time.'

He settled down to wait on one of the vinyl chairs. The reading material ran to three-year-old copies of *Readers' Digest* and City Sentry's promotional material. Maybe three per cent battery would be enough to check his messages. He flicked through the texts, ignoring the missed calls – no-one who knew him would leave a voice message.

Friend, business, business, friend, business, business.

His breath caught.

Gary.

It must have come while he was driving to his house. A final message. He paused for a moment, then opened it. A sagging moment of disappointment: there were no words, just photos. Taken from hip-height by the look of the angle. Why had Gary sent them? They were badly framed and lit: four men standing in a semi-circle, cardboard boxes behind them. The next couple of pictures panned across the men's faces. Grey-face; Petronin; a young man in police blues; the fourth man too shadowed to make out. None of them seemed to realise they were being photographed. He examined the surrounding boxes. Familiar brands on their sides: Benson and Hedges, Winfield Blue, Stuyvesant. Spoils from the warehouse robberies. He flicked through the remaining pictures. More boxes, a couple of blurred figures.

A gun.

The fourth man was holding it to the cop's head.

A frozen look of terror on the young man's face.

Caleb hesitated, then swiped to the next photo. Brain matter clearly visible, a slumped body.

He lowered the phone. Jesus.

'*Senior Constable Anthony Hobbs*... *killed in the early hours of June the twenty-fourth*.'

And Gary had been there to witness it. Had taken photos of it. And somehow Scott had found out about them. Easy to imagine what had happened then: Scott and his men hustling Gary through his house, holding him down. A matter of seconds to check his phone and see that he'd sent the photos to Caleb. A little longer making sure he hadn't sent them to anyone else: the ransacked house, the cutting, the broken fingers. A shudder rolled through him.

He enlarged the photo and examined the man holding the gun; a dark and pixelated blur. It had to be Scott. The evil fucking bastard. Medium height and weight, possibly blond, probably clean-shaven. Or was that darker spot a goatee? Maybe a good photo lab could run it through some whizz-bang software to enhance it. Send the photos to Tedesco? It couldn't make things worse, might make things better. Two per cent battery, might be enough. He typed a quick message and attached the photos. No problem remembering the Hotmail address.

He pressed send just as Sean appeared in his office doorway. He stood up, but Sean was looking at something behind him. A gust of air as the foyer door opened. It was a woman with long, honey-coloured hair. A little older than in the photo, but clearly Margaret Petronin. Someone coming through the door behind her – Grey-face.

'Caleb,' he said, flicking the lock on the door. 'Nice of you to make things easy for us.'

He ran. Weaving between the desks, towards the back of the room. A door at the end, maybe another way out. Footsteps pounding behind him. He flung open the door. A kitchenette. Fuck. Get a knife? No, he'd be cornered. Sean was bearing down on him, fists bunched. Back towards the foyer doors. Margaret and Grey-face were guarding them, the glint of steel in the policeman's hand. A weapon, he needed a weapon. Computer, phone, chair – chair. He grabbed it and hefted it above his head. Heavy. He ran at Grey-face, a scream building in his lungs. The policeman's eyes widened and he took a step back. Faster, nearly...

Something heavy slammed into his back. He crashed to the floor, the chair thudding in front of him. Someone kneeling on his back, wrenching his right arm up behind him. No air. Lungs squeezing. Hands going through his pockets, pulling something from it. The weight shifted slightly. He turned his head, sucking in lungfuls of oxygen. Margaret was scrolling through his phone. Hadn't locked it. Stupid. Stupid.

'The battery just died, but he hadn't texted them to anyone.'

She was so easy to read, like someone he'd spent hours watching. Someone from his childhood? No, that wasn't...

A fist in his hair, a flash of silver, and the cold touch of steel at his throat. He was going to die. Die like Gary: neck slit, blood spurting. Sean's bullish voice, Grey-face answering. Arguing. His head was released. Fuck. Fuck. He breathed heavily against the carpet as their voices rose and fell above him. A softer voice, Margaret.

Grey-face was beside him. '... evidence. Stupid.' He wrenched Caleb's arm out and anchored it with his knee.

'They broke his fingers. Every one of them.'

It would be OK. Pain was bearable. Better than a cut throat.

The woman knelt down. 'Plenty for a first timer. You are a first timer, aren't you, Caleb?' She pushed up his sleeve. 'Looks like it.'

Maybe his arm, not his fingers. God. But why? Evidence, Grey-face had said. Did they think he had more evidence against them? Margaret was laying something on the carpet. A spoon. Why would she...? A syringe.

His insides turned to ice.

Not questions, just a bloodless way to kill him. He heaved against Sean's immovable bulk. A band tightened around his arm, blood throbbing. He pulled away. Weight crushing his hand and back. A sharp prick, burning cold sweeping through his blood. And he was released. He struggled to his knees, rubbing desperately at his skin, scratching. Get up. Get help. To his feet. Nausea rolling through him, sending the room spinning.

The three of them were watching.

'What... think...?' Grey-face asked. '... minutes?'

'About that.'

Phone. Police, ambulance, someone. Yell until they came. They'd been too late for Gary. A phone on the desk, just there, close. Legs dragging. On the floor now, on all fours. Illness ebbing, leaving him light. The phone, what was the number? His body was liquid, sliding downwards, down onto the carpet. Soft.

Hands rolled him over.

'Well on the way.'

Up off the floor; light, like floating. He was going to... there was something important. Margaret was walking just ahead of him. Maggie for short, Kat had said when she'd put Margaret on the list of baby's names. How did you get Maggie from Margaret? Felt like it should be Marg, like getting Kat from Kathryn. Beautiful Kat. Down the stairwell, the air cool. And he was sitting with his back against a wall. Voices hummed around him, then flitted away. Alone. Warmth travelled through his body, up and out the top of his head. Weightless, like nothing at all.

Sudden light, cold air caressing his skin.

Frankie's face in front of him. 'Jesus, Cal, what are... been... wrong?'

Drifting.

'... hurt?'

No booze on her breath.

'Welldn.' Tongue not working. 'Welldone, Fnkie. Proudyou.'

She grabbed his face and angled it to the light. 'Oh shit. Shit, no.'

'S'OK.' The words fell away. Let them go. Let everything go.

'Ambulance.' Frankie spitting the words. '... OD... blue... hurry.'

Hands shaking him. His head lolled back and smacked against the wall. There was no pain.

None at all.

A slap. He opened his eyes. Frankie's face was wet.

'Cal.' Something hard rubbing his sternum. 'Cal. Breathe.' Another slap.

It seemed important to her. He concentrated, inhaled slowly.

'Good... and again. Caleb... Caleb...'

It felt like

30.

Awake like a slap in the face. A distant whining. Pain somewhere, everywhere. An unfamiliar face appeared over him. A bald man, wearing a dark-blue uniform.

What the fuck?

Something pressed against his face. He felt its shape: an oxygen mask. There were wires trailing from his bare chest. Where was his top? Hadn't he been wearing one? A red one, and a coat.

'OK there, mate?' the paramedic asked. A calm face, like a monk.

He nodded.

'You remember what happened?'

He shook his head.

'You... gave you... but it...'

He closed his eyes. Too hard: it had been better back in the stairwell.

The van doors opening jolted him awake. Frigid air gusted in. Pain in his chest, like thrusting knives. And he remembered: Margaret, Grey-face, Sean. That bastard, Sean. He'd held him down like a fucking schoolgirl and shot him full of smack.

A brief, arctic blast and they were inside the hospital. Down a corridor and into a curtained cubicle. A doctor appeared and conferred with the paramedics. Around thirty, with tired eyes and stooped shoulders. She checked him over with brisk movements. No eye contact, talking with her head down.

'Sorry, I didn't get that.'

She spoke again, still looking at the clipboard.

'Sorry, I didn't... I'm having trouble following you. Can you look at me when you speak?'

She looked up; surprised, irritated. 'You took heroin?'

'I don't know. I think so.'

'Anything else? Any dmmmm? Rmmmmm?'

'I don't know.'

'Any pain when you breathe?'

'Yes.'

She nodded absently, kept writing, talking.

'Sorry, what?'

Her lips compressed. 'That will be from the CPR. You may have a cracked rib or two, it's not unusual.'

CPR? Oh, God. 'Have you seen my friend, Frankie? She'll be worried.'

'No.' Still no eye contact. 'On a scale of one to ten, how would you rate the pain?'

'She'll be worried, she won't know...'

'On a scale of one to ten...'

'Five. It's a five.'

She wrote on the chart. 'I'll arrange... X-ray... ribs... IV.' Her hand was on the curtain, but he couldn't be bothered asking her to repeat anything.

'Can you tell Frankie...'

She was gone.

On a scale of one to ten, how would he rate her bedside

manner? He stared at the ceiling: a hard, white fluorescent that made his eyes flicker. He should have run straight at Grey-face, he should have pushed past the knife, he should have…

The curtains parted and a nurse came in, her movements quick and efficient. She was young, no more than twenty-three, with a little frown mark permanently between her eyebrows: the girl who'd always studied hard.

'You're Caleb?' A smile, actual eye contact. That was nice. 'I'm Susan. How are you feeling?'

'Fine. Is someone out there looking for me? Frankie?'

She wheeled the drip stand to the bed. Head down, talking.

'Can you look at me when you speak?'

Her face popped briefly into view, then lowered. '… important… you don't…'

Fuck it. 'I'm deaf. I need to see your face when you're talking.'

'Oh.' A blush rose up her neck. 'Interpreter? I'll get one.' She mimed walking away and speaking on a telephone.

'I don't need an interpreter. I'm fine as long as you look at me when you speak. Is there a woman looking for me? Tall, with crazy purple and grey hair. She doesn't know I'm all right. She'll be worried.'

'I'll. Keep. An. Eye. Out.' Miming again. God. 'A drip. Two. Hours.' She held up two fingers.

'OK.'

'Don't shoot up. Again. Today. Very dangerous. Understand?'

'I'm not a user.'

Her eyes went to the soft flesh of his inner elbow: there was a raised mark where the needle had pierced his skin.

'I'll get. Pmmmm. To. Help. You.'

'Get what?'

'Pam. Phhh. Leets.'

Maybe it was a name – Pam Fleets. Could be the doctor. Better not be a fucking interpreter.

'Wait.' She swished through the curtains and returned a moment later, carrying folded pieces of paper. Huh – pamphlets. She placed them in his lap, patted his hand and left.

Smiling, healthy people featured heavily on the pamphlet covers. Courses with patronising names like 'Fresh Start' and 'New Beginnings'. He used to leave similar things lying around the house for Ant. What an arsehole.

The curtains opened again and he steeled himself for more earnest do-gooding. It was Frankie. She stopped just inside the cubicle, one hand gripping the curtain. Her eyes were unusually bright, skin pale, as though she was feverish.

'Frankie. You found me.'

'You stupid fucking prick.' She left.

She returned an hour later, carrying two large bags from McDonald's and what looked like a bundle of clothing.

'Thought you might be hungry,' she said, dumping it all on the bed.

Still too pale, too twitchy. But definitely sober.

'Cholesterol police will be on to you, bringing that in here.'

'Nah, I got it from the Children's Hospital.' She busied herself undoing the bundle of clothing and threw him a T-shirt. 'Get that on. Don't want your manly physique sending the nurses wild.'

It was a strange collection of clothing: two pairs of undies and one sock, no warm jacket, but three T-shirts. An unwelcome insight into her current state of mind. He managed to get two of the T-shirts over his head before realising that threading the drip through the arm hole was going to be beyond his current range of movement.

Frankie wordlessly helped him to finish the manoeuvre.

She handed him a paper bag. 'Eat up before it gets too cold.'

He ate a couple of fries but they were dry and strangely tasteless. Frankie demolished her food without speaking, balled the wrapper and lobbed it impressively into a bin on the opposite side of the cubicle.

She caught his look. 'You like that?'

'Awed.'

'OK, tell me what happened. I'll try not to yell at you this time.'

'Well, City Sentry is involved.' He shifted to try and ease the pain in his chest but there didn't seem to be any comfortable way to breathe.

'Yeah, I sort of worked that one out.'

'Sean kept me waiting long enough for Grey-face to get to the office, then jumped me. Margaret Petronin was with him.'

Her hand paused halfway to her mouth.

'I don't know if she's using, or if they're dealing, but she had smack there, so... They held me down and shot me up.'

Frankie looked as though she were regretting the fries. She glanced at the packet and lowered it to her lap.

'I couldn't stop them,' he said.

'No.'

'I tried.'

'Yeah.'

'Staff here think I'm a smack-head.'

'Yeah, well, you're not. Fuck 'em.'

He gave a choked laugh. 'Thank you, Sensei, I feel much better now.'

'You're welcome, Grasshopper.' She shoved her uneaten fries back into the bag.

The shakes had gone, but she was still too pale. Should he mention their last conversation? Easier to pretend it had never happened. He opened his mouth, closed it again.

Frankie's face tightened. 'Just ask the damn question.'

'Did you get onto someone who could help you?'

'Yes, I did. Did I have a drink? I think you can see that I didn't. Am I going to? I don't fucking know. Maybe I'll never drink again, maybe one of these days I'll get some Johnny Red and a big bottle of pills and chug 'em all down. We done? Excellent. Now, should I be worried about you sitting around here? The whole tracking you through prescriptions, et cetera?'

Johnny Walker and a bottle of pills. That was way too specific a scenario.

'I won't be here for long,' he said. 'A couple of hours for the drip.' Get her out of here and into some sort of treatment program. Somewhere interstate. Hope Tedesco was straight. Hope everything was nearly over.

'Want to hear some good news?' he said.

'God. Please.'

He brought her up to date about Gary's photos and the warehouse shooting.

'Scott's in the photos?'

'Maybe – they're pretty fuzzy. I've sent them to Tedesco. Hopefully he'll be able to get someone to enhance them.'

'You sent them to Tedesco?' She shook her head. 'What if he's working with Scott?'

'Guess it'll make the ID easier. Either way, I've got a copy of the photos in my email now.'

'What about Margaret? Have you worked out where you know her from now you've seen her in the flesh?'

'No.'

'Guess it doesn't matter now. Oops.' She pulled out her phone. 'Forgot to turn it off after the ambulance.' She frowned at the screen.

'What?'

'Nothing terrible. Just hang on.'

Nothing terrible, but she was taking a long time reading the message. Re-reading it. Now thinking about it.

'Tedesco?' he said.

She began tapping the bed railing. And now she was re-reading the damn thing again.

'You trying to finish me off?'

'Trying to work out what to tell you. So, anyway, Kat's back in town.'

He shot forward, then doubled over, clutching his ribs. 'Kat? In Melbourne?'

She passed him the phone.

– *Back in Melb. Staying at Mel's studio. Her phone. No-one knows I'm here.*

No-one except Mel. Which meant Mel's friends, Mel's neighbours, Mel's boyfriend, Mel's boyfriend's friends.

He typed quickly.

– It's not safe. Lock the door and stay there. Frankie's coming to get you. C

'It's probably fine,' Frankie said.

'Mel's a talker, there's no way she'll be able to keep it quiet. And even if she did, they're too easily linked. They've had joint exhibitions, they lecture at the same uni. If Scott's smart enough to tap Kat's phones, he's smart enough to sniff around her friends.'

'Why would he bother? He's got your phone now.'

'Why kill Gary? Or Arnie, or Spiros? He doesn't like loose ends.'

The phone buzzed.

– *Was letting you know as courtesy, not a conversation. Turning phone off now.*

– NO. SCOTT WILL TALK TO YR FRIENDS. GIVE ME ADDRESS AND GO WITH FRANKIE. PLEASE.

Read it. Please read it. Still have the phone on and read it.

– *Why Frankie?*

What the fuck? That's what she took from the message? Why Frankie?

Frankie pulled the phone from his hand and typed.

– Caleb can't come. He's in hospital hooked up to a drip. Scott's work. He died twice. Dead. No heartbeat. Blue in the face. They're scary people. Give me your address. Frankie

'Frankie. Jesus.'

The phone buzzed.

– 241 Hampton St Carlton

'Sometimes you have to be blunt.' She passed him the phone. 'Now say something nice so she stops crying.'

His fingers hovered over the screen. No time to dick around, just say something. Anything. But make it good. Frankie was snapping her fingers.

– The Whitsundays. Tomorrow. I'll tell you everything.

He pressed send.

There was a slight shake to Frankie's hand as she took the phone from him. Sending her out in peak-hour traffic suddenly didn't feel like such a good idea. Cars cutting in front of her, the pressure building inside and out. Fuck the drip, he'd better drive. He sat up and a slicing pain froze him in place.

'What the fuck are you doing?'

'Getting. Comfortable.'

'Doesn't seem to be working. You need a nurse?'

He was going to slow her down if he went with her. Next best option?

'I'm fine. But listen, you should take a taxi.'

Her face closed. 'I can drive.'

'Taxi'll be quicker. And you won't get a park near Mel's studio this time of day. I don't want the two of you hiking blocks to the car.'

She gave a sharp shrug. 'Car's probably been towed anyway, it's in a loading zone outside Naughton's.' She turned towards the curtains.

'Frankie?'

'Yep?'

'I'm sorry you had to go through that. What you told Kat.'

She paused with her hand on the curtain. 'Yeah well, do better. There aren't many people in the world I love.' She disappeared.

He lay back and just breathed for a while. Shallowly. Everything was going to be all right. Frankie would have Kat here within the hour, Tedesco would get the photos, and it would all be over.

Susan bustled back in and fussed around him, checking his blood pressure and pulse.

She gave him a thumbs-up. 'How. Are. You feeling?'

'Good.'

'That's good. Your mum?' She pointed towards the curtains.

He laughed, imagining Frankie's reaction. 'More like a sister.'

Her eyes dropped to the pamphlets on the bed. 'Good. A sister will. Keep you. On track.' She gave his hand another pat and left.

Sister. The word tumbled around his brain. A sister. That's where he knew Margaret from. He'd seen her in an old wedding photo at Frankie's house. Two shy girls with honey-blonde hair and crooked smiles.

Frankie and her sister, Maggie.

31.

A fist squeezed his heart.

He swung his legs out of bed and ripped the cannula from his hand. Shoes. Where were his shoes? Forget them, just run. He sprinted from the cubicle, shards jabbing his chest. He pressed a hand to it and ran faster. Out past the nurses' station, through the doors: heads raising, startled looks. Down the corridor, out through the electronic doors. Dark. Later than he'd realised.

The car. Had Frankie taken a taxi and left the car? Near Naughton's, she'd said, the old uni pub. Not far. What could it be? Four hundred, five hundred metres? But parked in a loading zone. A loading zone in Parkville, home to the most enthusiastic parking inspectors in the world. Pain with each footfall. He fell back to a fast shuffle. Shit, shit. Had to move faster than that. He broke into a jog, knives stabbing him.

He had to be wrong; he'd seen a lone, yellowing photo of a teenage Maggie Reynolds. No reason to think he'd recognise her as an adult. He was wrong. Had to be wrong.

He wasn't.

There – the car. Thank God. He shoved his hand in his pocket.

No keys.

Like some kind of fucking recurring nightmare. Wire to jimmy the lock. Nothing. No time for it, anyway. He squatted and tugged at a broken chunk of bluestone in the gutter. A movement like a loose tooth. He stood and kicked at it. Should have looked for his shoes. Kicked again. Looser. Scrabbling in the dirt, tugging. It came free, sending him sprawling. Precious moments lost as the world pitched and spun.

He struggled to his feet and slammed the stone against the rear passenger window. It cracked and shattered into soft crystals. Into the car, across to the driver's side. He pulled the boot lever. Standard-head screwdriver should do the job. Ten-year-old Corolla, couldn't be too different from the Holdens and Fords he'd joy-ridden all those years ago. Petronin's gun was under the tool box. Take it? If Frankie led Scott to Kat's hideout, he'd need it. She wouldn't. She couldn't. All those hours they'd spent working together. All the times she'd been there for him. He picked it up. Heavier than he remembered. Heavier still once he'd snapped the clip into place. Into the car. No immobiliser; it should work. Please, God. He slammed the screwdriver into the ignition, turned it. A familiar shake, the engine rumbling into life. He threw the car into first and took off.

He doubled-parked outside Mel's studio and opened the high wooden gate. The small courtyard fronting the building was empty. The studio's arched door was closed, the windows shuttered. He pressed his hand to the door, but all he could feel was the thudding of his own heart. Maybe he'd got here before Frankie. Maybe Kat wasn't here.

Maybe he was too late.

He gripped the handle and flung open the door.

Frankie, alone. Crying. Sitting on the floor with one shoe off, a rubber tourniquet around her calf. Dark dots of needle tracks specked her toes. No. That didn't make sense.

She stared at him, her red-rimmed eyes wide. 'Cal.'

He snapped out of it. Frankie was using – deal with it later.

'Where's Kat?'

'She wasn't here.' She scrabbled to her feet and began packing away her kit: spoon, syringe, filters. Her hands shook as she slipped it into her backpack. 'Sorry you had to find out about this, this way. Don't worry, I'm not a junkie, I've got it under control. I don't do it often. It just helps me get through the...'

'I don't care. Just tell me where Kat is.'

'She didn't leave a note. Maybe she went out for a...'

'Stop. Just fucking stop with all the lies. I know you're Margaret's sister, I know you're working for Scott. So just tell me where Kat is.'

She raised her hand as though to deflect his words, then lowered it. 'Fuck.'

'Where is she?'

'I'm sorry, Cal. I didn't want any of this to happen. I've been trying so fucking hard to fix it all.'

'Is she...' He got the words out past constricted airways. 'Is she alive?'

She nodded.

His heart started again. 'But Scott's got her?'

Another nod.

'Where?'

'I don't know, probably at their warehouse, that's where they... Cal, you have to go. They think you're dead.'

He took a step towards her. 'Take me there.'

'I can't. You don't understand. Scott'll kill me, he'll kill us both. And it won't be quick.'

He raised the gun; it didn't feel heavy any more. 'Move.'

He tried to do the calculations as Frankie drove. He'd left the hospital ten minutes after Frankie, another five to break into the car, so he was probably twenty minutes behind Kat. Twenty minutes. What could happen in that amount of time? No, concentrate on why, not what.

'Why did Scott take Kat if he thinks I'm dead?'

'He wants to know who you emailed the photos to.'

'Shit, they checked my emails?'

'Of course they fucking checked them. Bring down half the fucking police force if they get out. Just took them a little while to charge up your phone. Lucky for you.'

He had a different idea of luck. 'Why didn't you tell them I sent them to Tedesco? Why drag Kat into it?'

'I didn't know who it was until you told me.'

'Why the fuck didn't you tell him once you knew?'

Her mouth moved, but she didn't look at him.

'Frankie?'

'I didn't want him to know you were alive.'

Giving up Kat to protect him. A strong chance he was going to vomit. He wound down the window and breathed in diesel fumes. They were stuck behind two lumbering trucks, traffic going nowhere.

'Go around them. Cut onto the wrong side.'

She changed down gears and squeezed past on the bike lane. More trucks. Parked cars. Jesus, fuck. What would happen if Kat told them it was Tedesco's email address? What would happen if she didn't?

'Give me your phone.'

She hesitated, then pulled it from her pocket. He searched for Tedesco's number and typed, hands slick with sweat.

– Urgent. Need help. They've got Kat

He sent it. Sent it again. And again. Pleaseseeitpleaseseeit pleaseseeit.

The phone buzzed.

– Who? Where?

'What's the warehouse address?' he asked Frankie.

Another hesitation, but she told him.

– Warehouse. 39 Arlington Avenue Footscray. It's Scott.

The reply was immediate.

– On my way. 15 mins

What else? Ring triple zero? And say what? Not as simple as at Gary's house.

They'd stopped moving. A green light, but no-one was getting through. A scream built inside.

Frankie was talking.

'... weren't meant to get hurt. Neither of you were. I thought if I fed him the right information...'

Realisation dawned, cold and unforgiving. 'You sent

Petronin to the Bay. What if Kat had opened the door to him? What if – God, you told Scott about her didn't you? The tapped phones, the photos. It wasn't smart thinking on his part, just good intel.'

'I didn't think he'd really go after her. It was just meant to distract you.'

'He's a fucking murderer, what did you think was going to happen?'

'What was I supposed to do? I told you we shouldn't take this job! But no, you had to sign the fucking contract, get Gary involved.'

Her words sunk in. 'You've been working for Scott from the start? I don't… What happened? Was it your sister? Did he threaten her?'

Her face twisted. 'Maggie? She's Scott's little helper. She's the one who introduced us in the first place, let him get his hooks into me. I've been dancing to their little tune for six fucking years.'

Six years.

Every day of their friendship had been a lie.

'Why? Was it the money? The thrill?'

She didn't answer, her hands clenched and unclenched around the wheel. Not just needing a drink, needing a hit.

'Jesus, Scott's your supplier. You gave me up for a fucking hit.'

She flinched. 'It wasn't like that. He owns me, Cal. Look at what he did to me!' She shoved up her top. A red scar ran along her side: the letter S. His stomach heaved.

'That's what happened at the house. He was pissed off because I didn't bring you to him. I tried to explain that you didn't have the photos, but he wouldn't listen. That's why I left. That's why I didn't call you. I did it to try and keep you safe.'

'Then why come back?'

She glanced at her backpack by his feet.

'Right. Because you needed a fix.'

'I was steady for years until the bastard cut me off. Bloody Gary and those photos. Six fucking years without grog or pills, just a little fix every weekend. OK, it crept up a bit. But I never did it in work hours. And it was better than the drinking, wasn't it? You didn't even know.'

No. He'd been oblivious.

'I couldn't…'

He looked away, unable to bear any more.

They were moving again. Finally through the intersection and onto Dynon Road. Not a big suburb, couldn't be much further. Turning onto a smaller road: Arlington Avenue. An old industrial estate, a handful of newer buildings, a wide, quiet road. Wide enough for trucks to reverse. No trucks here now.

Frankie was slowing down, pulling up in front of an old cyclone wire fence.

He pulled out the gun. 'Don't even think about trying to warn them.'

'Cal, I wouldn't.' Her face was haggard beneath the sheen of tears. 'You have to believe me – I didn't want any of this to happen.'

He climbed from the car without answering, hesitated at the sight of her backpack. Throw her kit away, make her suffer. But that familiar look of desperation – she'd shoot up immediately if he gave it to her. No fear of her alerting Scott if she was drooling in the front seat.

Frankie grasped his sleeve. 'Cal, I'm s–'

He wrenched his arm away, ran.

The gate was padlocked. No barbed wire along the top of the fence, though. He started to climb. Tearing pain in his chest, impossible to extend his arms. He clawed his way up with tiny movements. A brief moment of panic at the top, then a scrambling descent to the other side. He lay panting for a brief moment. No time, move. He staggered to his feet and ran across the weed-filled car park. A stab of panic – there were no cars here. Had Frankie betrayed him again? Brought him to the wrong address? It was all over if she had.

There was a cluster of tin sheds straight ahead, the shape of a larger warehouse looming beyond. Dark, only a sliver of moon. Anyone could be lying in wait. He reached the first shed and peered around it. There: a HiAce van with tinted windows. Ideal for transporting people without their consent. How had they got Kat into it? Kept her quiet during the trip? No, don't think about it. Stay calm and concentrate. Where now? The warehouse or one of the six tin sheds? The yard was gravel – that'd probably make a bit of noise, so choose well. He closed his eyes and started counting backwards from sixty to let his vision adjust to the darkness. He cracked when he got to twenty. Good enough; he could see pinholes of light coming from the warehouse roof. Any neighbours were hundreds of metres away. You could make plenty of noise there without fear of disturbing anyone.

He skirted around the sheds towards it. A solid brick building, with high, boarded windows. Old roof, but a new steel door. The framing looked solid. If it was locked, there was no way he was going to be able to get it open. He turned the handle. It twisted easily in his hand.

A shift of air behind him.

He whirled, gun pointing. Tedesco stepped back, the whites of his eyes catching the moonlight. Caleb suddenly realised he had the gun aimed at the detective's chest. He lowered it.

Tedesco followed the movement. '... fucking gun?'

'It's Petronin's,' he whispered.

The news didn't seem to reassure the detective.

'... how... use it?'

'Not really.'

'First rule.' Tedesco unholstered his own weapon. 'Only... someone... want dead.'

Caleb nodded and reached for the door handle.

Tedesco put out his hand to stop him. '...'

'What?'

The detective held an imaginary phone to his ear and mimed flashing lights. Help was on its way. Not soon enough. He shook his head and edged the door open. An anteroom: a single bulb burning, throwing long shadows onto the walls. Two doors led from it, both closed. He slipped inside, Tedesco close behind him. The detective tapped his shoulder and pointed to one of the doors, mimed people talking. He nudged the door open. A dark corridor, rooms leading from it. He followed Tedesco down it. Four doors, all closed. Which one? Tedesco seemed to know: he stopped in front of the second-last one and held up two fingers. Two people. Two was good – they could take two.

Tedesco gestured for him to wait, then stiffened. A

sound; high, just out of reach. Was it a voice? Something mechanical?

'What?' he mouthed.

Tedesco shook his head, but his hand had tightened on his gun. Fuck, what was happening? Was Kat crying? Screaming? He knelt and pressed his eye to the keyhole. A glimpse of long, dark curls: Kat kneeling on the floor. A man's fist gripping her hair. A sudden motion, the bright flash of a knife. Caleb was on his feet, reaching for the handle. Tedesco pulled him back, but he broke free and slammed open the door.

A cavernous space, filled with towering boxes, a cleared area the size of a tennis court. A single bank of lights threw the rest of the room into deep shadow. Kat was metres from him, Grey-face standing over her. Her mouth, her poor mouth. And her cheek – swollen and shining. The bastard had punched her.

He raised his gun. 'Let her go.'

Grey-face hauled Kat to her feet by her hair and pressed the knife to her throat.

'Put the guns down, or I'll fillet her.' He jerked his wrist and a trickle of blood ran down Kat's neck.

Caleb's hand lowered.

Tedesco waved frantically beside him.

Think. Grey-face wouldn't kill her. Not yet. Not while he and Tedesco both had guns on him. But if he put his gun down... He tightened his grip. Please, God, let him be right.

Kat was staring at him: her eyes huge. She raised her hands and signed, 'Another man in the...'

Grey-face yanked her head back. 'Hands by your sides or I'll slit your fucking throat.'

Tedesco was talking, his voice an even rumble, but Caleb kept his eyes on Kat.

'Behind you,' she mouthed. The words were only just recognisable from her swollen lips. 'Hiding in the boxes.'

'We need to check the room,' he told Tedesco.

'Go. I'll cover Grey-face.'

He didn't move.

The detective glanced at him. 'Go. If he moves, I'll shoot him.'

Tedesco looked like he had a steady arm. Could he do it? How good a shot would he have to be to hit Grey-face and not Kat?

'He's getting closer,' Kat mouthed. 'Got a gun. To my right. Second row from the door.'

He ran in the opposite direction, slowing as soon as he reached the cover of the towering boxes. Softly now, loop back around. A glimpse of Kat and the men through the towering boxes. No-one had moved. There, just up ahead, a flash of something white in the darkness: a man's shirt. He crept forward. Breathing too heavily. How loud was it? The man was edging around a row of boxes, gun raised, aiming at Tedesco. Caleb threw himself forward. They went down hard. Stunned immobility, then he struggled to his feet. He kicked the man's gun away.

'I've got a gun on you. Hands behind your head then turn over. Slowly.'

There was a pause, then the man rolled onto his back. Ginger hair and a heavily freckled face. A jolt of recognition – the detective from Ethical Standards, Hamish McFarlane. It clicked into place: the very Scottish name, the nickname, Scott. And he'd been there from the beginning; watching, waiting, manipulating. The accusations against him and Gary, the mysterious tapping of Kat's phone, the dead woman's photo. All wrapped up in a bow and delivered to Tedesco, the new boy in the department, with no connections or friends.

'He's got me,' McFarlane yelled.

There was sudden movement in the corner of his eye. Something happening where he'd left Kat. A snatch of that same high-pitched note he'd almost heard before, the one that had made Tedesco stiffen. Hold the gun steady, don't look away from McFarlane.

The detective grinned up at him. 'Can't you hear that? Doesn't sound too good. Maybe you should check if she's OK.'

His hands were damp. 'Get to your knees and crawl towards them.'

'You should hurry – that sounds painful.'

Don't look, don't look, just keep the gun on McFarlane.

'My hands are sweating. You'd better move before this goes off.'

McFarlane glanced at his trigger finger then rolled over and began to crawl. Caleb followed at arm's length, through the towering boxes. Another almost-sound scratched at the edges of his hearing. Out into the light. Tedesco was still aiming at Grey-face, Grey-face still holding Kat. But something was different – a rigid stillness to the scene. Kat's eyes were glassy, her mouth contorted in a grimace. God, her fingers, her beautiful fingers. Two of them bent and misshapen.

'Kat.' He stepped towards her.

Grey-face jabbed the knife. 'Stop right there.'

Caleb froze. Blood was flowing down Kat's neck, staining her T-shirt.

'Good, now drop the gun.'

Couldn't drop it. Had to drop it. Maybe if he...

Grey-face grasped Kat's ring finger and snapped it back.

Heat, then cold, flowed through him. God, oh God. He gripped the gun with suddenly weak hands. Grey-face grabbed Kat's forefinger. Her eyes were screwed shut, her breath coming in panicky snatches.

'Seven to go,' Grey-face said and twisted his hand.

A scream on Kat's face, in his heart and mouth. Jesus. Jesus. How could he stop it? Had to make it stop. Gun. Couldn't aim well enough. Why hadn't he learnt to shoot? Grew up in the country. Could have had a rifle. Why the fuck hadn't he learn to shoot?

And McFarlane was there, next to Kat. Fuck, hadn't seen him move.

'Come on, Caleb,' the red-headed detective said. 'Time to give it up now. Frankie told me all about you and the lovely Kathryn here. Childhood sweethearts, love of your life and all that.' He took hold of Kat's swollen hand and stroked it. 'So why don't you save me a little time, and her a significant amount of pain, and put the gun down.'

Tedesco was speaking. McFarlane's head jerked towards him, his smile fading. A moment's hesitation, then the smirk crept back onto his lips.

'Did you now? Then I'd better hurry things up a bit.' He pulled something from his pocket: silver and black, small enough to fit into his palm.

A knife.

Caleb's bowels turned to water.

McFarlane pressed the blade to Kat's wrist.

'Your choice, Caleb.' The detective raised his eyebrows. 'No? OK.' He slashed the knife up Kat's forearm.

'No!' The word ripped from his throat.

Noise, shouting. Blood. Blood everywhere.

McFarlane pressed the knife to Kat's wrist again.

Caleb dropped the gun.

32.

Kat sagged against Grey-face. Her clothes were dark with blood, a spreading pool at her feet. The smell, like a butcher's. How long did she have? Hours? Minutes?

McFarlane picked up Caleb's gun and pointed it at him. 'On your knees.'

He knelt, felt the cold burn of the gun as McFarlane pressed it to his temple. A strange calmness descended. Aware of many things: Kat's stillness, McFarlane's peppermint breath, the small pain of something hard under his knee. McFarlane was talking, yelling. Tedesco murmuring quietly in response, his voice as steady as the gun he had aimed at the red-headed detective. Caleb slowly moved his knee, glanced down at what he'd been kneeling on. A long nail. An old roofing nail. He edged his hand towards it, stopped as he caught a movement by the door. Someone was there. Frankie.

Her eyes were clear and focused. Not high. Fuck, what was she doing here? Come to pull the trigger? She called out and McFarlane turned towards her. The pressure against Caleb's temple lifted. No second chances. He snatched up the nail and rammed it into McFarlane's thigh. And he was standing, punching. Hands, feet, elbows. The gun flew across the room. Get it. A sudden pain in the back of his head. He stumbled, body suddenly weak. Another blow and he was on his knees, darkness edging his vision. Tedesco was running towards him. No, no, that left Grey-face alone with Kat. Get to her. Get up, move. A flurry of movement as Tedesco tackled McFarlane to the ground. Kat. Get to Kat. Grey-face was pulling back her head, raising the knife. Wouldn't get there in time. Please, God, no.

A bang, a spray of red. Grey-face crumpled to the floor.

Frankie was standing over his body, clutching the gun with white-knuckled fingers.

Her pale eyes locked on Caleb's. Neither of them moved.

She raised a shaking hand and signed, 'Sorry me everything. Ambulance call.' She dropped the gun and fled.

A blurred shape as McFarlane ran past him towards the door. Going after Frankie? No, the gun. Fuck. The detective scooped it up. He was turning, aiming. Nowhere to run, no weapon. This was the end. A vibration behind him: Tedesco stamping to get his attention, mouthing something urgent.

'Down. Get down.'

He threw himself to the floor. A rapid succession of shots. A percussive thud. Stillness. The smell of ancient dirt and iron. He slowly raised his head. McFarlane was sprawled on his stomach, one arm outflung, the back of his shirt a tattered, bloody mess. Beyond him lay Kat. Caleb staggered to his feet and ran to her. Her eyes were closed, blood darkening the floorboards beneath her. Was that a pulse? Hand trembling, too hard to tell. Yes, there it was, fluttering against his fingers. He inhaled on a sob.

'Kat? Sweetheart?' He stroked back her hair. 'Open your eyes. Come on sweetheart, wake up.'

Her eyelids slowly opened. Dull, unseeing.

'Good, that's the way.'

So pale, a marbled greyness to her skin. He stripped off one of his tops and began ripping it.

'I'm going to bandage your arm to stop the bleeding, OK?'

A slight nod and she closed her eyes again.

'I'm just going to... I have to move your arm.'

No acknowledgement this time. He eased her arm out straight, trying to avoid her mangled fingers. Long flaps of skin peeled back from a deep gouge. Valleys of flesh, glimpses of white, maybe bone. Jesus. He began to bandage. She inhaled sharply and jerked away.

'Sorry. Sorry, I'll be quick.'

Where the fuck was the ambulance? It should be here by now. How fucking long did it take to get to Footscray?

A tap on his shoulder.

'Let me do it,' Tedesco said. Blood dripped from a gash above his eyebrow. Unsteady on his feet, the unfocused look of mild concussion.

'Frankie called an ambulance. Go and direct it.' He stopped and thought it through. 'Give them another call in case she didn't.'

He began a new bandage as Tedesco turned for the door.

Kat pulled away. 'Cal, stop.' Her lips barely moved.

He tightened his grip. 'Hang on, sweetheart. Nearly finished.'

Blood oozed through the material and ran over his hands. They were sticky with it. Why the fuck wouldn't it stop bleeding?

'Cal. Please. It. Hurts.'

He began to cry: silent, wrenching sobs that threatened to tear out his throat. He wiped his eyes on his sleeve.

'Almost done.' Another layer. Still bleeding, but slower. He attempted to tie the material, but his fingers fumbled, thick and clumsy. He tried again, finally managed it.

'All done.'

She curled her arm protectively to her chest.

He lifted her head onto his lap and stroked back her hair. 'It's over now, the ambos will be here soon. They'll fix you up, give you something for the pain. They'll do some proper bandaging, too. You'll be good as new. Not much longer now. You'll be fine. You'll be fine.'

There was movement in the doorway, uniformed men and women. Not paramedics, cops. People talking, yelling, more guns.

Kat was shuddering now, her skin clammy. He gathered her in his arms and tried to warm her.

A searing pain stabbed with each breath. Hadn't felt his ribs until now, hadn't felt anything except blind terror. And finally the ambos were there, easing his arms from around Kat, pulling him away. Bandages, IV units, stretchers. So cold. Shaking. Someone wrapped a blanket around his shoulders and shone a light in his eyes, asked stupid questions.

Tedesco came over as they loaded Kat onto a gurney, speaking, maybe to him. Caleb nodded, not trying to follow.

'... Cal...'

'Yeah?' His eyes were on Kat: there was a terrible stillness to her body. Why wasn't she moving?

Tedesco moved in front of him and gripped his shoulders, holding him in place. 'You need... trate... You concentrating?'

'Yeah.'

Tedesco's mouth moved slowly. 'McFarlane had... gun... Understand?'

'McFarlane had a gun.'

'That's right, McFarlane had Petronin's gun, not you. You picked it up in the fight, but you didn't bring it. Got that?'

They were taking Kat out now. He had to go. Halfway out the door, he understood. He turned to Tedesco.

'Thanks.'

The big man nodded and turned away.

They took them back to the Royal Melbourne. A different doctor, thank God. More uniformed people talked at him, but he turned off his aids and eventually they left him alone. Kat was wheeled away, wheeled back much later, groggy and blank-eyed. She murmured something incomprehensible and drifted off. He sat watch next to her, still wearing clothes stiff with blood.

And sleep must have come at some stage, because the sun began to lighten the sky. He closed his eyes against it, unsure how to face the new day.

EPILOGUE

He went back to the Bay to see Gary buried, his body finally returned to his birthplace. They laid him to rest in the old cemetery on the hill, among the giant red gums and the graves of all the other local men who'd died too young. After the ceremony, the funeral party moved down to the gardens for the wake. It was a beautiful view: looking across the valley towards the sea. A boom box pumped out something with a driving beat and someone fired up the electric barbie. Caleb stood on the edge, watching it all. Kat was there, never looking his way. Her arm was in a sling and she was holding herself with the air of someone afraid of being bumped.

The surgeon had visited the afternoon after her surgery, words full of consonants tripping from his tongue. Caleb had made him repeat everything and then write it down, but his message could be reduced to one word – hope. We hope Kathryn will regain full function in her hand; we hope her career and life and dreams weren't destroyed while you stood by and watched, Mr Zelic. He'd tried to hold her when the surgeon left, but she'd turned her face from him and cried. When Maria arrived, he'd taken his cue to leave. They hadn't spoken since.

A presence by his side: Tedesco, looking like a

distinguished thug in a dark suit and white shirt.

'Uri. I didn't know you were here.'

'Least I could do after all the shit that was said about Gary. Struck me as a good bloke, a family man.'

Caleb nodded and looked across to what was left of Gary's family. The kids were clinging to Sharon, their eyes skittering away whenever anyone approached them. He'd only spoken to them briefly today: a toss-up whether that was from cowardice or kindness, although he had a bit of an idea. He was going to have to get over that if he was going to have a place in their lives.

He looked back at Tedesco. 'Is there any word on...'

'No.'

'Is anyone looking for her?'

'Not hard. We've got nothing on her except shooting Grey-face. Even then – killing a known murderer in self-defence?' He shrugged. 'She'd walk with a good lawyer.'

'She was working for Scott for years. Feeding him information and God knows what else. Probably while she was still a cop.'

'And if we find any evidence of that, we'll prosecute. If it makes it any better, I think she tried hard to keep you safe. Kat, too, until the end.'

'I think...' He said the words that had been burning his guts for the past ten days. 'I think she was the one who called Gaz from the public phone.'

Understanding flicked across Tedesco's face, but he waited for Caleb to voice the idea.

'I don't think she missed Gary's call that day. I think Gaz told her about the photos and she called Scott from the public phone to warn him. Then she rang Gary back and told him to wait for her.'

'So who was Gary warning you not to trust when he texted you?'

'Everyone. He just didn't take his own advice.'

The detective nodded. 'Could be. Or he could have been warning you about Frankie, and answered the door to one of the other eight cops we've rounded up so far.'

Nice fairy tale; pity he couldn't make himself believe it. Tedesco didn't look too convinced by it, either. He was looking worn: the pouches under his eyes were a little heavier, a patch of bristles under his chin where he'd missed with the razor.

'How are things?'

Something crossed Tedesco's face, quickly gone. 'Still on leave pending the investigation, but I think it's safe to say my popularity hasn't risen. Killing a fellow cop will do that. Even a bent one.'

Nicely side-stepped: just enough personal information to deflect the question. He thought back to those chaotic seconds in the warehouse, Tedesco wiping the blood from his eyes, trying to aim as McFarlane raised his own gun.

'I'm sorry,' Caleb said. 'I should have worked out that McFarlane and his mates were behind the first robbery, the buy-up of City Sentry.'

He'd known the company had new owners; Elle had mentioned it, Frankie had made a note of it, but he hadn't looked further than the company name. If he'd dug a little deeper he would have found McFarlane.

Tedesco shook his head. 'Seeing as it took a forensic accountant a while to work it all out, I wouldn't be too hard on yourself. And what would it have told you anyway? A group of cops buy a security company? Nothing strange about that. And McFarlane was careful not to put his name anywhere.'

'Did you know he was bent?'

'Played me like a fucking violin. Biggest shock of my life, seeing him crawl out in front of you. Even then, I thought maybe it was some kind of elaborate sting. If I hadn't seen what he did to Kat... Jesus.' His mouth twisted. 'The way he smiled when he cut her.'

He could see it still: the grin, the slicing blade. It was etched on his retinas forever.

'Fuck, sorry,' Tedesco said. 'That was thoughtless. How's she doing?'

'Surgeon's hoping for full function in her hand.' He forced himself not to look at her. 'Did you work out how Spiros and Arnie were involved?'

'Yeah. Like you thought, they did the second robbery – a nice little copycat of McFarlane's. Not quite bright enough to cover their tracks though. He found out and smacked them around for bringing unwanted attention to his operation. I guess he let them live because they were useful, then cut his losses when things got too heated.' His eyes widened. 'Is that someone you know? Or is she heading for me?'

Maria was striding across the park towards him. She looked immaculate: no breeze daring to disarray her perfectly styled hair and elegant navy pantsuit. He stood a little straighter.

'You're looking well, Maria.'

'I wish I could say the same, Caleb. You look appalling.

You need to get some of that weight back on. Now, you weren't very forthcoming in your emails. Should I believe what I've been reading in the papers?'

He hadn't read a newspaper since Gary's death. Had gone out of his way to avoid them. 'They probably got the basics right.'

'I'm sorry about your partner. That must be hard.'

The fact that Frankie had betrayed him? Or that he hadn't seen her for the traitor she was? How could he not have recognised the signs of her addiction? Everything that had happened, all the pain and death, could have been prevented if he'd looked a little harder. If he'd seen.

'Why haven't you spoken to Kathryn?'

'She doesn't want me to.'

A hesitation. Or maybe a sigh of relief. 'Did she tell you that?'

'Scott abducted her, beat her and tortured her, all while I stood by and let it happen. She doesn't need to tell me.'

Beside him, Tedesco stirred.

Maria's mouth tightened. 'You should take better care of yourself, Cal. I went to a lot of effort getting you well.' She strode away.

'Jesus,' Tedesco breathed. 'Who was that?' There was a hint of reverence in his expression.

'My ex-mother-in-law.'

'That must have made for some interesting family dinners.'

'She's not too bad. Once you get to know her.'

'I'll take your word for it, mate.' Tedesco's mouth moved, testing some idea. 'Have you considered counselling? It could help.'

'Yeah, she's getting some.'

'I meant you.'

'Me? I'm not the one McFarlane tortured.'

'You sure about that?'

He felt a flash of heat. 'Pretty fucking sure. And Kat's got the scars to prove it.'

'There's all kinds of pain, mate. Just because you can't see it, doesn't mean it isn't there.' He turned away before Caleb could respond.

Enough. He obviously shouldn't be in human company any more. He headed for the car.

Anton was sitting on the bonnet, wearing an out of date, too-loose suit that had to have been their father's. Clean hair, freshly shaven, normal pupils.

Caleb stopped in front of him, trying not to wince at the memory of their last meeting.

'Hey Ant, looking good.'

'You're not. Did you sleep in that suit?' Every word signed.

He relaxed a little: forgiven, although he had no idea why. 'Last time, at the house. Sorry I was such a prick.'

Anton shrugged. 'Another mark on the scoreboard – I also totalled your Camry.'

'My first fucking car? The one I saved ten months to buy? I thought that was the O'Brien brothers.'

Anton grinned. 'Mum was a wicked liar.'

'Jesus. Any more family secrets you want to tell me?'

Anton smoothed the lapels of his coat. 'Not a secret, but we're right now, aren't we? I mean you're sure I had nothing to do with Gary or that Scott guy?'

'Yeah, I'm sure.'

'The way you looked at me that night... Fuck. Listen, I've still got that message Gary left me. The cops've heard it and I played it to Frankie when she called. She said she'd tell you that she'd heard it, but I guess she probably didn't. I can make you a copy if you like. You can get someone to, you know, confirm what's on it.'

The sun felt too bright.

'No need, I believe you. Sorry, Ant, I shouldn't have let Frankie get in my head. I should have trusted you.'

Anton shook his head. 'I've done some bad shit over the years, I know that. I was clean yesterday, I'm clean today, but who the fuck knows about tomorrow?' He slid off the bonnet of the car. 'You staying the night? Let's get a drink.'

'No, I've got to get back to Melbourne. The business is a mess.' More than a mess; failing. Bad enough that he hadn't answered a message in weeks, but word of Frankie's betrayal had swept quickly through the old-cop network. He hadn't had a referral since and there was a good chance he never would again.

'Come on, Cal – a lovely cup of tea. I'll even wash a mug for you. You can drive back in the morning.'

'Next time.'

Anton's face settled into his usual, oh-well-fuck-it expression. He glanced over Caleb's shoulder. 'Guess I'll get back to the – fuck, what's Brad O'Brien doing here? He and Gary weren't mates, fucking hated each other.'

'Free grog.'

'Oh, look, he's brought his great-grandfather along, that's nice. Oh. Maybe not nice. The old fella's getting very friendly with Kat.'

He wasn't going to turn around.

'He's upped his medication, you know. Twice the recommended dose, but apparently it does the trick. You know what medication I'm talking about, right?'

'Shut up, Ant.'

Anton's eyes widened. 'Dirty old man, pawing her like that. Thinks he's in with a chance.'

He turned. Jeremy O'Brien was standing in front of Kat, one hand on her good arm, delivering a way-too-close monologue. He caught the odd word: beach, picnic, dress. Jesus, what was the old perve suggesting?

'You think she'll have him?' Anton said. 'You know she's got bad taste in men.'

Jeremy finally stopped talking. He smirked happily at Kat's brief reply and shuffled away. Caleb smiled at her suppressed shudder. She looked up, looked at him. His breath caught somewhere low in his ribs. What the hell was he meant to do now?

'Go,' Anton signed.

Her clear, blue eyes held his as she waited. For what? For him to leave? Go to her? Spontaneously combust?

'Go on, quick.' Anton gave him a little push. 'Before Jeremy wins her over.'

He began to walk.

'I'll come for that drink later,' he said over his shoulder.

His eyes locked on Kat's as he made his way towards her. The words were already flying from his hands. So many words, so much to say.

ACKNOWLEDGEMENTS

My enduring gratitude to everyone who made *Resurrection Bay* possible. Thank you to all my Deaf, deaf and hard-of-hearing friends for their honesty and for not laughing (too hard) at my Frankie-like attempts at Auslan. To the wonderful Janette Currie, who helped me find the book within the manuscript, and the WoMentoring Project for giving me the opportunity to work with Janette. Everyone at Pushkin Press, in particular Daniel Seton and Tabitha Pelly. Brooke Clark for her insightful editing, Kate Gorringe-Smith for her pink pen and Tom Sanderson his evocative cover design.

And above all else, to Campbell, Meg and Leni for their patience, love and support. You are my everything.

NEXT IN THE SERIES

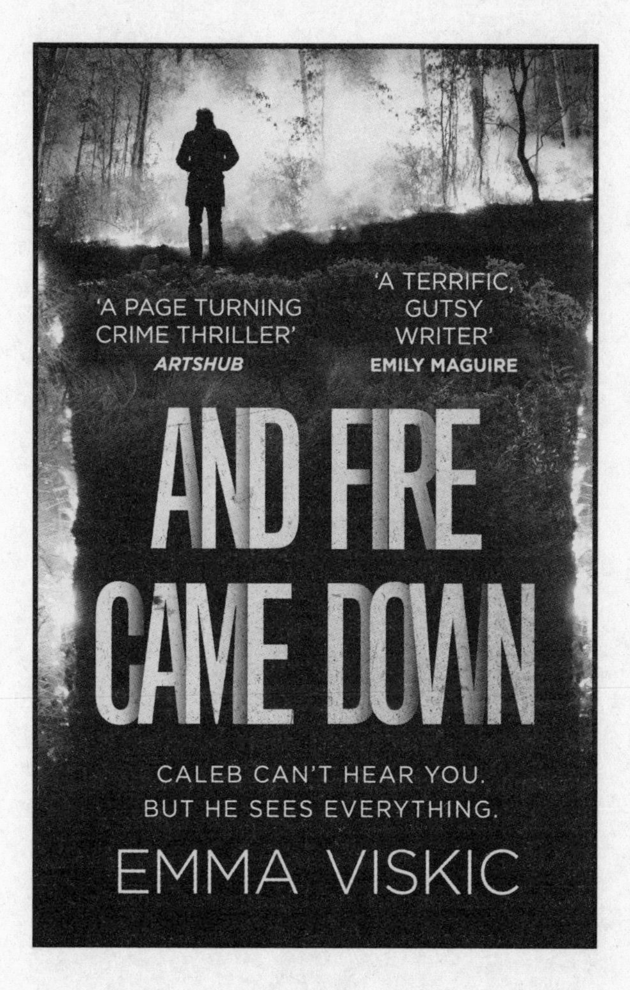

PUSHKIN
VERTIGO

1.

The man cornered Caleb at the lights. Twitching and sniff-ing, talking in staccato bursts. A skeletal face and pupils like voids.

Caleb gestured to the empty pockets of his running shorts. 'Nothing on me, mate.'

Sniffy kept talking and twitching. Caleb ignored him. Thirty more seconds and he'd be in his flat and under a long, cold shower. It was an hour after sunset, and the day's heat still clung to concrete and asphalt, the pores of his skin. Stupid to have gone for a run, but last night's dreams had slipped into his waking hours again, plucking at his thoughts with their bloodstained fingers.

And now Sniffy was waving a piece of fucking paper in his face.

Caleb tried to skirt around him as the lights turned green, but the guy did a little sideways dance to block his way.

'Piss off,' Caleb said.

Sniffy shoved the paper into his right hand. A receipt of some kind, sweat-stained and crumpled. Something written on the back in thick letters. He held it up to the streetlight.

Caleb

33/45 Martin St Nth Fitzroy

His name, his address. The words were scrawled in lipstick, but there was nothing flirtatious about their jagged letters, the strokes flecked with lumps of flesh-like pink. Something cold slid down his neck.

He looked at Sniffy. 'Where'd you get this?'

Words scuttled from the man's mouth and disappeared into the shadows. Was that a W? And an O? Definitely an M.

'A woman?' Caleb guessed. 'A woman gave it to you?'

Sniffy gestured down the street. 'She said… and I…'

'Slower. What woman?'

'Tall, black…'

Kat.

Fear gripped Caleb's bowels. 'Where is she? Show me.'

Sniffy headed along the street, talking the entire time. A shambling gait like a sleep-deprived toddler. Step, shuffle, step. Past apartment blocks and pizza shops, around a corner into an empty side street. So slow. Why the fuck couldn't he go any faster? Around another corner into an unlit alleyway of rusting corrugated iron and jumbled cobblestones, the stink of stale piss. Caleb came to a halt halfway down it. Dark, no overlooking windows – a good place to get jumped.

Sniffy made his way to the back of the alley, where a thin shape stepped out of the gloom to meet him. Not Kat. Nothing like Kat. The woman's skin was so pale it looked translucent, a startling contrast to her short, dark hair. Black hair – Sniffy had been describing her hair, not her skin. Caleb let out a shuddering breath. Of course it wasn't Kat. She was five thousand kilometres away in Broome, not in a stinking Melbourne alleyway. And if he'd stopped to think for a second, he would have remembered that.

A quick exchange of money between the pair, and Sniffy shuffled away. Just a delivery boy. So who was the woman? She was young, probably early twenties, carrying a brown handbag and wearing a red cotton dress that looked as though it would smell of incense. Dark alley, vulnerable young woman – it had to be some kind of a con. Walk away. But he glanced at the crumpled receipt in his hand.

Caleb

'How do you know my name and address?'

Red launched into speech, but her face was deep in shadow. It was brighter out on the footpath – he'd be able to see her mouth there. And her hands.

'Move onto the street,' he said. 'It's too dark in here.'

She shook her head and pressed herself against the wall.

Well, he wasn't waiting around for someone to walk up behind him with an iron bar.

'OK,' he said. 'Find yourself another mark.'

He turned away, and she darted forward and grabbed his arm. Her trembling hand was slick with sweat. Impossible to fake that kind of fear. Or for him to feel like more of an arsehole. She was gesturing urgently, pressing her hands together and pulling them towards herself. A familiar movement, as though she was signing the word 'help'.

'You know Auslan?' he signed.

Red stared at him as though he'd performed a circus trick. Not a signer, then, just someone who'd learned a word. Which meant she probably knew more about him than his name and address.

'Help?' he said out loud. 'You need help?'

A rapid nod. 'I... and... said you'd help.'

'Who said I'd help?'

'...and... you...'

This was hopeless; he'd have to get her to write everything. He reached for his phone, but his hand dug into the empty pocket of his running shorts. Shit: no phone. Just him and his stupid desire to be alone when he ran.

'Have you got a phone?' he asked. 'Something to write with?'

She shook her head and attempted another sign. It was the wrong hand-shape, but it looked a lot like...

'Do that again,' he said.

Two fingers against two fingers, a twist of her wrists: 'family'.

Family? A brother he barely knew and an almost-ex-wife avoiding him in Broome.

'Anton?' he asked. 'Kat?'

More headshaking, more incomprehensible speech. Something about bees? No, that couldn't be right.

He tried for a gentle tone. 'Look, I can't understand you. My flat's around the corner. Do you want to go there? Or I can take you to the cops.'

Her eyes widened, staring behind him. He spun around. A man was pounding up the alleyway towards them. Thickset, with short, blond hair and a dark swirl of tattoos up his arms and neck. Caleb threw himself backwards and caught the edge of the blow on his forehead. Falling. Down on his knees, head to the cobblestones. Up, get up. He levered himself to his feet. The man was dragging Red away, his arm locked around her neck. No thought, just motion: five steps and a fist to the man's kidney. Caleb's knuckles hit solid muscle. The man staggered and dropped Red, swung around. A calculating look as he took in Caleb's equal height but lack of kilos. His fist clenched. Caleb ducked the punch with reflexes born of a thousand playground fights. Quick, go for the kneecap. An awkward movement, mistimed, but his foot hit the side of the man's knee with a sickening jolt. Down like a felled tree.

Red. Where was Red? Caleb sprinted to the street. There she was, running towards Alexandra Parade. Good, there'd be people, lights, cars. He ran after her. Fitzroy Police Station was only a few blocks away – he'd get her there and work out what the fuck was going on. She was at the intersection, scanning for a break in the traffic.

'Stop,' he called, nearly at her side. 'It's safe here.'

Her head whipped around and she stepped back, her eyes focused behind him again. Shit, the blond man was only metres away, charging past him towards Red. She threw up her arms and stumbled backwards off the kerb.

Caleb lunged for her.

A fleeting touch of skin, then a flash of white, the smell of diesel and brake pads. She slammed against the van's bonnet. Into the air. Down.

An endless moment.

People were running. And he ran, too. Red was sprawled on the road, her arms flung wide. Blood. Blood everywhere. Bubbling from her lips and darkening her dress. He'd been here before, seen the spreading pool, smelled its iron sweetness.

Her lips were moving.

'...the be... got the be...'

He made himself touch her cheek. Cold beneath the slick warmth of her blood.

'It's OK. Help's coming.'

Her eyes held his: sea green and rimmed with pale lashes. A fierce brightness that flickered, dulled and faded.

Then nothing.

2.

He made his statement in a soulless grey room at the Fitzroy Police Station. Eyes gritty, a dull ache squeezing his temples. The young policewoman questioning him was a hard read, with rigid lips and a tight jaw. She wasn't too impressed by him, either. She'd been through his statement twice now, querying each sentence, her eyebrows drawing together at his answers. He didn't blame her for her wariness. His image in the two-way mirror looked like it should be on a wanted poster: hollow-cheeked and unshaven, a wildness to his dark hair and eyes. Probably slurring his words too, exhaustion stripping all those years of speech therapy from his tongue.

He was going through the events for the third time when the constable stood without warning. A moment of confusion until she strode to the door. Right, someone knocking. Hopefully someone with a couple of painkillers.

It was a large man with granite-like features and close-cropped hair. Uri Tedesco: friend, life-saver, cop. Caleb had texted him from the station's sticky-handled public phone to explain why he'd stood him up for Friday night drinks, but hadn't asked him to come. A flash of anger that the big man had assumed he'd need help.

Tedesco shot him an unreadable look, then spoke to the constable. The pair of them batted words back and forth, too fast for him to catch. Conversational ping-pong – his least favourite sport. He stared at the table until Tedesco waved to get his attention and said, 'You're right to go.'

The young cop wasn't looking too happy, but homicide detective trumped constable every time. Particularly a homicide cop who'd had the temerity to kill a bent colleague and stay in the job. Caleb gave her a nod and followed Tedesco through the station.

Outside, the air was like a sick dog's breath.

'You didn't have to come,' Caleb said.

Tedesco's gaze flicked across his bloodied running clothes. 'I was out of beer. Figured there'd be some at your place.'

Caleb showered while Tedesco got started on a beer. A long shower, with plenty of soap. He dressed and hunted for his hearing aids, finally found them under a book in the bedroom. They were small and pale, almost invisible beneath his dark hair. They amplified every unwanted sound and only gave hints of speech, had to be cleaned and replaced and adjusted and paid for. But without them there was nothing – no faint words or murmuring tones, just gaping mouths and guesswork. He never wore them on a run. Never took his phone or his notebook or even a fucking pen. Would Red still be alive if he did? Maybe. Probably.

Tedesco was out on the apartment's shitty balcony, halfway through a stubby of Boag's. Caleb slumped into a chair and opened a beer.

'Not your year,' the detective said.

'No.'

Seven months since he'd stumbled blindly into an investigation that had ended with his best mate murdered and Kat badly injured. Since his business partner had betrayed him. Understatement was one of Tedesco's stronger suits. Caleb took a long drink, then put the bottle down. Enough. People having very bad years didn't have the luxury of drowning their sorrows, not if they wanted some semblance of a life.

A sudden realisation that it was January and the new year had begun. God.

Caleb nudged the bottle further away. 'What did you find out?'

Tedesco paused, probably consulting his inner censor. 'Not much. No handbag or ID. And no one's reported her missing.'

'She had a handbag. I told them. Did they look for it?'

'Nah, just shrugged and went home.' Tedesco drained his beer and set the bottle on the table. 'You definitely didn't know her? Not an old neighbour or something?'

'No.' He had a fierce memory for faces, but he'd never seen hers. Not in the street or in a shop, not even in a photo. Which meant she wasn't a local.

His phone buzzed in his back pocket. A message from Kat.

—I've checked. No one thinks they know her. You OK? x K

Damn. He'd gone straight to his phone when he got home. Standing in the entrance hall, hands still crusted with blood. It hadn't taken long: one text to his brother, Anton, in Resurrection Bay, and one to Kat. A description of Red and a bloodless version of her death, a plea for them to tell him if they'd sent her. Neither of them had. Kat's ring-around of her family in the Bay had been his last hope.

He resisted the temptation to prolong the exchange, and sent a quick reply.

—Thanks heaps. All good. x C

Tedesco waved. 'Any joy?'

Only the sight of that 'x'. A sympathy kiss, but a kiss nonetheless.

He shook his head, and Tedesco reached for a second beer. 'Guess that's that, then.'

Caleb roused himself. In the seven months he'd known Tedesco, he'd discovered that the man wasn't a big talker, sharer of secrets or believer in late nights. Caleb probably had one more beer and four more questions before the detective took himself home to bed.

'Have they got any leads on the guy who was chasing her?' Caleb asked.

Tedesco paused for another ethics committee meeting. 'No. No one else noticed him. They'll get her picture onto the news and do another doorknock tomorrow, see if they can jog anyone's memory.'

'That's it? A doorknock and a photo?'

'More than usual for a traffic accident.'

'It wasn't an accident.'

'Mate, half a dozen witnesses, one of them a QC, saw her step in front of that van.'

'So Red just decided to play with traffic on a whim? Her death's got nothing to do with the big bloke chasing her?'

'Red?'

'Better than Jane Doe.'

Tedesco's grey eyes fixed on him. The detective was only a couple of years older than Caleb's thirty-one, but his Sphinx-like expression was aeons old. 'You're a country boy, you ever raise an orphaned animal?'

'I lived in town,' Caleb said. 'The only thing I raised was a rabbit.'

'I was eight the first time I did it. A spring lamb. He slept in my room so I could feed him. Did a good job of fattening him up, too. I called him Toby.' Tedesco tilted his head. 'Reckon you can guess how that story ends.'

Caleb stayed silent.

Tedesco drained his beer to the last couple of inches. 'Let it go, mate. It was a shitty experience, but the more I hear about it, the more I think you were just a mark.'

Tell him about today's break-in? The possible break-in, possibly today. A loose grip on time and specifics these days. There was no proof that anyone had been in his flat, just a bathroom door left ajar, a sense of stale air disturbed. He'd had the same feeling a few times over the past couple of weeks.

'She knew my name,' he said. 'Knew some signs.'

Tedesco lifted a shoulder. 'Good groundwork on her part. And everyone knows one or two signs.'

Not the people he met. A scant few people in his life knew any Auslan, and only two of them were fluent. His parents hadn't learned a word.

'You don't,' he said.

Tedesco smiled, the look of a smug student catching a teacher in a mistake. He circled a fist in front of his face and then formed a diamond with his thumbs and forefingers.

Caleb choked on a laugh. 'Jesus, where'd you learn that?'

The smirk slipped from Tedesco's face. 'What? Why?'

Ant, it had to be Ant. Who except Caleb's brother would have taught a member of the force to call himself a pig's cunt?

'First lesson.' Caleb slid two fingers across his forearm. 'That's the sign for "cop". Second lesson, don't trust Ant. What were you trying to say?'

'That I –' Tedesco coughed. 'Never mind.' He finished his beer and stood. 'Bedtime.'

Caleb checked the time: 12.14 a.m. Long, long hours to go before dawn. Be a bit pathetic to beg Tedesco to stay and keep the monsters at bay.

He walked the detective to the door and paused with it half open. Red had known she was dying. That look in her eyes: desperation and pain, terror. He'd seen that look before. The memory of it lurked just beneath his thoughts, leaching to the surface in unguarded moments.

'Can you tell me if you find out her name?' he asked.

Tedesco shook his head. 'As my mum'd say – that'd just end in tears and a nice Sunday roast.' He slapped Caleb on the shoulder. 'Take care of yourself. And tell your shit of a brother to watch his back.'

Caleb wandered into the living room. He'd caught Tedesco's quick frown at his surroundings as they'd walked to the door. It was hard not to see the place through the man's clinical gaze: the hand-me-down orange furniture and un-vacuumed carpet, the patchy coat of white paint that Caleb had slapped on the walls in a burst of 3 a.m. energy. The thick layer of dust. Only the neat filing cabinets and organised desk saved it from being a hovel, and they didn't lend much to the ambience.

Trust Works had been shaky in the months after Frankie's betrayal, with no new clients coming in and plenty of old ones leaving. For some reason companies seemed reluctant to hire a fraud investigator whose business partner had been a lying, drug-addicted criminal. So he'd given up the shiny office and set up in the flat, taken on more quick-turnaround work: background checks and due diligence cases. Jobs that required hours in front of the computer and minimal human contact. Jobs he could do alone. Nothing was lined up for the next few days, though. Just him in the flat with the endless, empty hours.

A familiar darkness uncurled and stretched, ran its well-honed claws down his skull.

Move. Keep moving. He could outrun it if he pushed himself hard enough.

He was doing up his runners when he remembered the piece of paper he'd shoved in his pocket. Red had written his name on some kind of receipt. It could have her credit card details. He picked though the kitchen bin, found his blood-stained shorts beneath the banana skins and coffee grounds. He pulled out the receipt and turned it over. Only a cash payment for a train ticket, but written at the top was the station of origin – Resurrection Bay.